The

iSpeaker

MIKAEL CARLSON

WARRINGTON
PUBLISHING

Warrington Publishing
Danbury, Connecticut

The iSpeaker
Copyright © 2014 by Mikael Carlson
Warrington Publishing

WARRINGTON
PUBLISHING

Printed in the United States of America
First Edition
ISBN: 978-0-9897673-4-7
978-0-9897673-5-4 (E-Book)
978-1-944972-06-6 (Hardcover)

Cover design by Veselin Milacic

Novels by Mikael Carlson:

– The Michael Bennit Series –

The iCandidate

The iCongressman

The iSpeaker

The iAmerican

– Tierra Campos Thrillers –

Justifiable Deceit

Devious Measures

Vital Targets

– Watchtower Thrillers –

The Eyes of Others

The Eyes of Innocents

– America, Inc. Saga –

The Black Swan Event

Bounded Rationality

Boiling the Ocean

Dedicated to all the young people in this world we entrust to do a better job than we have.

While the exploits of Michael Bennit in *The iSpeaker* can stand on its own, a reader will get far more out of his story by starting with the beginning of his exploits. To that end, I encourage anybody who purchased this book to read *The iCandidate* and *The iCongressman* beforehand.

"With the evolution of social media that includes blogging, Facebook, and Twitter, who and how information is delivered has changed tremendously. The landscape for news is a different place, and people have to accept that."
— Michael Eric Dyson

"Technology and social media have brought power back to the people."
— Mark McKinnon

-PROLOGUE-
MICHAEL

I feel the impact even before hearing the sound. The force is enough to spin me ninety degrees and knock me off balance on the staircase leading up to the east entrance of the Capitol. My left ankle slams into the step behind me, and I lose my battle to remain upright. I crash hard onto the stone steps and roll down them, sprawling out when I reach the bottom.

People are screaming all around me. My vision fills with a blur of motion as those gathered for the press conference scatter. The sense of knowing what's unfolding clashes with thoughts that it can't be possible…not here…not now. I try to push the thoughts out of my mind and focus. Chelsea, Vince, and Vanessa are here. Peyton and Emilee are here. Kylie is here, and they're all in grave danger.

The gunman is standing only a few feet away from me, and there is no cover to hide behind. Adrenaline is dumping into my bloodstream by the gallon. The seconds that have elapsed feel like an eternity. I'm hit, but I can still fight, still survive, and still protect. I don't waste time staring at the wound in my shoulder and reach for the Beretta 9mm I keep on my body armor to return fire.

I hear more pops as the shooter engages more targets. I keep reaching for my weapon. It's not there. It's always there. I check to ensure it is clean, serviceable, loaded before every mission we go out on. I do the same thing with my rifle. Where's my rifle? Only then do I realize I am not wearing body armor. There is no army-issued Beretta or SOP-modified M4A1 carbine to fight back with. I'm not lying in the sands of Afghanistan—I am in Washington, D.C.

Only then does the gunman notice that I'm still alive. He looks at me with cold, calculating eyes. I am not going to die lying on the ground like this. I need to force myself to my feet and close the distance between us before he can bring his handgun to bear on me. It's a race against time, and

I'm lagging behind. Another second or two more, and he will have me in his sights. "Come on, Michael, get it together and move!" I hear my mind screaming.

I push up hard from the squatting position and start to lunge forward when I see the first volcanic eruption of red from his chest. Then a second burst, and a third. I catch his arms as I lunge toward him, using my inertia to redirect the weapon he's holding towards the sky. It discharges twice, the slide locking to the rear, indicating he's out of ammunition. We tumble to the ground. I roll off him, immediately assuming a combat stance as I look for other targets. There are none.

I glance down at him as he clutches at the three wounds in his chest. He cocks his head to stare up at me with dark, black eyes filled with pure hatred. I want to watch the life leave his body but am ordered back by a cadre of men shouting as they advance toward us.

One of the worst kept secrets in Washington is that there are plain-clothed law enforcement officers everywhere. One such member of the Capitol Police approaches the shooter with his weapon expertly trained on him. Several others, both uniformed and not, approach with their guns drawn. I may be in my nation's capital and a world away from the Middle East, but it feels like I'm in combat again. I do a threat assessment on each before surveying my surroundings.

Cisco is down, grabbing at his leg as he writhes in pain. Blood spurts into the air in broken streams from a wound on his thigh. Viano is lying prone on the steps near where I was standing and isn't moving. Blake is lying face down on the ground at the base of the stairs. Two dark holes are evident in the back of his suit jacket. Chelsea is next to him, lying on her side and not moving.

"Chelsea!" I shout, taking several tentative steps towards her.

Vince seems to recover from his own shock over what just happened and scrambles over to check on her. Vanessa joins the two of them a couple of moments later.

"Michael!" Kylie screams, tears flowing from her eyes. "Oh God, are you okay?" she yells over the din.

"I'm fine. Where are Peyton and Emilee?"

"I don't know. Has Chelsea been—"

"I'm not sure, but Vince and Vanessa are over there with her. I need you to find the others."

"I'm not leaving you!" she bellows in response. I notice that no one is working on Cisco yet.

"Kylie, listen to me," I demand, trying to get her to focus. "Kylie! Are you listening?"

"Yes," she sobs, finally locking eyes with me.

"Cisco's been hit, and I need to help him. Find the others. Do that for me, please. Can you find them?"

"Yes, but—"

"Please, Kylie, go!"

People are rushing everywhere, adding to the feeling of chaos. Some are still running away from the Capitol, others running toward it. Sirens urgently wail in the distance, and I know more help is on the way.

Kylie frantically scans the chaotic scene and rushes up the steps toward the entrance of the building. I turn my attention back to the spot on the stairs where Chelsea and Blake are lying. I want to run over there, but there is already a growing gaggle around them. Cisco needs my help, and he needs it now. Paramedics are starting to arrive, but he can't wait that long.

"Hang in there, buddy," I tell him when I make it over to him, doubting that he is hearing me over his own agonizing screams. He has already lost a lot of blood and is slipping into shock. Once again, after more times than I care to remember, I find myself performing battlefield triage.

I rip open Cisco's pant leg at the wound and recoil as a spray of blood almost hits me in the face. The bullet must have hit the artery, and he's going to bleed out in a matter of minutes. I yank at my tie as a gutsy photographer rushes over, a camera dangling around his neck.

"Can I help?"

"You have a towel or extra shirt or something?" I demand, the knot of my tie finally coming loose. I rip it from my neck and look around.

"Yeah, I have a small towel," the guy says, digging through a camera bag and presenting it to me. Not ideal, but I don't typically walk around with sterile dressings like I did while in combat.

"Put it on that wound and apply as much pressure as you can."

I get up and rush the short distance over to a microphone lying on the ground. I snatch it up and race back to my fallen friend, fighting increasing light-headedness every step of the way. The pain in my shoulder grows worse as the adrenaline rush subsides. I work through it as I use the necktie and microphone to fashion a crude but effective tourniquet on Cisco's upper leg.

"Keep his leg slightly elevated," I say as calmly as I can to the shell-shocked photographer. "He's going into shock."

I'm worried that the bone might be broken, but that's the least of his concerns. Shock is as deadly as excessive blood loss is. I twist the tourniquet a few times and then tell the photographer to lift the towel. The bleeding has decreased to a slow trickle out of the wound. Good enough.

I secure the microphone with the free ends of the necktie so it doesn't spin loose. Soldiers in Iraq and Afghanistan were issued a small tourniquet that they kept on their body armor for medics or comrades to use if they were severely injured in battle. Despite that, learning to improvise the device is a part of any soldier's basic first aid training.

I need to get to Chelsea. "Stay here. Keep pressure on the wound until the paramedics get here," I say to the journalist.

Metro and Capitol Police have joined forces and are streaming onto the scene now, their squad cars screeching to a halt and men forming a hasty perimeter. I step past Viano, taking a quick measure of what I see. It doesn't look good. Paramedics are already tending to Blake, and Vince is kneeling next to Chelsea. She's still not moving.

My shoulder and arm have gone completely numb. I'm starting to get woozy. I make it over to Vince before being pushed back by a cop who doesn't seem to know who I am.

"Stand back!" he shouts, still winded from having just raced over.

I immediately swell with anger and try to push past him to no avail. I'm getting weaker and find it hard just to keep my balance. After a moment, several other police officers and first responders join the huddle around her and Blake. I can't see her. A few seconds later, they shove Vince away.

"Vince! Are you okay?" I ask him, doing a quick once-over with my eyes searching for wounds. I move aside his suit jacket and search for any bloodstains on his shirt, but my vision is getting fuzzy and, despite my efforts to refocus, it's getting worse.

"I...I think so," he stammers, giving himself his own cursory visual check for signs of injury.

"Is Chelsea okay? Was she hit?"

"She's not responsive. I...I don't know. I didn't...I didn't see anything, but..."

Vince is starting to show signs of shock, more in a mental sense than a physical one. He may be uninjured, but his brain is having a hard time processing what's going on around him. It's pandemonium around us in the most fundamental sense of the word, and as much as I want to help snap him back into the present, I know I have a bigger problem.

One of the first things they teach you when you train for combat is to tend to your own wounds before looking after others. I chose to ignore that rule and am paying the price. I can feel my shirt is wet and sticky. In a rush to ensure Cisco, Chelsea, and the others were being taken care of, I didn't realize how much blood I'd lost. I lose my equilibrium, and I collapse against the stairs when gravity takes over.

"Congressman!" I hear Vanessa call out as she runs to my side. Where did she come from? Was she with Chelsea? Suddenly, I can't remember.

"Oh, my God!" Kylie screams, the urgent concern echoing in my head as she reaches me with Peyton and Emilee in tow.

Thank God they are okay. She cradles me in her arms and screams at the top of her lungs as I stare into the empty sky.

"Somebody get over here! He's been hit! Are you going to let a congressman die right in front of you?"

The pain is searing now as the adrenaline rush begins to ebb. I know I won't get any pain medication until reaching the hospital, assuming I stay conscious for that long. The woozy feeling is overpowering, and my vision completely blurry.

"Congressman Bennit? Are you still with us?"

I see a man in a uniform. Is that a cop or a paramedic? Is that the guy who pushed me? Why are they fussing over me? Look after Chelsea...and...Cisco...

"Michael! Please, hang on!" I hear Kylie plead.

"You need to move out of the way, ma'am," a guy in a white shirt says as he kneels beside me. I can't see who he is.

"No, I'm not leaving him. Michael! Michael!"

"Ma'am, you need to let go of him," the guy says more insistently. The wails of the sirens and sounds of men barking orders become distant and muffled.

I feel the darkness closing in. The deep blackness steadily creeps into my vision from the periphery. The commotion, sirens, and wails seem to fade until they are like a distant memory.

"Congressman? Congressman? Stay with us..."

PART I

ABUSES AND USURPATIONS

-ONE-
KYLIE

The George Washington University Hospital has one of the premier Level One trauma centers in the country. Located blocks from the White House, it is the primary receiving center for emergencies that may occur in and around downtown Washington's government complexes, museums, and monuments.

This emergency department played a significant role in saving President Ronald Reagan's life after an assassination attempt in 1981 left him severely wounded. More recently, they took care of two victims of the tragic shooting at the United States Capitol in July 1998. There is a long history of treating the casualties of some of the capital's most traumatic shootings, and they'd better be on their game today.

The man they wheeled in here on a gurney is not just a United States congressman. He's a brilliant teacher, respected mentor, and a man I could not imagine living my life without. I've fallen in love with him as deeply as one ever could, and I simply cannot lose him now. I refuse to.

I bury my head in my hands, trying to stifle my tears when I feel a tap on my shoulder. I look up to see Vanessa standing over me and offering a cup of coffee. Petite and powerful, she was an incredible three-sport athlete in high school with a competitive spirit and a no-nonsense Latina attitude. Add all that to her savvy intelligence, and you get a force to be reckoned with. Right now, she's an angel of mercy sent by Juan Valdez himself.

"You're a saint, thank you," I say, graciously accepting the aromatic liquid.

It's hospital java and undrinkable under normal circumstances, but these aren't normal circumstances. I'm drained but won't permit myself to rest. I am too emotionally strung out to sleep. Even if I wasn't, I would infuse an intravenous drip with caffeine to ensure I'm awake when news about Michael arrives.

"He's going to be okay, Kylie. Mister Bennit has been wounded in combat before. If he can survive the deserts of Iraq and mountains of Afghanistan with nothing more than battlefield medicine, he can survive in Washington with the best medical care on the planet."

I know she has a point, but I'm not in the mood to hear it. Somehow sensing that, she gives me a squeeze on the shoulder and sets off to find a seat in the crowded waiting area. That's not going to be an easy task.

Despite the efforts of the hospital to limit the number of people allowed to wait in here, the room is still packed. Vince, Vanessa, Peyton, Emilee, and I were all checked out in the ER and permitted to stay. There are other concerned parties here, but for whom I'm not sure.

Scanning the room, I'm drawn to the decorations hung to mark the holiday season. Today was the last day of the congressional term and four days until Christmas, so it would otherwise be a happy time for Michael and me.

Stuck in this cramped waiting room, nobody visiting here would ever be in a festive mood, present company included. Regardless, the hospital staff saw fit to bedazzle it with politically correct decorations ranging from snowflakes to plastic gingerbread men. Yeah, we're sorry your loved one is fighting for his life, but Merry Christmas anyway.

Misery loves company, and there is plenty of both here. Peyton is a hot mess right now. The blonde goddess with movie star qualities was a big reason that so many young male volunteers flocked to work for Michael's campaign once their race against incumbent Winston Beaumont became a national obsession. If she looks that emotionally and physically worn, I can only imagine what I look like.

Emilee isn't in much better shape. She and Chelsea grew close during their senior year in high school, and I was sure she would join Michael's staff along with her best friend. Deep down, I think Emilee knows that politics is not her thing. It didn't stop her from doing a fantastic job during the first campaign or in the time she has worked with us since.

Police rotate through periodically to take statements or corroborate some tiny piece of information, but mostly we just sit, wait, and occasionally look at the coverage on the news. The shooting is being covered on every station except the History Channel. They opted to run a documentary on political assassinations. If that was planned programming, it's one hell of a coincidence.

"Let her through, damn it! I said, let her through!" I hear Vince shout from the entrance to the room.

A wrestling match is starting to break out as everyone turns their heads towards the commotion. A few uniformed officers rush over to support their brethren as Vince starts shouting at the top of his lungs at the men.

Vince Orsini was one of the most hot-headed and difficult students Michael said he had ever taught. What he lacks in physical intimidation he makes up for in sheer force of personality. His father walked out on the family years ago, and as a result, Vince is fiercely independent and vocal. It also means he never learned boundaries. Pair that with a strong Italian heritage, and you have an unpredictable yet devoted and loyal consigliere.

"Officer, she's with us. Please let her in," Vanessa pleads after rushing over and joining the fracas.

I can't see who it is that they're lobbying to get the police to let in. It obviously isn't Chelsea's father, who I know is still in transit down here and could never be confused as a "she." The question answers itself as Amanda squeezes in the entryway.

Vince has a couple of parting words for a couple of the police as they go back to guarding the doorway. They're exercising considerable restraint, understanding that we are emotionally frayed and hanging on the ragged edge.

He is taking this especially hard and is looking for any target to vent it on. It makes no matter if the objects of that rage wear uniforms and carry a badge and gun. Mister Bennit became something akin to a surrogate parent to Vince when he taught him in high school. Growing up with no father figure for most of his life, he needed the guidance Michael was happy to provide.

Vanessa immediately hugs an emotional Amanda, who appears even more distraught than I am. Mascara colors the river of tears flowing down her cheeks. I'm sure I look just as bad, not that I give a damn right now.

I think I know why Amanda is so upset—she wasn't there. Not happy with our chosen tactics to win the rules vote, she got in her car and left for Connecticut while we were getting shot at on the steps of the Capitol.

Peyton, Vince, and Emilee all join in the group hug with Amanda. If there is any animosity towards her for leaving, it isn't evident in this scene. I can't help but think about how much these kids have been through. A smear campaign in the first election, watching their mentor fight for his political life all this year, a hard-fought race to get the icandidates elected…the list goes on.

As much as I want to join them, I let this close-knit group have their moment. I deal with stress in my own way. Right now, it's a desire to find an empty room somewhere in this hospital and just cry my eyes out alone.

My longing for solitude is not to be. Amanda sees me and walks over when the group hug breaks up. I get up out of the seat, and she shares a fierce embrace of her own. Her sobs start my own waterworks up again.

Peyton was the knockout blonde of the gang, but Amanda was the girl-next-door cutest of Michael's campaign staff. She was also the most astute when it came to numbers, explaining why she is a business major at the University of Connecticut. When we release our hug, I can see her hazel-green eyes are as puffy red as mine are.

"Do we know…I mean…have the police said…?"

"They aren't telling us much, Amanda. Michael was hit and is in surgery. Cisco was hurt badly, too. I'm not sure if he is going to make it. Michael was working to save his life before the paramedics arrived."

Congressman Francisco Reyes has been the closest thing to a friend and political ally Michael has in the House. Winner of a special election of his own, the flamboyant Texan also ran as an icandidate, and the two have become the most visible leaders of the independent movement in the country.

"And Chelsea?" Amanda whimpers.

"She's still unconscious. She hit her head pretty hard on the steps, I guess, but she should be okay."

"Any others?"

"We haven't heard anything about Viano or Blake. I know they were both critically wounded. I think there are a couple of others, but I really don't know. It's been chaotic since we got here."

Marilyn Viano. I can't stand that woman, but I don't want to see her hurt either. Despite her duplicity toward Michael and the icandidates in the last election, the truth is it never would have come to fruition without her help.

Blake Peoni is more of an enigma. The man who was once responsible for creating a scandal that cost Michael a win in his race against Winston Beaumont had become an integral part of our own efforts this past election. It has taken Chelsea the better part of two years to warm up to him, and now she may even be dating him. Go figure.

"Did they catch the guy?" Amanda asks, bringing me back to the present.

"Yeah, they caught him with a few well-placed bullets," Vince states defiantly. "He's dead and burning in hell, right where he belongs."

I feared something like this would happen. From the moment Michael almost got clipped by that taxicab in Manhattan, I was scared someone would try to take a shot to silence him. I dismissed it as being irrational up until Terry Nyguen showed up. He warned us before the election that something like this could happen. Then we had the anthrax scare, and my fears had become more of an obsession.

This is not the country I want to live in. I know assassinations are nothing new—four presidents have been killed. Several others barely escaped with their lives. A couple of congressmen have even been targeted over the years. Most of those gunmen were unbalanced loners with a weapon and an agenda. At least, that's what we've been led to believe. Every fiber in my being tells me this is different, and my years as a journalist have taught me to trust that feeling.

All Michael is guilty of is trying to make this country a better place. Unlike so many men and women who get elected to serve in this town, he doesn't want fame, power, prestige, or money. Michael only wants the government to work for the people again. Now he's on an operating table, fighting for his life along with his colleague and closest political ally, solely because they dared to challenge the status quo.

Something needs to change, and I'm going to help to change it. I'm going to root out who is behind this if it is the last thing I ever do. I owe that to Michael.

He made so many sacrifices to take this job and has asked nothing in return. It's about time he understands just what he means to this country, the people of the Sixth District, to his former students, and to me.

It's time to step out of the shadows and back into the light. I got kicked hard when I got fired from the *New York Times*. Once I got up off the ground, I made Winston Beaumont pay for what he did to me. I found the most wonderful man I have ever met in the process, and now we're together while my arch-nemesis rots in a jail cell. The shooter may be dead, but whoever is responsible for cutting him loose will join him.

The room falls quiet when a dour-looking man in a white coat enters. Those sitting down stand, and we all brace ourselves for the news we know is coming. He surveys the room for a moment, taking stock of all the concerned faces gazing back at him. Only a few seconds elapse, but it feels like hours.

"My name is Doctor Zeigler. I have some news."

-TWO-

JAMES

Anyone who's ever seen a crime scene on *Law & Order*, *CSI*, or any other police-themed television program knows what one looks like. This one is no different, only much grander in scale.

Police have much of the area on the east side of the Capitol cordoned off. Yellow police tape surrounds the area in front of the grand stone stairwell that leads up to the chamber of the United States House of Representatives. The blue and red flashing lights of police and medical vehicles are everywhere. I'm not sure why the latter is here, considering the wounded and deceased were removed hours ago.

It's been just over three hours since the shooting. Despite my best efforts, the closest I can get is far across the grass from the Capitol on First Street in front of the National Archives. The visitor area that handles thousands of tourists a day is closed, as are several other public landmarks in the Capitol Hill area. A large crowd has gathered to watch the scene, and a few shrines have even begun popping up just outside the restricted area.

I walk by one of them, the yellow candlelight flickering and creating eerie shadows on the handwritten notes scrawled and taped on the half wall that separates the field from the street. From 9/11 to the Sandy Hook massacre, these shrines are a way for people to show their sympathy and support. This one is growing larger by the minute.

Do these people even know why? Do they really know who Michael Bennit is or understand the threat he poses to the way their government works? If they do, do they care?

I step off to the side of the burgeoning makeshift memorial to keep out of the people's way. Bennit had this coming to him. He was messing with influential people and never understood the ramification of his actions. It all finally caught up with him. He was going to be removed from the political picture one way or another.

I listen as a couple of people discuss the latest news reports on the shooting. Not much is being released, but they have confirmed that the assassination attempt failed. Michael Bennit and Francisco Reyes were wounded in the attack, but both are still breathing. At least they were when they got loaded into the ambulance and rushed to the hospital.

There are reports of other various injuries to bystanders, and there is speculation as to who may have perished. I don't put much stock in what the media is reporting. Like with all tragedies, they fill all the airtime by taking scant details and injecting their own speculation. It's why they're wrong so often.

Bennit should be grateful he's alive. He may be a jacked, athletic, tough ex-Special Forces soldier, but even they are susceptible to gunfire. Bullets don't discriminate, and the shooter could not have been more than eight feet away when he pulled the trigger. How do you miss at that distance? Hell, even I could kill a man with a handgun from that close. Of course, there are YouTube videos out there of an assassin missing at point-blank range, so anything is possible.

I'm about to leave the lovefest when another lemming joins the small group discussing the news on Bennit. I hear him exclaim that the media are reporting that police have initially called this a random shooting. The others scoff at the notion. Let the media keep saying that because all it will do is add fuel to the fire that conspiracy theorists will be eager to ignite. The truth is all too obvious to me.

Bennit was almost killed because he's a maverick wanting to change how a system of government operates when others like it just the way it is. From what I know about him, he values people over prestige and power and his relationships with his girlfriend and former students the most. Now he's been sent a loud and clear message. Only time will tell us how hard he's listening.

-THREE-

CHELSEA

I was awake for all of thirty seconds before my room flooded with doctors and nurses. My head feels like it was split open and is pounding. It's so hard to focus.

"Look straight ahead," I hear the doctor tell me as he waves a small light in and out of my vision. I should say "doctors," as in plural. I see two of them. "How are you feeling, Chelsea?"

"Nauseous...and a little light-headed."

"That's normal for someone with a severe concussion. Do you remember what happened?"

I'm in a haze and haven't been able to remember how I got here. I remember the vote in the House, and then we moved to the bottom of the stairs where the Congressman was speaking. And then...

"Oh, no!" I blurt out as I try to sit up in bed.

"No, don't move too fast, Chelsea. It's okay."

I feel an instant rush of overpowering nausea and dizziness that almost causes me to vomit. A pair of nurses grab my shoulders and attempt to ease me back onto the bed. I fight them every inch of the way.

"Congressman Bennit! Blake...where are they? How ar—"

"You need to take it slow, Chelsea. The answers are coming."

"No, tell me now!" I bark, regretting it in an instant. The sound of my own voice makes my head pound even harder.

"I don't know much. Everyone is being treated by different doctors. I can find out, but my responsibility here is for you," the twins in the matching lab coats say.

I make an impatient face but realize the fastest way to get what I want is to cooperate. I don't know why everyone is making a big deal over a concussion. I'm alive, but I need to know who else is. I need to know if Mister Bennit is okay. And Vince, Vanessa, and the others. And Congressman Reyes. Wasn't he next to the congressman? And Blake. Oh my God, Blake! He had to have been hit.

"Your father is on the way, and your friends are in the waiting room," the doctor continues. "If you let me finish my examination, I can let them see you."

I'm having problems paying attention to what he's saying. I can't think. Everything hurts, and I don't have the energy to fight him on this. Resigned to do things on his timetable, I nod my head and let him finish poking and prodding me.

The sooner this is over, the sooner I get the answers I need. All I can think about is my mentor, Congressman Reyes, Blake, and my friends. The thought of losing them hurts more than I can bear. I feel the tears streak down my cheeks and hope they help speed this up.

* * *

"Is the congressman okay?"

They're the first words out of my mouth once the tears stopped and hugs ended. Vince was the first one through the door. I was relieved that he was unhurt. He was standing right in the middle of it all with us.

Many of the most cherished people in my life followed him in — Vanessa, Peyton, my close friend Emilee, and the matriarch of this little group, Kylie. The last through the door was the one I least expected to see.

My relationship with Amanda became strained in the days leading up to the rules vote. She was adamantly against playing the Republicans and Democrats against each other. Through it all, she has remained the most idealized amongst us and argued against playing political games. She was so upset over the whole thing that she decided to skip the vote and headed home. She's visibly distraught, and I assume it's a consequence of that choice.

"He just got out of surgery an hour ago. He lost a lot of blood, but he's going to be okay," Vanessa reassures.

"Thank God," is all I manage to mutter, the relief sweeping over me.

"How are you doing?" Vanessa asks, inspecting the bandage wrapped around the top of my head.

"Dizzy, nauseous, and suffering from the worst headache ever, but otherwise okay, I guess. What about the others?"

"Congressman Reyes is still in surgery. He was shot in the leg. Congressman Bennit probably saved his life at the scene," Vince says.

How is that possible? I need to hear the story, but I need to find out about a certain someone first.

"What about Blake?"

Vince and Vanessa share a glance, and I begin to fear the worst. Tears well up in my eyes as I ready myself for the inevitable bad news I know is coming. If he were okay, he'd be here with them.

"He was hit twice in the back. They've been working on him since we got here, too. The doctor says they'll put him in a medically induced coma for a short while. We don't know much more than that. I'm sorry."

Emilee leans over and awkwardly tries to console me as I begin to sob uncontrollably, but I soon force myself to stop because it makes my head hurt that much more. When I get a handle on my emotions, I notice Kylie in the corner of the room. She hasn't spoken since she entered.

"And the shooter? Is he alive? Do we know who he was?"

"They're still investigating, but it's going to take time. He was killed at the scene by the Capitol Police."

"At least the only one killed was the bastard who deserved it most," I state with conviction. I know I might have jumped to that conclusion when everyone exchanges wary glances. "What? What did I miss?"

"One person didn't make it, Chels," Peyton adds sheepishly from the foot of my bed. The room suddenly floods with an unease I'm not used to.

"Who?"

"We only found out a little while ago that she was pronounced dead on arrival here," Emilee whispers, rubbing my shoulder as she does so.

I glance over at Vince and plead with my eyes since nobody else wants to tell me. He doesn't want to say it either. The usually brash and brutally honest Vince averts his eyes to the floor, trying to avoid my stare.

"Vince, who got killed?"

"Senator Viano."

-FOUR-

MICHAEL

"Welcome back to the world," Kylie says as my eyes flutter open and focus on her. My God, she looks good, even under these circumstances.

Kylie is so much different than Jessica or any of the other women I've ever dated. Most of them were all glamour and no substance. That type of woman sufficed when I was a soldier in my twenties. I didn't care anything about love back then, so long as I had an impressive-looking woman to bring to the military ball.

Kylie is different. She is bright, passionate, driven, and kind. She'll never be the hottest girl at the party but will always be the one men want to leave with at the end of the night. She's enchanting that way.

"It's good to be back," I croak.

My mouth is still dry, and it feels like I ate a bag of kitty litter. I reach for a cup of water, but she grabs it first and helps me insert the straw into my mouth. The first sips are like liquid heaven.

"How are you feeling?"

"Like I got shot," I respond with as much of a smile as I can muster. "What did I miss?"

"A lot."

Kylie proceeds to tell me all the gruesome details about how everyone's doing. I'm grateful that former students are physically okay, but I'm already starting to worry about the scars this attack will leave on them mentally. Extreme trauma can take its toll even on the uninjured. That problem is for another day, though, as I force the thought out of my mind. The biggest concern in the here and now is for Cisco's well-being.

"Any news on the shooter?"

"He's dead. That's about it. They haven't released a name yet. I guess they are waiting for the morning."

I look at the clock on the wall. A little after eleven p.m. is too late to release much of anything to the media. I shift my gaze over to the television, where they are showing footage of candles and handwritten notes along the sidewalk.

"They're popping up everywhere," she says, following my gaze before looking back at me. "Communities around the country are holding impromptu candlelight vigils for the victims here. Everyone is worried about you."

"How are you holding up, sweetie?" And that's when she loses it.

No man ever wants to see the woman he loves cry. When the tears come with a sense of palpable anguish, it hurts me more than the hole in my left shoulder does. She buries her face in my chest, and I wrap my only working arm around her back, trying to console her.

"I thought I was going to lose you," she cries out between sobs.

"I'm okay, honey. I'm okay…"

The knock on the door prompts her to try to stifle the rest of her tears. She rubs her cheeks in a futile effort to dry them off. I know it's about trying to show them strength, but I don't think she's going to fool anyone.

"That's probably the gang. They all wanted to see you and weren't going to take no for an answer. Come on in, guys," Kylie yells loud enough to be heard on the other side of the door.

On cue, Vanessa, Peyton, Emilee, and Amanda enter the room. When did Amanda get here? We all exchange little hugs, each of them careful not to aggravate my shoulder or get tangled up in the wires and tubes that are snaking all over me.

"You guys are a sight for sore eyes," I say, thrilled that my prized pupils came through relatively unscathed. A commotion from the hallway interrupts our reunion.

"Well, she's already out of her bed, so you might as well let us do what we came here to do," I hear Vince shout.

"She can't be out of her room. She needs rest," another voice I don't recognize hollers back.

"Nobody in this hospital knows what my daughter needs more than I do," the unmistakable voice of Bruce Stanton follows. "So, I suggest ya get the hell out of our way!"

After another moment, Vince comes in pushing a wheelchair, followed by Bruce. Chelsea looks like crap. Her head is wrapped in a bandage, and her eyes are puffy red. Despite her physical appearance, she is radiating that defiance most redheads are known for.

"Look who we sprung free with a little effort," Vince says proudly.

There is no doubt in my mind that he's causing the staff of this hospital heartburn. Vince doesn't like to play by the rules on an average day, and that tendency is heightened when he's under stress.

"Hey, boss," Chelsea whispers. She looks like she wants to get up and try to hug me but thinks better of it.

"Hi. You know you're going to turn that bandage into the next big fashion trend," I say, trying to elicit a smile. I almost succeed when the room fills with a couple of beefy orderlies and some severe-looking nurses.

"Ya look like shit," Bruce says, walking over to the edge of my oversized hospital bed while ignoring the intrusion of the ward's Gestapo. I extend my hand. For once, it was not one of those handshakes that left the blood needing to rush into my lower extremities when it was over.

Bruce Stanton is your typical tough-as-nails former Marine. Hardworking, patriotic, and fiercely protective of his only daughter, he would single-handedly take on an army if he thought the cause was just. When he first heard the lie about my affair with his daughter, it included trying to knock my teeth out in his living room. We only ended up with cuts and bruises, but his lamp and end table were collateral damage in the brawl.

"Thanks, Bruce. That's comforting," I say with a slight laugh. I can always count on an honest appraisal from Bruce Stanton.

"I thought you were Superman, Mister B. Aren't bullets supposed to bounce off you?" Vince asks, sporting the smug grin on his face that makes me want to smack him on the back of the head. Fortunately, Peyton does it for me.

After a few minutes of playful banter, it almost feels like we are all back in the classroom and not huddled around my bed in a D.C. hospital room. Amanda goes on to explain how she heard what happened and then raced back to Washington. She broke every traffic law ever passed on the drive to the hospital after prodding the police at the scene into divulging where we were taken. Emilee explains that Xavier and Brian will be here tomorrow and that they are not taking the news of the attempt on my life well.

Trading notes about what happened is a kind of therapy for me, knowing that nobody in the room will want to dwell on today's events. Kylie hasn't left my side, still holding my hand. We start chatting about what we remember when the head nurse bursts into the room like a Kansas tornado.

"Enough is enough. You folks shouldn't be in here. You can all catch up on things tomorrow, but until then, everyone out. And you, Miss Stanton, need to get back to your room," she barks at Chelsea. "You shouldn't even be out of bed."

Vince and Bruce give her a hard stare, which she eagerly returns. Like most veteran nurses, she has seen it all and dealt with far more challenging patients and family members. To that end, Bruce, who is tough enough to chew on steel rebar like it's a stick of Wrigley's, doesn't challenge her authority. Neither does Vince, who takes every opportunity he gets to do just that.

We say our goodbyes, and everyone starts to pile out under the watchful eye of the orderlies and Nurse Ratched. Kylie looks like she has no intention of leaving.

"You too, Miss Roberts," she demands.

"Five minutes."

"No, now."

"Five minutes. Please," Kylie pleads. I don't know why she caved, but the otherwise unmoved warden acquiesces to the request.

"Okay, five minutes, but not a minute longer."

-FIVE-

KYLIE

"I know that look you have," Michael says to me after Helga the Horrible closes the door.

"The media are reporting that the police think this was a crazed lone gunman..."

"But you don't believe that."

"Do you?" I ask in reply, looking into his eyes. I shudder to think how close I came to never having the chance to do that again.

"I haven't had much time to think about it."

"I have. While I was waiting for someone to tell us whether you would live or die, I had nothing but time to think. I love you with all my heart, Michael. You're the best thing that has ever happened to me. Someone tried to take that away. I need to find out who."

"I'm tired, doped up on...whatever they put in that IV bag, and very sore, so don't take this the wrong way. Could it be possible that the police are right? I mean, I looked into his eyes. All I saw was some crazy who was looking for his fifteen minutes of fame."

"You're right," I agree, getting a nod in return. "You are drugged up."

"Kylie, let's be—"

"I don't believe for a second that's the case. I do believe that whoever planned this wants everyone to believe that."

"Kylie, you're starting to sound a little insane. Please don't make this your white whale."

I'm not about to indulge the love of my life by letting his *Moby Dick* reference get to me, but he is right. I am Ahab right now. Just as the whale took a part of him and launched his journey for revenge, so someone took something from me. Michael may be alive, but the gunman stole something from us today—confidence in our security and well-being. So long as he stays in politics, I will always wonder if someone else is hunting him.

"I won't. I'm not monomaniacal, just driven."

"Kylie, I saw your determination to take down Beaumont firsthand. I'm not sure there's a difference in your case."

"Just what does that mean?"

"It means that when you set your mind to something, you have a hard time letting it go."

"Sound like anyone else you know?"

"Touché."

There's an awkward silence between us for one of the first times ever in our relationship. He knows deep down that I will not relent but doesn't want to fight about it tonight. Not that I can blame him after being shot in the shoulder eight hours ago.

We both look up at the television where the reporter is live somewhere outside the hospital. Reading his mind, I turn up the volume.

"And there is still no word from Michael Bennit or any of his staff on any social media outlet. Sources at G.W. have confirmed that he is out of surgery and resting, and we can only wait until he reaches out to the legion of followers eagerly awaiting word of his condition."

"Do you have your phone with you?" he asks as the reporter throws it back to the studio.

"Yeah," I say, digging it out of my purse. "Do you want Twitter or Facebook?" Yeah, I know him that well.

"Twitter, please."

I bring up the Twitter app and sign in under his account. Not that I ever imagine he would, but God help him if he ever cheated on me. I know every password he uses and would have no problem living up to the whole "hell hath no fury" mantra. I prop the phone up on a pillow in his lap so that he can type using one finger on the hand of his only working arm.

I read the note before I hit send. All it reads is:

Thanks for all your prayers and support. I'm doing okay. Pray for Francisco Reyes and Blake Peoni. #DCshooting

"Short, sweet, and to the point. I like it."

A loud knock at the door precedes one of the orderlies coming in.

"I'm afraid your time is up, ma'am. I gave you an extra minute or two."

"Thanks," I say, turning back to Michael. "I'll see you tomorrow. Try to get some rest."

"I don't think that's going to be a problem," he says before I lean over and give him a kiss.

We say our goodnights, and I leave the room. I instantly feel alone again. I don't like the nights we are forced to spend apart, but it's far worse in this situation. I feel vulnerable, and that's a feeling I am neither used to nor enjoy. When we get through this, it'll be a long time before I let Michael ever spend a night away from me.

I know it's going to be a long night. Sleep is not going to come quickly for me. I'm exhausted, but my mind continues to race about the events of the day. I feel like I've lived a lifetime in the last sixteen hours. So much has happened, yet so much still needs to be done.

I'm going to spend some time with my love tomorrow and then start to get some answers. Michael may not be interested in the truth, but I became a journalist because of my compulsive need to uncover it. The difference this time, just as it was with Winston Beaumont, is it's personal. He was right— I am going to go hunting for my white whale. Tomorrow, my quest begins. When the line pops into my head, I can't stop myself from murmuring it.

"Call me Ishmael."

-SIX-

JAMES

K Street is both a physical location and a derisive term used to describe my chosen profession. Located a stone's throw away from the White House and Capitol Building, the thoroughfare used to be home to the preeminent think tanks, lobby groups, and advocacy organizations in the country. Many of them fled for greener, less costly pastures in the 1980s, leaving only two large lobby firms still located on the block. Mine is one of them.

Lobbying has earned the scorn of many Americans who unfairly pin the ineptitude of government on us. They think we buy votes when the opposite is true—sending generous donations to politicians never guarantees they will vote as we wish on an issue. In fact, some of the senior legislators in town pride themselves on spurning us every opportunity they get.

Regardless, many pundits use "K Street" as a derogatory metonym for the industry. The pejorative doesn't matter to me. I wear both my occupation and the physical location of my office as a badge of honor.

My office is located on the top floor of a modern twelve-story building that offers a majestic view of Franklin Square. Technically it's a high-rise building, although there really is no such thing in Washington by my standards. Manhattan is the home of the skyscraper, and because of the Height of Buildings Act, there's a cap on how far skyward a developer can reach in the nation's capital. The twelfth floor is the top of the world in Washington.

I am a kingmaker in this town—the money I provide challengers and incumbents often dictates whether they are called to serve the people here or not. All of them eagerly accept my generosity. All of them welcome my input once they are elected—all of them except one.

Michael Bennit has been a thorn in my side since the moment he stepped off the plane in Washington. He went from being ostracized to the champion of a political movement. Because of him, the House of Representatives is flooded with independents beholden to no party or lobbyist. In doing so, he has become one of the loudest voices in a city where everybody talks.

The shooting yesterday afternoon will only make his voice stronger and louder, but it also creates an opportunity for me. While he's recovering from his wounds and concerned about his colleagues and staff, he won't be paying attention to me. I have a small window of opportunity to act and need to make the most of it. All that's required to gain the control I so desperately want in Congress is finding the right person to manipulate.

"Sir, your eight o'clock interview is here," my secretary announces over the intercom. These archaic systems have fallen out of use in both the business and public sectors, but I still like mine. Call me old-fashioned.

"Please send him in, Marcy," I order after punching the button.

I rise and put on my suit jacket, taking time to button and smooth it as I file my previous thoughts in the back of my mind. I'll return to planning later, but right now, I need to deal with this distraction. A moment later, my "interviewee" enters the spacious office, my secretary closing the door behind him.

"Nice digs," he says, admiring the artwork, cherry furniture, and expensive décor. "You aren't much for decorating for Christmas, are you?"

"My staff has better things to do," I respond, believing that holiday cheer for the office should be reserved for the annual party and not during work hours.

"Should I be insulted that I'm nothing more than an interview? I thought we had an arrangement."

"We do have an arrangement. Have a seat."

He accepts the chair, and after declining my offer of coffee, I sit across my huge desk from him. The man before me is barely competent, despite the swagger he exhibits. He's a cheap suit, and by his attire, I mean that both figuratively and literally.

"Then why lie about the reason I'm really here?"

"Our relationship has been cloaked with a shroud of secrecy from the outset," I explain, annoyed that I need to. "To meet with you here in the office without a cover story may raise eyebrows in light of yesterday's events. However, it is common for former congressional staffers, and especially former chiefs of staff, to look for employment with lobby firms."

"Okay," he says, placated by my explanation. "I'll get to the point. I've fulfilled my end of our arrangement. Now I'm here for you to fulfill yours."

I figured that's what he's here for. Buying him was easier than I had anticipated. In a town full of egos, most congressional staffers like to inflate their worth. Gary Condrey was no different; only his worth could be purchased at a dollar store.

My arrangement with him was a simple one. He was tired of working for a useless congressman doomed to be defeated in the November election and decided to work with Marilyn Viano in her quest to help Michael Bennit. She was a longtime friend of mine, so I knew I could not trust her motives to stay aligned with mine if another opportunity presented itself.

As an insurance policy, I recruited him to report back on what Marilyn was up to. The only price for his allegiance was a measly financial stipend and the promise of a job if things went south.

"That's a bold statement coming from a man seeking employment with the firm I run," I say, intending to put him on the defensive. "What makes you think you fulfilled your obligation?"

"Marilyn Viano is dead, and unless she's Robin, the Human Torch, or Captain America, she's not getting resurrected. With her gone, there's no more information to report back to you with. I have no relationship with Bennit, and even if I did, he'd be very guarded about who gets invited into his inner circle after someone tried to kill him yesterday."

"I don't expect you to get close to Bennit," I say, knowing full well that even if I did, it would be a fool's errand. While I don't consider the iCongressman an intellectual giant, he's a behemoth compared to Gary. "And you don't seem too upset that Marilyn was shot and killed. I thought you two were close."

"She was a boss who treated me like a common employee. Despite her posturing, Viano would have been nothing in her term as a senator without me. She never realized that."

Is this guy for real? I made Marilyn Viano, and Viano made him, not the other way around.

There is a shocking amount of disloyalty in this world. It's on display in Washington every day. One of the reasons I don't lose sleep over my job is because I recognize that politicians aren't loyal to their countrymen, constituents, or even their party. They're devoted to money.

If corrupt politicians are cast into Dante's Eighth Circle of Hell, then a man like Gary Condrey resides in the Ninth Circle for his treachery. He betrayed Marilyn for a pittance and the promise of employment, with no assurance I would uphold my end of our bargain. He stabbed his former boss in the back by working with Viano and against him in the last election. Rumor has it that he's even betrayed his wife with some local low-rent hookers.

Given his track record, why would I believe he would ever remain loyal to me? I was sincere with my offer of a job when I made it, but I have since rethought that proposition. I needed information at the time, so using Condrey made perfect sense. Now I wonder if the promise was worth the benefits. Keeping him around could open me up for a similar betrayal.

"I'm not prepared to offer you a job at Ibram & Reed at this time, Gary," I say, folding my hands as if in thought. "I am willing to financially compensate you for your services, but employm—"

"That was not our deal. I don't want handouts, James."

"I'm changing our deal," I state in a manner that implies it is not up for discussion.

"You can't do that!" Gary bellows. I guess he didn't correctly infer the statement.

"I can, and just did."

"You son of a bitch," he spits. "You used me just like you used Viano. Is that why you had her killed? She was no longer of use to you, so you changed the deal with her, too?"

"I beg your pardon?" I say, anger rising in my voice despite my attempt to control it.

"You heard me. The shooting on the steps of the House was no more a random act than my chances of buying a cape and flying out of here."

There would be a chance if I threw him out the window, though I suppose that would be considered falling, not flying. I don't respond well to threats and accusations against me, especially from a washed-up, third-rate political hack.

I'm about to lash out at him when it dawns on me he may be bugged. He could be recording this conversation to use my own words against me. Would he dare try to blackmail me? This is Washington, so anything is possible. The Ninth Circle of Hell is precisely where he belongs.

"I'm not in a position to know what the motivations of the shooter were, *Mister Condrey*. I leave the speculation for the police. I am in the influence business, not an investigative one. What I do know is this *interview* is over." I punch the button on my intercom. "Marcy, please come in."

A moment later, the heavy oak doors to my office swing open, and my secretary waits for Gary to get his pudgy ass out of the chair.

"This isn't over, Reed. I won't forget about this. I'll make you regret making an enemy out of me." Hollow threats make me smile, but I suppress this one.

"Can you please show Mister Condrey out?" I ask my secretary, ignoring Gary's parting shot. There is nothing to be gained by responding to it.

"Of course, sir. Mister Condrey," she says, gesturing toward the door. Gary gives me a stern look and obliges, saying nothing as he exits.

"Thank you, Marcy," I say as she swings the doors closed behind her.

I stand up and look out the window at the park below. Gary Condrey. He's pond scum. I think back to our conversation, trying to recall if I said anything that could be interpreted as incriminating. There was nothing illegal about hiring Condrey to spy on Viano for me. If he was recording me, he has nothing of use. Regardless, I need to begin planning for the possibility that this will not be the last time I hear from him.

-SEVEN-

MICHAEL

Once they start to hurt, gunshot wounds really *hurt*. Never let anyone tell you that the 9mm is an ineffective weapon. The heavy dose of morphine dulled the pain nicely yesterday, but I don't like that stuff. I tried not to use it after I got wounded overseas either.

The simple through and through gunshot wound is in the upper part of my pectoral muscle, inches below my shoulder. The bullet the gunman used was a hollow point and tore my soft tissue up, but had the courtesy of missing any bone, arteries, and critical organs. I suppose that provides some solace, at least.

Of course, there is more going on in that part of the body than just bone and muscle. Blood vessels and the most concentrated collection of peripheral nerves below the neck make their way through that area, explaining why I went so numb. This deep penetration wound will earn me a surgery or two, months of immobilization, tons of physical therapy, and some permanent impairment. It could have been much worse.

I'm happy to be alive because I know how close I was to death. I never would have reached the gunman in time. A few seconds was all that stood between me and the afterlife until the Capitol police intervened.

It's not the first time I've had a brush with death. I know the road to recovery from gunshot wounds well because I've traveled it before. It wasn't much fun then either. But that was combat in Afghanistan — a third-world country where people toting AK-47 assault rifles was as common a sight as commuters armed with cups of coffee are in the U.S.

"Michael?" I focus back on Kylie and then notice that everyone in the room is looking at me. "Did you hear that?"

"Uh, no, sorry, I was lost in my thoughts."

I look up at the television where one of the morning shows is playing footage of a small but growing protest that sprung up. People are angry at the whole incident and are now beginning to vent it. It's one thing for Americans to post their frustrations in a Facebook status and something entirely different when they rally in the streets.

Kylie wasn't injured in the attack, but she's bearing the same emotional scars as the rest of us. She wants answers to what happened, but, most of all, she wants justice. Just like the people in the streets, she isn't buying the lone gunman story either.

Conspiracy theories grew out of the JFK assassination for a couple of reasons. Eyewitness reports vary, as they often do. Details were slow in being released to the public because they usually are. When the facts don't add up, purveyors of myths fill in the holes and provide the most sinister face they can to the events. It is hard for people to accept that one man planned and perpetrated such a heinous act of such evil on his own. As a result, others had to be involved, or so many theorized. In many cases, the government, namely the CIA, is the favorite target of opportunity.

I know I'm not going to be able to convince her yesterday's attempt on me was nothing more than the desperate act of a deranged individual. She believes it was much more, thanks to the notion Terry Nyguen planted in her head last November. That idea is growing in her mind like a virus. There is nothing anyone is going to say to stop that.

"Did you hear the news?" Vince queries as he and Vanessa rush in with steaming cups of coffee in their hands.

For a fleeting moment, I thought he was referring to either Blake or Cisco. Both of their conditions are weighing heavily on my mind. Cisco lost a lot of blood, but he's stable. Blake is another story. The bullets that tore through his back did a lot of damage, and he'll require multiple surgeries. We're all concerned about how well he'll come through this.

"That they released the shooter's name?" Kylie replies, accepting one of the cups. "Yeah, it's on every station."

"Jerold Todd Bernard," I mumble, echoing the name of the man who came close to planting me in a flag-draped coffin. "You guys ever wonder why assassins almost always have three names?"

"What do you mean?" Vanessa asks, handing me the other cup of steaming java. It's not great, but I'm going through major caffeine withdrawal. I'm sure my personal pack of overwrought nurses would protest if they knew, but what the hospital staff doesn't know won't hurt me.

"Seriously, Vanessa? You just invited him to give us another history lesson," Vince scolds.

"Lee Harvey Oswald, John Wilkes Booth, James Earl Ray, Mark David Chapman… They all have three names."

"Plenty don't, honey, including John Hinckley," Kylie corrects, trying to stuff the genie back into the bottle.

"Not to cut you off before you really get rolling, Congressman, but we have more news. Congressman Reyes is responsive," Vince says, effectively ending what would have been a great lesson on assassination attempts.

"Cisco's awake? How's he doing?"

"He's not faring too bad for someone who got hit in his femoral artery and almost bled out."

"I need to see him," I state, leaving little room for discussion.

"He's still in the ICU," Vanessa answers. "They may be moving him later, but they say we should be able to get in there this afternoon if he's up to it. The doctor says he's pretty out of it right now. He doesn't have your experience with morphine."

I hope she's implying the treatment of my previous war wounds and not that I'm a heroin addict.

"No, we are not sneaking you out of your room," Kylie states emphatically as if reading my mind. "It can wait."

"It wouldn't do you much good anyway, Mister B. After what Chelsea pulled last night, they're watching all your rooms like hawks," Vince laments.

"This is getting ugly," Vanessa comments after turning her attention back to the television. "I think the people need to hear from you, Congressman."

She's right. I need to address the public, but I don't want to do it through social media. They need to hear my voice and see me, not just read what I write on Facebook and Twitter. Unfortunately, I don't think I'm being left an option.

"I think he needs to heal up before doing any of that," Kylie warns.

That is a little uncharacteristic for her. As a journalist, she knows exactly what the people want and usually advises us to give it to them.

"Kylie, I have to do this."

"No, Michael, you were shot and have to rest. This is not up for discussion, debate, or compromise. And that means all of you," she finishes, warning my former students and current staff in the room. She knows I could convince them to sponsor a jailbreak and is reminding them that her wrath is the consequence of them doing so.

"I can rest when I'm dead," I say, probing to see just how serious she is.

"You almost were," she deadpans, "and absolutely will be if you so much as set one foot out of that bed. You'll have plenty of time to address your legion of fans, but right now, you are going to take care of yourself. The world can wait another day or two to hear from Michael Bennit."

-EIGHT-
CHELSEA ·

I fled to the quiet confines of Blake's room in the ICU, only a short distance from where Congressman Reyes is recovering from his injuries. After checking in with the receptionist and washing my hands, I take up my post at Blake's bedside.

"Hey, Blake, how are you feeling?" I ask, gently rubbing my hand against his cheek.

I know he isn't going to respond, but I have read studies claiming coma patients reported after waking that they heard and understood conversations that took place while they were unconscious. I want him…no, I need him to know I'm here.

I give him the good news about Cisco and Mister Bennit's recovery. I've already told him about his aunt. I wonder how he'll respond to that when he wakes up.

"Knock, knock," I hear the voice behind me say.

I turn to see Amanda waiting in the doorway.

"Hey," I say, taking Blake's hand and kissing it a few times.

"We've been looking for you. The nurses would only let one of us in, and even that took some explaining."

"Yeah, they only let two people into the ICU at a time, and it's usually restricted to family. I almost had to fight my way in to see him the first time."

"Your redheaded temper pays dividends, I see," she says, coming up beside me.

"Why were you looking for me? Is everything all right?"

I know my concern that something may have happened to Mister Bennit or Congressman Reyes is irrational. If it was something serious, there would be a lot more urgency in her voice. Not that I am thinking straight these days. I'll blame it on the concussion, but I know it's much more than that.

"Yeah, everyone's fine. You left Mister Bennit's room a while ago. We got concerned about you when you didn't come back."

"Sorry about that," I say, sincere in my apology. "I never meant for anyone to get worried. When Kylie flipped the news on, I was afraid the conversation would turn to the politics of the shooting. I don't want to deal with that right now."

"You're going to have to deal with it eventually. You're the chief of staff. The congressman is going to need you."

"Actually, I resigned as his chief of staff not long after the election."

"What?" she asks in unadulterated surprise. I forgot that I hadn't told anyone yet—damn concussion.

"I resigned. I'm set to start at Harvard at the end of next month."

"Do…does anyone…?" She can't even finish the question, so I answer it for her.

"No. The only people who know are the congressman, my father, probably Kylie, and anyone who works in the Harvard Admissions Office. I was going to tell Vince and Vanessa after the vote until…" Until we got shot, was what I was going to say, without being able to bring myself to utter it.

"Chels, why would you resign?"

"For the same reasons that you left the day of the vote."

I can see from the look on Amanda's face that my words cut deep. I know she's been harboring tremendous guilt about not being on the steps with us yesterday. I didn't mean it like that, but it's too late as her eyes fill with tears.

"I'm sorry I left you guys," she cries. I let go of Blake's hand and get up to hug her.

"I didn't mean it like that, Amanda, I promise. We don't blame you for not being there. We all understand, me most of all."

Her sobs begin to subside after a few moments. After everything I have been dealing with over the past eighteen hours, the last thing I want is to add to Amanda's feelings of guilt. She may not have been there, but I understand the reasons why she left all too well.

"What did you mean when you said it was because of the same reasons I left?" Amanda is letting me off the hook as we break our embrace.

"It's hard to explain," I deflect, taking my seat next to Blake's bed. I don't really want to talk about this right now. Unfortunately, it doesn't look like she will let this one slide.

"Please tell me," Amanda replies, pulling up the other chair.

I think about it for a moment, really wanting to direct my attention to Blake. In the end, I suppose this talk with Amanda is long overdue. I should have had it before she left. Of course, then she would have ended up in harm's way, just like the rest of us.

"Congress...well, the government, in general, is a huge embarrassment. We've lost the capacity to make the simplest decisions, let alone the most essential ones. I watched for a year while the congressman tried to get *something* accomplished. *Anything* accomplished. There wasn't a single man or woman elected to the House interested in talking to him. All they wanted to do was force him out of office. I got frustrated, and when you factor in all the lies and games they play, I'd had enough."

"Don't you think that you may see some progress with the icongressmen joining you in the next congress?" Amanda asks after digesting what I told her.

"Maybe," I say without any genuine enthusiasm. "But we still have nothing approaching a majority. I don't think that we'll see any traction on things that are important to Americans. Look at the list of issues that never get resolved.

"We have bloated and inefficient bureaucracies making it impossible for average Americans to do anything without a massive hassle. We have an incomprehensible climate policy, no agreement on immigration, stagnant economic growth, and food that is too expensive and downright unsafe. Our financial system has already sunk the economy and easily could again.

"The list goes on, and those are just items where there is at least some consensus. It's daunting to think about the number of things in this country that are broken."

"But that's why the people elected Mister B in the first place, Chels. He's the best hope for helping to fix that mess, and he's going to need your help to do it. You guys finally have the power to make a real difference in people's lives."

I understand what Amanda is saying, but I don't care right this instant. It's amazing how getting shot at changes your perspective. Even more so when some of the people you care about most are lying in hospital beds because someone tried to kill them. It sends a shiver down my spine.

Congressman Bennit rarely talks about the time he was in Afghanistan. One time, a few months after I got to D.C., he did confide in me that all he cared about in combat was the person next to him. The political reasons he was there no longer had any meaning. It was all about survival—for him and the men he served with. He lost his best friend to enemy fire and still can't explain why he died and what it was for.

"Amanda, for the last two years, I've listened to everyone here talk about power like it has any real meaning. Typical politicians are sociopaths obsessed with it. They're lying if they say otherwise. None of them fulfill their promises to the people, and God himself cannot pry them from the marble halls of the Capitol once they get into office.

"You know what has meaning to me? People do. The people closest to me; you guys, Mister Bennit, Kylie, Blake…"

Here come the tears again. I feel like I've been crying nonstop forever now. I'm tired of feeling this way.

"And that's precisely why we need you here," she says, as I engage in the typical struggle with my emotions, "because you still care in a world where few others do. Mister Bennit doesn't have the luxury of quitting. He's feeling guilty for putting you all in a situation where you could've been killed."

"It wasn't his fault."

"It doesn't matter. He still feels responsible, just as I feel responsible for walking out on you guys and not being there on those steps with you. Hell, I still feel guilty going off to college while you were all down here trying to make this work."

"I thought you were having fun in college?" I ask, confused at her statement.

"I am, but remember back in high school when we all sat around the table in the cafeteria after the election? We felt out of place because we had grown so much running the campaign. It's no different in college. All my friends want to do is go party every night. I want to stay in, fire up my laptop, and find a way to help you guys. I miss being a part of something bigger than going to just classes and hanging out in the dorm."

"Is this your way of talking me out of leaving?"

"No. I've learned firsthand what overwhelming guilt feels like. I don't want you to have the same experience I've had when you go to school while everyone is down here, still struggling to make a difference. You'll miss it far more than you know."

With that, Amanda gets up and returns her chair to the corner of the room. She has given me a lot to think about, although I really can't think straight about anything right now. I really wish Blake was awake so that I could talk to him about it. As infuriating as I find him sometimes, he knows me better than I know myself.

"I'll go out and tell the others you're okay."

"Thanks, Amanda."

I wish I was okay because I feel anything but.

-NINE-
KYLIE

Like most men, Michael is insufferable when he's sick. I have found that if you take that and multiply it by a factor of a thousand, you get how unbearable he is when he's wounded. I feel so sorry for the staff at Walter Reed when he got back from Afghanistan.

It's been a little over twenty-four hours since the shooting, and he's already going nuts being cooped up here. The morphine drip may be helping him manage the pain in his shoulder, but it does nothing for the irritability that comes with the lack of freedom from being hospitalized. When he's not terrorizing the staff or pining for caffeine, he's spending time communicating with his followers on social media. Long live the iCongressman.

America is going crazy over this. A veteran of countless media frenzies, I'm used to circus environments that accompany traumatic events like the tragic shooting at Sandy Hook elementary. Despite that track record, I have never seen the public react the way they have to this. People aren't mourning anymore. They're not even angry – they are livid.

The vigils that popped up around the country in the wake of the shooting are morphing into something else. Once the people realized Michael would survive the attack, they channeled their frustration at the other politicians they feel are responsible for attempting to silence him. Right or wrong, the country's general mood is a dark one, and the news channels are not being bashful about feeding that ire to boost ratings.

CNN was reporting from Seattle. MSNBC was getting an update from the field in Manhattan's Central Park. The reporter from FOX News is in the middle of an interview with an angry citizen at a demonstration in Texas when Michael seizes the remote and clicks it off.

"You know, your enemies will feel even more threatened by you with these protests happening all around the country. They're going to come after you and come hard."

Michael just looks at me for a moment before lowering his eyes. I think he agrees with me, but it doesn't look like that's what is weighing heaviest on his mind. It could be his concern for Blake or Cisco, or maybe something else. Whatever it is, he's taking his time sharing it with me, and I'm getting annoyed.

"How has it come to this?" he mutters after what feels like an eternity. "If I had only known…"

"Are you doubting yourself, Michael? Are you wondering if this is really worth it again?" I ask, trying to determine if he is experiencing the same emotions he did during his first race. This reminds me of the conversation we had at the Perkfect Buzz coffee shop when Winston Beaumont went on the offensive and launched a smear campaign that targeted Michael's students.

"No, not this time. My students are adults now, and as much as I don't want them in harm's way, they just learned a valuable lesson that many Americans who live in their comfortable lives forget: sometimes bad things happen to good people. It's random and sad, but it's also a part of life."

I'm a little surprised by his answer. It may be logical, but I don't want him to be rational right now. I want him to be emotional, and by that, I mean angry. I need him to be as mad as I am.

"So, you're just willing to let it go?" I ask, letting the tone of my voice seep with disbelief.

"I have a job to do, Kylie, and so do the police. I am going to do mine and let them do theirs."

"But they won't do their job, and you know it. Police are already calling this a random shooting, and we both know that's not true! What happens when they bury this investigation, and whoever is responsible tries to kill you again and succeeds? What happens if Chelsea, Vince, Vanessa, or one of your other students gets shot or killed? Will you be able to live with yourself?"

Once again, there's a long, awkward silence between us. Michael stares at me blankly, expressing no emotion. I have enough for both of us, but I want a reaction from him. For such a passionate guy, he picked a lousy time to lose his balls. Where is the former Green Beret I fell in love with?

"You're not going to say anything?" I probe, starting to sound like a mother reprimanding her teenage son after catching him raiding the liquor cabinet.

"I have nothing to say, really."

"You're not scared someone will try this again?"

"No, Kylie, because I can't control it," he says, violently shifting in the bed to try to get comfortable. "I refuse to live in fear. I can't comprehend why people don't fly because they are afraid of crashing or... Look, when my number is up, it's up. I will live every day to the fullest until that happens, whether it's tomorrow, next week, or when I turn ninety-eight."

I roll my eyes at his response. How do I get him to understand? I'm about to unleash another tongue lashing when a knock at the door beats me to the punch.

"Ho, ho, ho, Merry Christmas! I hope I'm not interrupting anything," Bruce Stanton comments, entering the room wearing a red Santa hat and toting a large sack with "U.S. Mail" stenciled on it.

"No, come on in, Bruce," Michael says from the bed with the eagerness he displays when he wants out of a conversation.

"Yes, please, come in so he can explain to you why he doesn't want to find the person who was responsible for your daughter getting knocked unconscious on the steps of the Capitol yesterday." Okay, that was hitting below the belt, but I don't care.

"What? Did I miss something on the news?"

"No, you didn't, Bruce. We're just indulging Kylie and her paranoid fantasies. And I don't mean running into the Ghosts of Christmas Past, Present, and Future."

Michael goes on to provide a quick, albeit one-sided, rehashing of our argument. Bruce listens intently to him and then to me as I plead my own case. It takes Chelsea's father a couple of moments to respond.

"I'm sorry, Kylie, but I'm siding with the congressman on this one."

"What? Why?" I sputter, sure I had connected with him during my impassioned argument. He has an unyielding fatherly instinct, so I'm shocked that finding who may actually be responsible for Chelsea's injury is not the first item on his to-do list.

"Don't get me wrong, I want to get to the bottom of this shooting, too. I stand with the millions of Americans who think there's no way this Bernard guy did this on his own. I need my congressman to lead, though, not run around like Mark Harmon on *NCIS*."

"I'm not saying—"

"Let me show ya something, Kylie." He opens the sack of mail and pulls out an open letter. "The FBI and Capitol Police are temporarily opening your mail, at least the non-official stuff. They want to see if any other threats are coming in. Anyway, read this."

"I'm guessing this wasn't addressed to the North Pole," I remark sarcastically.

"No, but they're all asking for something for Christmas."

He hands me the envelope, and I pull the letter out and read it. It's from an older woman named Elaine who lives in Cedar Falls, Iowa, and says how much she admires Michael and how she hopes he recovers soon so he can bring positive change to Washington. I look up when I'm done reading the short but sweet note.

"I'm pretty sure this sack, and the half dozen just like it they're going through, all say the same things," Bruce says with a grin before handing me another letter.

"She thinks you should be the Speaker of the House," I state after reading it, handing the second note to Michael, who scans it quickly.

"She's not the only one," Bruce claims. "I heard it mentioned on CNN when I was downstairs. The American people are counting on you to lead now. It's not enough that you're a good representative anymore. Everyone has lost faith in this country. They all want someone they can trust to step up and restore that faith. That is what these protest rallies are all about."

"They want me to run for Speaker of the House? I don't think so. I don't know the first thing about that job."

"You can do anything you put your mind to, Michael," I argue. He can, and sometimes I find that infuriating.

"I thought you wanted me to help you catch Professor Moriarty," he retorts, evoking the persona of Sherlock Holmes's old antagonist.

"I do, but since you've already made up your mind that you're not going to help me—"

"I don't want you involved either," he commands. "I want you to let it go and let the authorities do their jobs."

I bristle at the comment. I loathe being told what to do. It's the big reason I got fired from the *New York Times* and am in hot water with my current employer.

The *Washington Post* hired me not long after Michael won the special election that followed Beaumont's indictment and subsequent resignation, and the editors at the paper have done everything they can since to keep me on a short leash. Because of my temperament and the lies perpetrated by my former editorial staff in New York, my current boss considers me a powder keg that flames should be kept away from. The result is, I get a paycheck, they get good investigative reporting, and we both clash over my independence and what my role at the paper should be.

"What do you think, Bruce?" I ask, not wanting to react to my boyfriend's mulishness in front of Chelsea's dad.

"I voted for ya, Michael," he says, instantly informing me I'm not going to like the next words that come out of his mouth. "I would be angry if ya don't see this thing through. If that means ya find a way to become the next Speaker of the House, then damn it, that's what I want ya to do."

-TEN-

JAMES

I hate traveling during the holidays, but a lobbyist's work is never done. While the time between the adjournment of one Congress and the start of another is typically considered downtime during most years, this isn't one of them. With a slew of independents set to start work in just over a week, plans need to be made.

The only two members of the House still in Washington, D.C., are Bennit and Reyes. The only reason they're still here after Congress adjourned is that they're hospitalized, and their doctors won't release them. Thus, meeting any other member of Congress requires a trip to their district. That's what brings me to Columbus, Ohio, three days before Christmas.

Congressman Stepanik is too conservative to ever win the metropolitan area of the state capital. However, more than enough Republicans in one of its affluent suburbs guarantees it as a safe district. Harvey moved his family there when he decided to enter national politics and won the seat with ease. He has risen quickly through the ranks of the GOP ever since. He may have gotten a scare in the recent massacre Bennit led against the extreme incumbents in both parties, but the former House majority leader lived to fight another day.

For this meeting, he picked a nice steakhouse not far outside the Columbus city limits. The restaurant is tastefully decorated for the holidays with lights, a tree, and a menorah. That's fortunate because I hate it when places are decked out with enough discount rack holiday trinkets that it looks like Christmas threw up.

We made small talk over our before-dinner drinks, the conversation eventually turning to the shooting. We traded notes on the rumors going around, Bennit's and Reyes' condition, the public reaction, and Viano's death. It was only then that the question everyone is asking inevitably escapes the lips of the former majority leader.

"Do you think someone planned the assassination attempt on Bennit?" he asks, studying my face for a reaction. I purse my lips and look up in mock thought.

"No, because I can think of a dozen easier ways to do it. If someone wanted Bennit dead, they all could have done it anywhere. Walking up to him with a gun on Capitol Hill? It's too risky, especially with security everywhere in a public place like that."

"I guess," he agrees, wanting to end the discussion. "The larger question is where we go from here? I assume that's why you wanted to meet with me." How astute.

"The election of the Speaker is going to be a national embarrassment. It will be ugly and tough to watch on television, let alone from the front row. It will be like watching…what was the name of that reality TV show?"

"Which one, James? There are a few dozen on now."

"The one in New Jersey with that girl, Snooty, or whatever her name was?" By his laugh, I can tell I'm not even close. I should have avoided trying to make a pop culture reference.

"Snooki is her name. The show was *Jersey Shore*."

"That's it, thank you. Anyway, these reality shows will have far less drama than the circus coming to the House unless someone puts a plan in place ahead of time."

The first order of business in a new term of the House of Representatives is to elect its Speaker. Since 1839, the election has been by roll call instead of a ballot, but that is a mere formality. The party caucuses have traditionally predetermined the result by meeting and selecting the candidates to be voted upon. The successful candidate must obtain the majority of votes cast by the full body, and in a two-party system, that means the party with the most seats always wins. Once you introduce a few dozen independents into the mix, however, all bets are off.

"And you're that someone?" Harvey inquires, a little too glib for my taste. I don't think I'll bother responding to his question. He can answer one of mine instead.

"Who is the GOP planning to nominate? I know it won't be Albright."

Stepanik's derisive snort informs me I'm right on the money. In a way, it's too bad. I have rented a lot of politicians over the years, but I owned Johnston Albright.

He was easy to manipulate, given the tenuous hold he had on his position. His nomination was an act of desperation by his party, and he spent much of his time trying to solidify support for his leadership. That desperation was easy to turn to my favor, and by the end of this latest Congress, he was my lap dog.

He's now more radioactive than Nancy Pelosi was for the Democrats. The members of his party view him as a liability now and would never support his return to the rostrum. Losing his position isn't the worst of his problems if the rumors are true. Scuttlebutt has it that he's getting pressured to resign his seat "for health reasons" at some point during this term.

"I don't know. It's a crapshoot. I suppose I'm a leading contender, but there will be a lot of support for guys like Thomas Parker and a few others who have been around for a while."

Thomas Parker. Curse that man. One of the most conservative Republicans in Congress, anyone would think he'd be the typical GOP cheerleader. Unfortunately, when Bennit was a single vote away from packing his suitcase, Parker's Christian conscience got the best of him. He changed his vote, and Bennit survived. Parker went on to score a blowout victory in his race that November as a result.

"There doesn't have to be this much uncertainty. Y'all don't have to wait for your colleagues to choose."

"What do you mean?"

He's playing dumb. Harvey Stepanik is politically astute enough to understand where I'm going with this. He torpedoed Albright to put himself in a position to become Speaker, and I'm willing to bet my ridiculous salary that he was close to making that dream a reality.

The attempt on Bennit might be screwing that plan up. Many moderates are willing to cast a sympathy vote to make that upstart third in line for the presidency. The far-right members will be looking for an appealing candidate to keep them from breaking ranks for Bennit. Harvey Stepanik is not that guy and won't get the Republican nomination without help. I wonder if he knows that.

"I can ensure you get nominated for Speaker. I may be able to even secure your victory."

"Oh, I doubt that," he says, taking a sip of the expensive scotch.

"Don't," I respond, putting my lips to the tumbler and having a drink of my own. After a satisfying draw, I set it back down on the table, fold my hands, and continue. "The icongressmen are new and impressionable. My sources tell me that your efforts at swaying a couple of them over to you have failed spectacularly."

"You're well informed. We have managed to convince a couple, but not enough to make a difference. We can also assume the Democrats have done the same. There may or may not be a tie heading into the session. Regardless, choosing the next Speaker is going to be a nightmare for both parties."

"You don't think you can sway any more of them?" I probe.

"Bennit is the new golden boy. It will be hard to keep the ones we have enticed, let alone convince others to join us. Even members of my own party aren't sure who to vote for." There's the answer to my question. He knows his plan is foiled, so it's time to go in for the kill.

"Don't underestimate my influence with the incumbent members who are left—on both sides of the aisle. I can get you the nomination for sure. We'll see about the rest."

Influencing modern politicians is about as simple as breathing. They have agendas to advance, want to win elections, accumulate power, and best of all, they need money to do any of that. To be a successful lobbyist in Washington today, you only need a big stick and some carrots. I have the biggest stick in town and a truckload of carrots to get what I want.

"I don't see how you think you can pull that off."

"Trust me, I can."

"Enlighten me. You have no sway with the icongressmen, so I know you aren't going that route." I would have if Viano hadn't completely screwed it up. "Tell me the plan, or I don't see how there is anything further for us to discuss."

I had every intention of telling him anyway, but I make it look like I am apprehensive. When I reluctantly disclose my idea to him, it will appear like

I caved and that he won the round. Giving a shark like Stepanik the perception of winning is the easiest way for me to get what I want.

"Harvey, the first couple of ballots will be meaningless. The House will be deadlocked, and people will start going out of their minds trying to make deals. Who do you think the Democrats would rather see running things? The choices will be a cooperative Republican from Ohio who knows the rules of the game and a maverick independent from Connecticut who can't spend a year in office without getting censured twice."

I suppress a smile. Both of Bennit's censures came from the pressure I put on Albright. The way he is looking at me, I'm willing to bet Stepanik had a hand in helping that along too.

I'm going to take Michael Bennit down, with or without Stepanik's help. I've concluded that his election to Speaker is the easiest way to make that happen, but it's not the only way. If Stepanik declines, I will move straight to plan B, C, or any other letter it takes to destroy Bennit. He won't, though, despite his histrionic performance of appearing to ponder my offer.

"What do you want in return?" is all he asks.

I smile and inhale deeply. Yup, it's exactly like breathing.

-ELEVEN-
MICHAEL

It is two days before Christmas, so, understandably, everyone needs to go off in separate directions. Xavier got a leave of absence from the Syracuse men's basketball squad to visit, but they have a tournament during Christmas that he needs to meet them at.

Peyton is going home to visit her parents before returning to school during the break to get ready for a fashion exposition she's helping to work on. Amanda, Brian, and Emilee can stay until tomorrow, but they have parents demanding to see them as well. Chelsea will be discharged from the hospital today and might be sticking around since her father is already visiting Washington. A blue-collar machine, this may be the first time he's ever missed consecutive days of work.

Vince and Vanessa were going to return to Millfield, but they feel obliged to carry the water for the rest of us since they weren't injured. As for me, I have no place to be except wherever Kylie is. All I know is I cannot bear being cooped up in this hospital for another day.

Christmas is a wonderful time, and I love the holidays because of it. The weather is typically cold, at least in my neck of the woods, but not frigid like you see in February. The pace of the country slows as most Americans can finally exhale and relax after another long year. It's a time meant to be spent with those closest to you. I'm grateful those closest to me are here, although I wish it was under different circumstances.

Visiting hours start at nine a.m., and there was a knock on my door one minute later, followed by the entire gang piling in. We spend the next hour or so chatting. Brian, Emilee, and a couple of others took to checking in on my social media sites. I look like hell, but they insisted I post a pic to

Instagram and Facebook. My tirade about how horrible I look caused a fit of laughter amongst the group, interrupted only by another rap on the door.

"I hope I'm not interrupting anything," the deep bass voice of Thomas Parker says. He's holding a large vase of flowers. The arrangement had to have set him back a few bills.

"I'm sorry, Thomas, that's very sweet of you, but I'm taken," I say, giving a wink to Kylie. "And I'm straight."

Okay, that wasn't the most appropriate thing to say to an ordained minister.

"Ha, ha. I'm glad you are feeling better," the congressman says, entering the room and places the flowers on a table.

He walks over to the bed, and I extend my hand. He gives me a firm yet gentle handshake that most veteran politicians have managed to master, while his eyes give me a once-over.

"I thought you Green Berets were tougher than this," he says, looking at me and my morphine drip with a sarcastic grin.

"What can I say? Washington has made me soft. What brings you back to D.C. before Christmas, sir?"

"You do. I wanted to stop in to see how you were faring. Besides, you're the most coveted photo op in the country right now."

"Oh yeah? Where's your camera?"

"I thought we could take a…what do the kids call it? The picture you take of yourselves?" he asks my twenty-something chief of staff, whom he correctly assumes is savvy about such things.

"A selfie," Chelsea responds, unable to hold back a smile. She must be warming to him. A year ago, Parker was public enemy number two in her eyes. Albright held the top spot.

"I hope you're not serious, Thomas, because I've had enough of seeing grotesque pictures of myself in a hospital gown."

"I bet. Photo ops aren't my style, anyway," Parker says with a hearty laugh. "No, this visit is on the down-low, so to speak. I was wondering if we could have the room for a moment to speak privately."

"Uh, yeah, sure. Guys, could you give me a moment with the congressman?"

"Coffee break?" Vince asks Brian, Vanessa, and the rest of the gang. They accept. "We'll be in the cafeteria if you need us."

"I'm going to go visit Blake," Chelsea says, reserving her spot in the line to exit the room. "Good seeing you again, Congressman Parker."

"You too, Miss Stanton."

"I really should go check in at work," Kylie offers.

"I'd like you to stay for a moment if you can, Miss Roberts," Parker requests. "I think you may be interested in hearing this."

"Okay, you have my attention now," she says, offering a chair to the congressman, who declines. She takes the seat next to my bed.

"Were the flowers your idea?" I ask once everybody leaves and the door is shut.

"Honestly, I have a remarkable wife who has the uncanny knack of reminding me what the customary behavior is for such circumstances."

"I know what you mean," I say, almost earning a smack on the shoulder from Kylie, who thought better of it at the last moment. I only have one good one, and she tends to hit hard.

"First, I'm glad you, Francisco Reyes, and the rest of your staff are okay. How's Blake Peoni doing?"

"He's still in a medically induced coma and hurt pretty bad, but they think he'll pull through."

"That's a relief. I'm sorry about Marilyn Viano. I was never a fan of hers for a lot of reasons, but she didn't deserve that."

I nod. Nothing more needs to be said. Parker is sincere with his concern and condolences. He may be a couple of shades too conservative for me politically, but he's a decent man, and we do share some similar views.

"The country is just sick over this. My staff is telling me there are all kinds of rants that have gone viral on social media over the past two days. Every interview I see on television tells a similar story. Even protests are popping up. The one thing I don't see is you fanning the flames."

Parker leaves the statement hanging in the air. He sees the country tearing itself apart just as I do and likes it even less. He may be a distinguished, longtime politician, but at heart, he is still a holy man and servant to the people of his district and his country.

"Is that why you're here? To ask why I'm not making political hay out of this tragedy?"

"No. Although you should already know that the president, powerful members of both parties, and the financial interests behind them will be very threatened by you and what this shooting means to your political popularity. They're going to target you when Congress reconvenes, and you need to be ready for that."

"Please tell me you didn't brave long security lines at the airport just to fly up here to give me political pointers," I say, knowing full well he wouldn't do that.

"No, of course not," Parker laughs.

"Then why travel all the way up from Alabama two days before Christmas, Congressman?" Kylie prods impatiently, wanting him to get to his earlier point.

"Do you believe the gunman acted alone?"

Of all things, he had to ask about the most sensitive subject between us. I know where Kylie stands on the issue, but I'm not there yet. I cannot grasp the idea that someone wanted me dead simply because I was a political threat.

Americans try to find meaning in great tragedy. They want to turn it into a lesson or a source of inspiration. Every time one person or small group of people inflicts so much pain and suffering, the nation rallies to turn it into a positive. That's precisely what I am trying to do, much to the chagrin of my beautiful girlfriend.

"I don't know what to think," I offer, looking over to Kylie. "For now, I want to have faith that the police are doing their jobs, and if any information is uncovered that disproves their lone gunman theory, they will act accordingly."

I don't subscribe to most conspiracy theories. If I've learned anything in my life, it's that people can't keep a secret. The larger and more complex the conspiracy, the more likely information will leak into the open. Of course, I don't trust our government entirely either, so anything is possible.

"I will say that taking a shot at me only moments after we defeat a rules bill meant to restrict the political power of independents, and before the start of a contentious new Congress, is damn convenient timing."

"For the record, I don't think it was a lone wolf either. As much as it pains me to think someone orchestrated this to get you out of the way, I believe that is the case," Congressman Parker concludes.

"Do you have any evidence of that?" Kylie asks eagerly. Parker's words are an affirmation of what she's believed all along, and any information he has will bring her one step closer to putting someone's head on her platter.

"No, I don't. If I did, I would have turned it over to the police already. I do know someone who might, though."

"Who?" Kylie and I say at the same time.

"You're not going to like the answer one bit." He looks at both of us, letting the tension build throughout his dramatic pause. "Johnston Albright."

"How would he know anything about this?" Kylie probes.

"He was working closely with Reed."

"You think Reed had something to do with this?"

"I don't know for sure, but if anyone does, it's the former Speaker." He takes a moment to exhale, noticing the same gleam in Kylie's eyes that I do. She is about to embark on a mission, and she just got her first operations order.

"Miss Roberts, I know you're an investigative journalist, and I'm sure you want answers more than anyone. Let me tell you, this isn't Hollywood. There won't be a smoking gun here. You aren't going to find the Watergate tapes or a chain of e-mails ordering a hit. It will be a classic case of he said, she said, and I doubt you will ever be able to prove any of it."

"Then why are you here telling us this?" she shoots back.

"Because if it were me lying in that hospital bed, I'd want to know why. I'd also want to know if someone was pulling the strings of the man who tried to kill me and those closest to me."

"To what end?" I question, not sure what good any of this is going to do.

"Michael, there is more than one way to take down corruption and evil in this world. Justice is not always rendered through the legal system or the barrel of a gun."

"Implying what, exactly?" Kylie interrogates.

"You're both about to learn firsthand how the dark side of Washington works."

TWELVE

CHELSEA

"Hi, honey," I mumble as I adjust the blanket draped over him on the hospital bed.

I work gingerly around the tubes and wires running between his body and various machines, intravenous bags, and oxygen canisters. I stop and stare at him. My heart aches. He looks like the subject of some twisted medical experiment.

Despite the tubes and wires, he looks so peaceful yet so wounded. I pull a chair up next to his bed and hold his hand. I hate this room.

Why do hospitals use this color on their walls? It's an ugly blue that I suppose is meant to be soothing but belongs on a decorator's color wheel for a funeral home. With cold tile floors and a stack of machines and monitors that look like something out of Doctor Frankenstein's laboratory, there is nothing comfortable or soothing about the ICU.

"I have some bad news. I wanted to be here to spend Christmas with you, but Dad has other plans. He's laying a serious guilt trip on me and dragging me home to Millfield. I guess after almost losing me, he at least wants me home for a couple of days. I hope you understand."

How did we come this far? Back during the first campaign, we would have shelled out big money to see him like this. I would have run him over with a garbage truck myself to make it happen. He deceived the media, which in turn reported his lies. To this day, some people still believe I had an affair with the congressman when he was my teacher.

I hated Blake for that. He might not have been the architect of Winston Beaumont's final scheme to win the election, but he was the executioner.

Now I find myself falling in love with him. Life is a crazy thing. I find myself wishing it was me in that bed and not him.

"When you said you'd take a bullet for me, I didn't think you meant it literally."

Tears roll down my face. I remember that day like it was yesterday. I channeled all my frustration from the past year into jamming him up against a wall. He told me he loved me and would take a bullet for me. Who knew then he would get the chance to back up those words by proving it to me.

"I'm scared, Blake. I'm scared of everything. I've been that way since long before you met me. I put on a brave face, but I'm terrified of being here in this town. I'm terrified of the job I've been asked to do. I know you would tell me that I'm stronger than that, but I'm not. I'm really not."

I try to suppress the tears that refuse to stop, but it's futile. Not that it matters. Blakes's in a coma, and with no one watching, I can drop the façade I have put up for so long.

"I'm so tired of being scared. I'm so tired of believing I can't do this. So, you know what? I'm going to stop being scared. I'm going to prove to all the people who think I'm in over my head just how wrong they are."

I feel stronger and better just saying that. It needs to be more than words, though. Just feeling stronger is useless if I don't act that way. Washington, D.C. is a town full of people who like to talk. Precious little of what happens here ever translates into action. I need to change that. I need to change myself.

"How do I do that? I'm too young to do this job. Everybody thinks so. How can I convince them I can do it? How can I assure them that I deserve to be here?

"Wait, why should I convince them? People who think they have all the answers are wrong more than they're right. What if they're wrong about me? I know I can do this. I need to just start doing it and leave people to whisper whatever they want."

I have been the scared freshman that wandered the halls until a new teacher took me under his wing for too long. Mister Bennit saw my potential even though I didn't. Now it's time to show him that he was right all along. It's time to prove it to myself. I wipe the tears from my eyes and take a deep breath.

"I'm going to make you proud of me, Blake. But I'm not just doing it for you. I need to do this for me."

-THIRTEEN-

KYLIE

The *Washington Post* has its main office on Fifteenth Street in the Northwest quadrant of Washington. Tourists will say it's a historic building and part of the lore of the nation's capital. I think the eight-story brick building looks like it was made of Legos. I guess it's a lot like Fenway Park—an iconic piece of Americana and just as dumpy. Sorry, I'm a New Yorker.

I should feel blessed that I work for one of the oldest and widely circulated newspapers in the country after getting canned from the *New York Times*. The *Post* emphasizes national politics, earned over fifty Pulitzer Prizes, and is a coveted employer for any political journalist. It's the old stomping grounds of Bob Woodward and Carl Bernstein, whose reporting of the Watergate scandal in the early 1970s resulted in the resignation of President Richard Nixon.

Unfortunately, I don't feel particularly blessed as I ride the elevator to the floor where my cubicle is located. Working for the *Post* is like swimming with a battleship's anchor tied to your feet. If this current crop of editors had been running the show in the seventies, I'm not sure my journalistic idols would have ever gotten their stories printed.

As I walk onto the spacious floor jammed with cubicles, the feel of the room is all wrong. Offices across the country have a different atmosphere around Christmas. Aside from the decorations and uninterrupted supply of cookies, there is a noticeable difference in people when you get close to Christmas. All that is absent here.

The drama that accompanied the defeat of the rules bill was quickly replaced with the fallout of the shooting of a pair of U.S. congressmen and former senator on the steps of one of America's most treasured buildings.

The coverage of every detail and harried search for answers begged for journalists to fill the pages of the paper with countless articles for the public to devour. As a result, this year's holiday cheer has been replaced with the stress of deadlines, fresh angles, and struggle for exclusives. Merry Christmas.

I'm sure I have a few dozen voice mails and hundreds of e-mails to sort through, but I eschew stopping by my workspace for the more direct route to my editor's office. I've been given time off until Michael is out of the hospital, so there is no pressing need to return to work. My mission here is a simple one. I need to get on any investigation the *Post* is conducting.

To do that, I need to have a chat with my boss and hope he takes my side. Carl Ackerman is my editor and is in charge of the dwindling personnel and resources that once comprised the mighty investigative arm of the paper. He's a reasonable man, but right now, all bets are off. Over the last couple of months, the events are driving even the most grounded men to the edge of insanity.

A quick knock on the door is all the notice I give him before waltzing into his office. It's never closed, so I decide to seize that subtle invitation. Carl likes to think of himself as approachable by the people who work for him. We're about to see how true that is.

"Kylie? Didn't I gave you some time off?" he asks, now concerned that I'm here because something grave has happened.

"You did, and I wanted to thank you for that. There's something I need from you more than a vacation."

"Oh yeah? What's that?" he says over his reading glasses.

Carl is the ultimate journalism success story. He began his career delivering papers. After his editor-in-chief stints for both his high school and college newspapers, Carl went to work as a small-time journalist himself. Cutting his teeth on Reagan's Iran-Contra scandal, he rose through the ranks to lead the division he dedicated so much time working for.

Now in his mid-fifties, he's in good shape for a man always under severe pressure and stress. Rumor has it Carl is up before dawn every morning for a run, although nobody has ever seen him exercise. Regardless, he has managed to maintain his athletic build and most of his hair, both of which are feats in the newspaper industry.

"I want on the Bennit shooting."

"Not going to happen, Kylie," he declares after an emphatic sigh. "You have a serious conflict of interest, which means—"

"No, Carl, I have *an* interest, which means I'm the perfect person for the job. I'm going to get you better results faster than anyone else you assign, and you know it."

"I am not denigrating your talents, Kylie, but you're too close to this thing. With so many eyes focused on Washington, I cannot afford the appearance of impropriety. Worse, it would be calamitous if you did manage to interfere with the investigation. I don't need you grilling the police about every detail at press conferences or asking them why they haven't done this interview or that one."

"Isn't that our job?" I'm astounded by his lack of logic.

"No."

"Seriously?"

"I cannot allow you to jeopardize the reputation of this newspaper or call into question my judgment for allowing you to work on a story you are so clearly emotionally involved in. The police want answers, the same as you do. We'll let them do their job and take it from there."

Welcome to our modern media. Investigative reporting in the United States was not invented with the Watergate scandal during the Nixon administration, but it spread across the country and the world because of it. With the expediency of the digital age and daily newspapers struggling to cling to life, editors are unwilling to dedicate the resources or take the risks they used to.

Unfortunately, this is a losing battle. Carl is reasonable, but once he has decided, the result is not open to debate. Going head-to-head against him is about as futile as trying to derail a locomotive with a penny. Fortunately, I have a backup plan.

"Fine, then how about letting me investigate the investigation?"

"What?"

"You don't want me getting in the way of investigators by getting in front of them, so let me follow them. I want to ensure they're doing their jobs. The American people will want to know that too. What better paper to do that than the one who set that standard in 1972?"

If you ever need to convince an editor of anything, appeal to increased circulation. Woodward, Bernstein, and their colleagues were the only ones reporting on the story for months following the Watergate burglary. Doubted by the rest of the media and under attack from Nixon's White House, they gambled with their credibility and risked the newspaper's future.

The result was a significant one. The *Post*'s reporting until Nixon's resignation in 1974 prompted a judge, prosecutors, federal investigators, and even Congress to hold the White House accountable for the crimes committed at the Watergate.

"That was a long time ago, Kylie. A lot has changed since then."

"It has, but if we aren't willing to do this type of investigative work, then why do we even bother printing a paper? Are you willing to cede that ground to the blogosphere? Carl, if there was ever a time to devote our resources to a story, it's now."

"Okay."

"Okay?" That was easier than I thought.

"Yes, at least on a trial basis. Report on how the Capitol Police conduct their investigation and report everything you find back through this office. Do not, under any circumstances, get in their way. I mean it."

"Deal."

"I mean it, Kylie. I'm going out on a limb with this. This story is radioactive, and this paper can't even appear like it's interfering in the investigation. Do you understand?"

"I heard you the first time, Carl. You have my word."

Yup, a lot has changed since the days of Woodward and Bernstein. I understand why, but it's a shame. I have my marching orders and can only hope that he didn't notice me cross my fingers when I made that promise.

-FOURTEEN-

JAMES

"Diane! It's great to see you again. I'm glad you were able to meet with me. I know you must be busy with the transition and preparing for the holidays."

"Good Afternoon, James," she replies with her trademarked tone. "I appreciate you thinking about me. Yes, things are hectic, but I'm happy it worked out that we could sit down for a chat."

I point her over to the sofas. Unlike my meeting with Condrey, Diane Herr rates much higher on the political food chain. Most chiefs of staff for the president-elect of the United States do.

"How are things?"

"This Bennit shooting is a messy business. The fact that he was shot on the steps of the Capitol Building has the Secret Service in a tizzy."

"I bet," I say with a laugh.

The Secret Service is no joke. Aside from reports about some agents canoodling Colombian hookers, they are consummate professionals who are deadly serious about their job of protecting the president. They examine security down to the minutest detail to minimize the possibility of an assassination attempt on the commander-in-chief. Less than a month away from the inauguration, they will spend countless hours analyzing how a U.S. congressman was shot mere yards away from the House chamber.

"Have you heard any news on the shooting?" she asks, probing me for information.

"Only what is being reported by the media."

"A national tragedy," she laments. "Although I suppose it could have been much worse. Did you know Senator Viano?"

"We crossed paths a few times," I lie.

Diane Kerr is one of the most astute political operatives in the country. A longtime friend of the incoming president, she turned his fledgling governorship in New Mexico into a national juggernaut that came out of nowhere to snatch the nomination in a wide-open field. It was reminiscent of Barack Obama's brilliant primary run when he stunned Hillary Clinton to earn the Democratic nomination in 2008. The general election should have been a coronation for his opponent, but seizing on the strange mood of the electorate, he went on to an Election Day upset.

Diane was the force behind him all the way. A slender forty-five-year-old, she has disarming good looks and short black hair that lets everyone know she's all business. She is going to be a terrific White House chief of staff.

"How's the transition going so far?"

"Pretty smooth, actually. The Bennit saga is distracting the media, so we're not getting hounded over every nomination we make."

"I suppose that's one benefit of it," I offer, trying hard not to appear indifferent to the attempted murder of Bennit and Reyes.

"It's a double-edged sword. We aren't getting any coverage on our agenda. The lack of attention will make it more difficult to get traction once the president-elect assumes office. For now, we're just focusing on securing enough votes to win Speaker of the House. We'll have a much better chance to advance the president's agenda if we have Congress solidly behind us."

Yeah, about that. "You know, as nice as that would be, I'm not sure it is going to be a reality."

"What do you mean, James? Not only could we end up having the majority in the House if we sway enough of these independents into our camp, but we have just as good a chance as the GOP to win the election for Speaker."

"You don't really believe that, do you?"

"Do you think differently?"

"Diane, y'all don't have a reliable representative to lead that chamber after getting decimated by the icandidates. Dennis Merrick was your only real option, and he's gone. The minority whip would have been a distant second choice until he lost.

Merrick was the minority leader of the House before losing the election in his district to one of Bennit's upstarts. He wasn't the only high-profile casualty in November. Bennit ran one hundred icandidates, not including himself and Reyes, against entrenched incumbents and won seventy-seven of those races.

The resulting tie between Republicans and Democrats provided the media plenty to report on for weeks, culminating in the lame-duck session where Albright tried to pass the rules bill that would have forced the independents to join a caucus. The bill was defeated, and the world knows what happened at the resulting press conference.

"There are plenty of other strong Democrats that could take the reins of leadership," Diane insists, offended at my remarks.

"Name one." She doesn't take the bait.

"What would you have us do?"

It's time for me to throw my Hail Mary down the field. "You need to consider throwing your support behind a Republican."

"You've lost your mind."

"I'm serious."

"So am I," she retorts. "In case you've been asleep for the past decade, our relationship with the right is the most toxic it has ever been. The nation is as divided as we were before the Civil War."

"And what better way to mend the divide than a show of presidential leadership by reaching across the aisle. Call it a bipartisan initiative to heal the wounds of our nation. The common folk will eat that up."

"No way. That's political suicide. He'll alienate our base right out of the gate. Glenn will never go for it."

Using the president-elect's first name is designed to show me how close they are and that her words might as well be his words. Smooth political operators deal in subtleties, and Diane just reminded me why she's one of the best. Fortunately, I have some moves of my own.

"Is our relationship a one-way street?" That question earns me an angry look. She knows exactly what I am implying.

"Of course not."

"It's beginning to feel like one."

"You were a big part of getting us here, James. All the money your political action committee funneled into our campaign made a huge difference down the stretch, especially considering how much free airtime the icandidates managed to hog. We will repay you for that someday."

"I need you to start repaying it now."

"I'm sorry, that's not going to happen," she declares, shaking her head. Now it's time to reel her in.

"Fine, how about a compromise then? Since you won't come out in support of a Republican in the name of bipartisanship, get your boss to stop exerting pressure on the Democratic members about who to vote for."

"Why would I do that?"

"Because I asked."

"James, do you really want to cost us any chance of having a cooperative Congress? The president-elect is willing to rule by executive order if he must, but we all know that will drive the right and good portion of the center nuts. We want Congress's blessing on our agenda, and having control of the House goes a long way—"

"You aren't going to control the House regardless," I interrupt. "Even if you get a Democrat elected Speaker and own the most seats, the best you can hope for is a plurality in the chamber. A majority made up of Republicans and independents are not going to be eager to work with you if you use strong-arm tactics to seize the leadership."

"We'll make it work," she says dismissively.

"No, you won't."

"Excuse me?"

"Diane, you were involved in a presidential campaign that stayed far away from the independent movement Bennit spearheaded, so let me explain. Bennit almost beat a longtime incumbent using nothing but social media and by spending no money in his first campaign."

"James, I'm familiar with what Bennit and his students did, so I don't need a history lesson," Diane says pleasantly, her body language sending a completely different message.

I have no love affair with Diane, the incoming president, or his party. I don't hold Stepanik and the Republicans in high esteem either. This is politics, and for me, politics is business. Independents at any level of politics are bad for that business.

I see the future White House chief of staff making the same mistake I did this past summer—she is underestimating Michael Bennit and his team. Bennit is like a jug of good Kentucky moonshine. It looks innocent enough until you take a big swig and feel it burn all the way down. I don't want her to learn that the hard way, too.

"Okay, I'll get to the point. If you take the icongressmen head-on and expect to win, prepare to be disappointed. Michael Bennit is a strong leader. The assassination attempt stoked his base into being as fired up as they were during the election. Bennit's social media following measured in *millions* of Americans."

"In case you didn't notice, we have a pretty good following ourselves," the defiance evident in the tone of her remark.

"Not like his. Look, we could debate this all day, but neither of us has the time. You can do as you see fit but take the advice I gave you. Bennit owns the American public right now. They like and respect him."

"I don't really care. The president's priority is executing his agenda the first hundred days he's in office. If Michael Bennit gets in his way, he's directed us to do anything in our power to neutralize him."

"That sounds overtly threatening," I admonish. Talking like that in the wake of an assassination attempt is amateurish and could be easily misconstrued by a sensitive public. Diane should know that.

"James, you know as well as I that men who have occupied the White House have had their presidencies destroyed over an uncooperative Congress. We *are not* going to let that happen."

"My plan gives y'all what you're looking for while limiting the president's political exposure -- a chance to neutralize Michael Bennit and his allies in a way Albright couldn't. Instead of being too aggressive during a sensitive time, your boss will be a hero to his party during the next midterms. With Bennit marginalized, the people will see how inept the independents are, and the icongressmen will be swept from office.

"The social media election phenomenon will be tossed into the dust bin of history and labeled a colossal failure. Their defeat will give you a major victory going into the second part of the president's first term. That should carry over to an easy reelection run as the public turns to the strongest leader left in Washington."

I see the gears turning in her head. She's on the ropes. Old-school lobbyists like myself used to be called influence peddlers, but more realistically, we are Jedi. Leveraging the power of money usually gets the results we want, but the good ones still use mind tricks. The best ones, like me, use both.

"And if we don't support your plan?"

"Lobbying is a business, and we like to support winners. If you don't, the tough economic times may force us to curtail spending by supporting the party we think will win."

"Are you making a threat?'

"No, just explaining the reality of our situation. The choice is yours. You can do me this small favor now or face bigger consequences later. Don't make the decision yourself. Bring it to the president-elect and see what he says. I think he will understand the value of my proposition."

The backhanded insult was not lost on her. Diane can narrow her eyes at me all she wants, but she knows she needs to bring this to him. He will agree to the plan, and Diane would be wise to be on the right side of his decision. After a moment of silence, that dawns on her as well. She sighs loudly. Yup, again, it's just like breathing.

-FIFTEEN-

MICHAEL

It feels good to be mobile again, even if that means being pushed in a wheelchair by an orderly. My world has been a hundred-square-foot hospital room for two days now. A roll down the hall is a small victory that feels like freedom. I really need to get out of here before I lose my mind.

Cisco is out of intensive care and has moved into a room half a dozen doors down the hall from me. Despite it being close to dinner, I managed to leverage the nurses' pre-Christmas Eve generosity to let me visit him to take the call they were informed was forthcoming. I'm elated to be getting wheeled into the room for the long-awaited reunion with my friend and colleague, only to have it spoiled by a surprise guest.

"Really? You've been allowed to have visitors for all of ten minutes, and Mister Dark and Mysterious beats me here?"

"In your defense, I didn't need to arrive in a wheelchair," the small but powerful Terry Nyguen says as the orderly leaves me next to the bed and exits the room.

"You look like you got run over by a lawnmower," I tell Cisco, channeling the self-effacing and ethnically disparaging humor he uses. "How are you, man?"

"I'm okay, thanks. I've been out of the ICU for twenty minutes, and three people have already tried to hand me a mop. I told them I wasn't a janitor, but most of the nurses have already measured me up for a gray uniform."

Same old Cisco. Trauma has widely different effects on people. Other than the wound, and the distinct possibility someone was coaxing him toward a white light, he doesn't seem fazed at all.

"I see getting shot hasn't cost you your sense of humor."

"No, but I am a little bitter and upset after learning that I owe you a life debt."

"Yeah, you're my bitch from now on."

"Well, there's something to look forward to," he says with a laugh. "What do I owe the pleasure of your calling on me, my liege?"

"We have a lot to catch up on, and then we have a pair of calls to take from the president and president-elect."

"Aren't we the big men now?"

"I know, right? In the meantime, I'm hoping Terry here is going to explain if this was what he had in mind when we met back in Millfield."

I found his initial warnings a little too surreptitious for my taste, but he got inside Kylie's head. Now I find myself wanting to borrow his crystal ball. If the lone gunman theory doesn't pan out, his earlier caveats about what the political power players might resort to will turn out to be prophetic.

"I am, sort of."

"All right, let's have it, oh wise and powerful Zoltar."

"I don't believe Bernard was a lone gunman acting alone."

I wince at the sound of his name. When I was in combat in Afghanistan, I didn't know who the bastard was that shot me. It was better that way. Now, Jerold Todd Bernard is my Lord Voldemort and should forever be referred to by the epithet "He-Who-Should-Not-Be-Named."

"Kylie would love to hear those words come out of your mouth," I say, shifting my thoughts to her as I often do. "She thinks there is a better chance of O.J. finding his wife's real killer than of Jerold Todd Bernard acting alone."

"But you're not convinced?" Terry quizzes.

"I don't know what to think. I guess I'm hoping the police investigation leads me to a conclusion."

That causes Terry to wince. I guess he doesn't have a lot of confidence in what the Capitol Police will find. The truth is, I don't want to feed into Kylie's unhealthy obsession with proving the shooting was not the random violence perpetrated by some sicko. I want to put this behind me and focus on the next session of Congress when it convenes in a week and a half.

"Have they briefed you?" he says, checking the length of his fingernails. He reminds me of one of the suits you would see on an old episode of the *X-Files*. He is the Smoking Man, only Asian and not serially puffing on Marlboros.

"Yes, they did. The detectives maintain they haven't found anything to refute the original story."

"Then, I'm wrong. If the police don't have reason to believe otherwise, I must be mistaken."

Yeah, right. My BS meter pegs to the red line as an imaginary klaxon wails the alarm in my head. He's not being straight with us. I'm about to ask that when he pulls a note out of his pocket and hands it to me.

"The Capitol Police are taking this investigation seriously. The shooting happened in their backyard, so they will leave no stone unturned," he says aloud as I read the note and show it to Cisco. He nods and hands it back to me. I reread the short, handwritten scribble to commit it to memory.

The room may be bugged.
Need to meet Kylie in private to discuss.
Baltimore. Fort McHenry.
Noon tomorrow.

Choosing to meet at a national landmark outside of Washington on Christmas Eve is clever. It will be open but almost devoid of people. Man, this guy is as paranoid as they get. Of course, I thought that a few months ago when he warned us of danger, and now Cisco and I are in a hospital. I guess the spook deserves the benefit of the doubt this time. There's no doubt in my mind he is one.

"How's life at the think tank?" I ask, passing him the note.

I learned a little tradecraft as a part of Special Forces training as we were not immune to working with the CIA. If you get passed a note, you either destroy it yourself or give it back. Since I'm not about to light it on fire in a hospital room, I'll just let him take care of its disposal.

"Boring. The recent excitement in this town hasn't managed to penetrate our walls."

The telephone next to the bed rings and Cisco picks it up. *"Hola. Paisaje de Francisco. Por favor, la hoja de un mensaje."*

I had to brain dump what I learned in high school Spanish class to make room for the crash courses in Arabic and Pashto that the Defense Language Institute crammed into me. If he said what I think he did, it was funny.

"Hi, Francisco's Landscaping. Please 'leaf' a message," I translate for a bewildered Terry. He just shakes his head. Cisco and I share a sense of *Spaceballs* humor. We still laugh hysterically at the "comb the desert" shtick. Mel Brooks was the best.

"It's the White House. They are looking for a translator," he says with a laugh. This is the reason our government can't seem to get out of its own way. The president's staff should know Congressman Francisco Reyes speaks perfect English and is just screwing with them, but they either don't or are too politically correct to assert otherwise.

"I will leave you both to your call," Terry says, rising. "I hope to see you both on your feet soon. Merry Christmas."

-SIXTEEN-
CHELSEA

I wanted to see Congressman Reyes before we left, but he wasn't released from intensive care in time. Dad was eager to get me home before the holiday traffic made this drive more unbearable than it already is, so we left the hospital right after I was discharged and said goodbye to Mister Bennit, Kylie, and the rest of my friends.

Interstate 95 in southern New Jersey is one of the most boring roads on the East Coast. Considering the shortest day of the year was only a couple of days ago, the darkness enveloping the unlit highway negates peering out the window as a source of entertainment. At least it has given me time to think.

I haven't been able to stop thinking about what Amanda said to me in Blake's room. I didn't realize that she was struggling so hard to fit in at college. It makes me wonder if the others all feel the same way. It does explain why they were so eager to work with us last summer while the congressman was fighting for his political life.

Another part of me is curious about what Blake would say about it if he wasn't in a coma. I know he wouldn't want me to leave, but would he be supportive if I did? I mean, we are dating, sort of. If I decided to stay, would I be doing it because I want to, or would I be doing it for him?

The congressman didn't bring the subject of my resignation up. Either he doesn't know I'm having second thoughts or is giving me space to make the decision myself. I would stay if he asked me to. I'm sure he knows that too, or so he told me at Briar Point when he told me he knew about my acceptance to Harvard.

I've been plagued by the need to see this thing through to the end. I did it for the congressman's first election after our disastrous announcement when the whole staff gave up. I did it for his entire first term when all I wanted to do was run away from Capitol Hill and never look back. I even did it after the election when the rules bill threatened to undo everything we worked to accomplish. Can I really give up now?

The challenges in the next Congress will be tougher than they ever have been. As scary as that is, I know people believe in me. The congressman and Kylie both believe in me. Blake does too. Even the Three Amigos, the chiefs of staff, all named Chris, who work for moderate Democrats from New York, have been prodding me to reach my potential. I need to stop listening to the voice in my head that keeps saying I can't do this and pay more attention to those who believe I can.

"You're awful quiet, Snuggle Bear. Something on your mind?" How does Dad always seem to know when something is wrong? The man's intuition is incredible.

"No, nothing really," I say. "I didn't realize I was quiet."

"Are ya kidding? Ya haven't said a word since we passed through Baltimore."

He's right. I lost track of how long I've been mulling things over. Well, no time like the present to break the bad news to him. I might as well get this over with.

"I'm going to tell you something you aren't going to want to hear, so don't drive off the road or anything."

"No promises," he grumbles, not taking his eyes off the road in front of us. I take a deep breath.

"I'm not going to Harvard next month. I'm going back to work for the congressman for a while." There I said it.

My father doesn't react immediately. He shifts uncomfortably in his seat but doesn't unleash the verbal assault I expected. Instead, he sits there and drives in silence—an eerie, quiet, brooding silence that is even more unnerving.

"Why not?" he finally asks, after what feels like an eternity.

"I thought I had accomplished what I set out to do in Washington. Leaving to attend school just seemed like the next step. The more I think about it, the more I realize all I'm doing is running away. I want to go to Harvard, but I want to finish this first. I'll regret it if I don't."

It's not the most eloquent argument I have ever made. I'm sure I was more persuasive back in eighth grade when trying to convince him to let me sleep over at my old friend Cassandra's house.

"Okay," is all he says in response. Wait, what?

"That's it? All the lectures you have given me about the importance of getting an education and all I get after hours of obsessing over telling you this is a lousy 'okay'?"

I know how bad he wants me to go to school. I have an opportunity he never had, and he reminds me of that on each of my visits home. His biggest fear is that the longer I wait, the more likely the opportunity to attend an Ivy League school passes me by.

"Yeah, that's it," he says, glancing over at me for the first time. "Do ya want me to start yelling or something?"

"No, but I thought you would. Or at least ask me why."

"Are ya staying for that boy Blake?"

"No."

"Then I figure I already know the why, and ya don't need to explain any further. You mentioned regret. Well, I know a few things about having regrets in life, and I don't want ya to have to live with that feeling."

This was not the reaction I expected, and it's thrown me for a loop. On cue, my emotions start to run amok as they're prone to do. My father can be stubborn, opinionated, and sometimes even pushy, but you can never say he isn't in my corner.

"I am going to go to school eventually," I blurt out. I'm not sure why I just said that. I guess I'm at a loss for anything else to say.

"I know ya will, Snuggle Bear."

"How do you know, Dad?"

"Because you're a Stanton, and we're always true to our word. It's how you were raised."

My father is the most honorable man I know. Mister Bennit is a close second. Blake, for as much as I care for him, is a distant third. He has potential, though.

"Do you think I will succeed?" I finally ask, hoping I already know how he is going to answer.

"If you say you're going to help Michael Bennit restore confidence in our government, then God help anyone who stands in your way. Chelsea, you've turned into an amazing young woman. You're driven, tough, and above all, you're a redhead."

"Why does that matter?"

"Your mom was one, too. Ya have the same fire in your eyes that she once had. She would be very proud of you, Snuggle Bear. I know I am."

With that, my eyes fill with tears again.

-SEVENTEEN-

MICHAEL

Sneaking out of the hospital proved to be insanely easy for two reasons. The first is the Capitol Police officers who stood vigil outside my door were eventually reassigned to other duties, leaving only a few disinterested security guards to creep around.

The second reason is that this is Christmas Eve morning, and the nurses have plenty of other things to worry about other than me making a break for it. The timing was perfect. When the clock struck six a.m., I got out of bed, dressed, and made my move before the staff began their morning rounds.

My shoulder still hurts like hell, but "armed" with a sling, I'm mobile. Getting out may have been easy, but getting to my destination proved more difficult. Taxicabs aren't as prevalent in Washington as they are in cities like London and New York. I had to request an Uber and wait in the shadows for the driver to show up.

Fortunately, the journey across the Potomac River was a mercifully short one. I'm sure it won't be long before my absence is noted, and the alarm sounded for half of D.C. to come hunting for me. I'll deal with that when the time comes.

Until then, I want to enjoy my constitutional in the Garden of Stone. The twenty-four-acre Arlington National Cemetery is my favorite place to retreat to, finding comfort among so many who gave so much. Enjoying every second of my newfound freedom, I meander slowly to my destination. Although it invokes a tremendous sadness in me, being surrounded by men and women who I know died for many of the principles I cherish fills me with the quiet ease I rarely find anywhere else in modern society. This section does that more than any other.

Section Sixty is filled with those who gave their lives during the Global War on Terror, including the old friend I'm here to visit. Sergeant First Class Leroy Charleston and I grew up in different worlds. Our love of country and dedication to duty brought us to the United States Army, then to Special Forces, and a final traumatic mission in Afghanistan.

"I see you've been busy," I say, placing the deck of cards I always leave on his grave marker in homage to our prowess as a team of card sharks in The Stan. "You were my guardian angel the other day. I know it had to be you. Nobody misses a shot from eight feet away. Thank you for keeping us all safe, especially Chelsea, Vince, Kylie, and the gang."

I fight to hold back my tears. Now I know how my prized pupil and current chief of staff feels. I'm not a crier, but I've had all these feelings bottled up inside since the shooting. The emotion surfaces whenever I think about losing my students or Kylie. The dam finally breaks, and in this final resting place for so many, I begin to weep uncontrollably in hopes it brings me some peace.

* * *

"Hey, buddy, you okay?" I hear the man ask, startling me. I raise my head to find a rotund man with long, white hair and a matching beard leaning over me. The "Vietnam Veteran" baseball cap is adorned with pins, including the Combat Infantryman Badge. That tells me all I need to know about this American hero.

"I'm fine," I say, getting up and brushing myself off with my only working arm. I have no idea how long I've been sitting on the cold ground next to Leroy, but I do know I'm shivering. "I was just spending some time with an old friend."

"I'm sorry. I didn't mean to disturb you."

"No, that's quite all right. I appreciate your checking up on me." I glance back at his hat. "And thank you for your service."

"And yours, Congressman."

"You recognized me," I say reflexively, forgetting that I've become a national sensation for a second time. The sling might have given it away too.

"Are you kidding? The news is obsessing over what happened to you. Speaking of which, what are you doing out of the hospital?

"I snuck out." He laughs, more out of amusement than anything. I extend my hand. "Michael."

"John," he replies, taking off his glove and rewarding me with a good, firm shake. "It's typical of a Green Beret to sneak out of a hospital. You serve with him?" he asks, gesturing to Leroy's grave marker.

"Yeah, we fought together in Iraq and Afghanistan. What brings you here so early in the morning?"

"An annual pilgrimage. The son of a buddy of mine is buried right over there. He was a gunnery sergeant in the Corps with over fifteen years of service. He got killed in an ambush on Christmas Eve in Fallujah in 2004. I make it a point to pay him a visit every year."

I give him a nod out of respect. There is nothing more that needs to be said. Warriors have saluted their fallen brothers since cavemen were beating each other with clubs over the carcass of a slaughtered mammoth. The way they are honored has changed, but the act of doing so is both timeless and universal across cultures.

"What do you think of Congress?" he asks. That's a loaded question.

"Congressmen are a lot like lieutenants I used to serve with. They love to be flattered, are insecure about everything, can't navigate out of an open coat closet, and are most effective when they aren't around."

"I hear that. I admire what you're doing here in Washington," John comments, removing his hat and stroking his hair.

"Thanks, but I'm not sure it will make a difference."

That's true. America forgot the lessons of 9/11 less than five years later, and that was one of the most tragic events in our history. How long before they forget the lesson I tried to teach during my first race?

"Hell, son, it already has. Your first campaign woke people up and showed them the power of the voices they have. Your second campaign in that special election validated that power. Last November, you showed the country there are viable alternatives to the usual lousy options. All you have to do now is get to work and show them that government can work for the people again."

"I wish it were that simple, John. There's a dark underbelly of American politics the public never sees outside of Hollywood movies and political fiction novels. I never realized how dark it all was until I got here to see it myself."

"So?" Yeah, John is a typical veteran. He doesn't like excuses, and I suddenly feel like that's what I'm making.

"Did you know no other major democracy in the world permits unregulated spending on elections by the private sector?"

"No, I didn't, but isn't that what makes us a free nation?" he asks. He has a point.

"I thought so, but then I realized something. The only chance the American people have for a government which acts in their best interests is to ensure that politicians need the support of voters more than the financial backing of wealthy individuals, corporations, and special interests."

"Isn't that what you accomplished?"

"Yeah, I guess. For the short term, at least, we have some momentum," I say, with no evident enthusiasm. "The icongressmen are viewed as the greatest threat to the elites in the system in generations. There is a lot of money and power aligned against us now. I just don't know—"

"There was a lot of that aligned against the North Vietnamese too. I know because I was there. They had no business being on the same battlefield as us, but they were tough. They were dedicated. They were fighting for their *country*, for their *home*, and when it was done, they sent the country that defeated Nazi Germany home beaten and bloodied with our tail between our legs, despite us never having lost a battle."

I want to point out that we had more than a little help in the Second World War but choose not to. His history may be a bit skewed, but I get his point. John conveys the message with his eyes as much as his words. *The Art of War.*

Sun Tzu was a Chinese general and military strategist who lived in ancient China. His views on warfighting are captured in *The Art of War*. It's widely regarded as one of the most influential books on military strategy ever written. It has been quoted during everything from insurrections and guerilla movements to hostile business takeovers.

"Confront them with annihilation, and they will then survive; plunge them into a deadly situation, and they will then live. When people fall into danger, they are then able to strive for victory," I quote, from memory.

I have read his seminal work a hundred times. The United States military may base its doctrine on von Clausewitz, but the Special Operations community lives for Sun Tzu.

John smiles and then nods off to the distance. "Is that somebody you know?" he asks. I turn to see what he is looking at. Uh, oh.

"Yeah, my fiancée is coming to retrieve me," I inform him, noticing the determined gait of her walk and clenched jaw as she makes her way up to us from the road.

"Damn, she looks pissed."

"You don't know the half of it."

"Well, then this is where I bid my farewell. I fought in the jungle four thousand miles from home and would rather go back than face the wrath of an angry woman. You take care of yourself, Michael."

"Thanks, John, you too. Have a Merry Christmas."

-EIGHTEEN-
KYLIE

Words cannot describe how angry I am. I answered the frantic call from the hospital as I was leaving the condo and thought something terrible had happened. I transitioned from panic to rage when they told me my obdurate boyfriend was nowhere to be found.

Fortunately, I had a good idea where he went and immediately drove there. Arlington is his sanctuary, so I'm not surprised to see him chatting with a vet next to Leroy's grave. I'm even less surprised to see a man who has seen combat run away like a three-year-old at a circus who's terrified of clowns. I'm that pissed.

"What the hell are you doing sneaking out of the hospital? You were just shot three days ago!" I scream, letting him know that his recalcitrance is not a laughing matter.

"I needed to get out for a while."

"Without telling me?"

"I don't need your permission any more than you need mine," he asserts, breaking eye contact with me and looking at the Pentagon off in the distance. His snarky response almost sends me over the edge.

"What the hell does that mean?"

"Nothing. Forget it."

"Don't play that game with me, Michael. If you've got something to say, say it."

"I asked you not to investigate the shooting. I don't want you digging up the bodies in this town and making me more enemies than I already have."

"You don't want answers?"

"Not if you're going on a witch hunt, no. Not if you're digging for something that may or may not exist comes at the expense of doing what I came here to do. I can't focus on both."

"I'm not asking you to focus on anything. I'll do it for you."

"I don't want you to."

"Why not?"

"Because I don't want you in harm's way, that's why. You could spend a year digging for answers and find out the official statement was right all along, or you could find something that could get you killed. Either way, it's a lose-lose proposition. I don't want you wasting your time on it."

"You're asking me not to do my job," I defend.

"What are you talking about? The *Post* doesn't even want you working on this."

"Seventy percent of the country isn't buying the 'lone gunman' explanation. The other thirty percent are idiots. Aren't you wondering why one of our country's most prestigious newspapers doesn't want to investigate the official story?"

Michael doesn't respond, but he doesn't have to. He has never been shy about questioning authority, even when he was in the army. I can't believe that he's suffering from the same lack of curiosity my employer is.

Unfortunately, he is right about one thing—my editor at the *Washington Post* made it a point to tell me that he didn't want me anywhere near this story. I may have succeeded in convincing him to let me follow the police investigation, but he was clear what the ramifications would be if I began looking into this on my own. As if his threats, hollow or otherwise, are going to stop me.

"If you didn't want me involved, then why did you tell me about Nyguen's note?"

I ask the question because I want to know, but I also use it to break the deafening silence between us.

"Because you would have found out about it eventually anyway and gotten pissed off."

"I'm pissed now!" I shout, losing the battle to contain the raging anger inside me. The fact that he was shot is the only reason I'm not beating him senseless. "If this was anything other than a lone gunman, you could still be in danger. I'm just trying to protect you. Can't you see that?"

"I don't need your protection, Kylie. I need your support."

I bristle at the comment. He doesn't think I'm supporting him? All I have done since the moment we met is dedicate myself to making him successful in any way I could. For him to think otherwise is a slap in the face, and it stings.

Words can hurt. As a journalist, I am more acutely aware of this than anyone. For that reason, I bite my tongue because I can't find anything to say that will make this situation any better. He doesn't seem eager to add to the conversation either, and the resulting long pause only increases the tension between us. I glance at my watch and decide to put this conversation out of its misery.

"I'll need a helicopter to get to Baltimore by noon if I don't leave now. If you want a ride back to the hospital, you'd better keep up with me on the way back to the car."

Michael doesn't say anything on the walk from Section Sixty to the parking lot. We're beyond the awkward silence we felt in the hospital room., I feel a real strain between us for the first time in our relationship, and it's scaring me to death.

-NINETEEN-

CHELSEA

"While I'm all for the nostalgia of this place, it's way too friggin' cold to be meeting here in December, so this better be good," Brian says as he walks up to the picnic table.

Briar Point State Park is the most picturesque site in all of Millfield. Nestled along the bank of the river that runs through town, it's a favorite spot for locals longing for a hike or a place to spread a blanket and have a picnic. Of course, that only happens during the summer months and not the dead of winter. It was much warmer when we launched the congressman's campaign from this table than it is now.

Brian is the last to arrive and is no less vocal about his reluctance to brave the thirty-degree temperatures on Christmas Eve morning than the rest of my peers were. Out of the core group that put Mister Bennit in Congress two years ago, only Xavier and Peyton couldn't attend this meeting.

"You know, Chels, Bri has a point. There is a really nice coffee shop we used to frequent only a couple of miles away," Emilee adds, shivering despite being bundled up like Ralphie's brother in *A Christmas Story*.

"I need your help, and I don't want to explain it anywhere people could be listening," I explain to the group.

"A little paranoid, are we?" Brian mocks.

"According to the boss's text, maybe we all should be."

I pull up the text message on my phone and hand it to Brian. He reads it, makes a face, and passes it around for everyone else to see. They each wear a mix of surprise and apprehension on their faces.

"That's crazy," Amanda says, handing me the phone back, which I promptly pocket before putting my glove back on.

"I thought the same thing, but considering the past year, I'm not taking any chances."

"I don't trust Nyguen," Vince states outright. "He's getting the congressman all worked up over nothing."

"Who cares?" Vanessa says, trying to speed us along. "It is what it is. Can we talk about whatever we're here to talk about, so we can go someplace warm?"

"Yeah, what do you need from us, Chels?" Brian asks.

I take a deep breath. Mister Bennit asked a lot from us when we agreed to run his campaign after losing the bet. He doubled down during the spring of our senior year to usher him to victory in the special election. Vince, Vanessa, and I went to work for him, but we asked a lot in enlisting everyone else's help while they were attending college.

Every step of the way, Emilee, Brian, Peyton, Xavier, and Amanda did everything they could for Mister Bennit. This is different, though. In the past, he was the one who asked for their assistance. This time, it's me.

"I need your help in Washington getting the congressman elected as Speaker of the House."

The group all looks at each other like I'm crazy. Considering what we've been able to accomplish so far, I didn't think the request was that outlandish. That's a minority opinion.

"Poor thing," Emilee observes, touching the abrasion on the side of my forehead. "You hit your head hard, didn't you?"

I let out a nervous laugh.

"Uh, Chels, I thought you were done working in Washington?" Amanda asks, trying to tread lightly. She doesn't know who I told about leaving and who I didn't.

"What?" Vince asks, confused. "What does she mean by 'done'?"

A look of regret creeps over Amanda's face now that she realizes I hadn't told any of the others. "Sorry," she whispers under her breath.

"It's okay," I say before addressing the others. "I was going to resign as chief of staff after the final vote. I would have told you all after the press conference, but we all ended up dodging bullets."

"You were leaving us?"

"I was planning on attending Harvard this spring, Vanessa."

"But you're not going anymore?" Vince asks, correctly surmising that I changed my mind.

"No, college can wait."

"I bet your dad just loved hearing that," Amanda remarks, knowing the history of the ongoing struggle with my father about going to college. I wonder how aware she is that her pep talk in Blake's hospital room probably contributed to this new epiphany of mine.

"He handled it better than I thought he would. I explained how the shooting made me take a step back and think about what I really want. I realized leaving Washington without accomplishing what we set out to do would be the worst mistake of my life. I'm tired of getting kicked around down there. It's time to stop playing the victim and start going on the offensive. The first step is to put the congressman in a position where the elites cannot afford to ignore him."

"Having a small army of icongressmen isn't enough?" Vanessa asks.

"Not enough for me."

"Chels, you realize there is almost no chance of getting enough votes to make him Speaker."

"*Almost* no chance," I say with a wry smile.

"Assuming for a second we have a shot of pulling this off, what's the plan?" Emilee posits.

Her petite build offers nothing in the form of insulation from the chilly weather she abhors. She was really meant to live someplace warmer.

"First, we're going to use social media to build public support."

"That plan is getting a little tired, isn't it?" Vince despondently questions. He's been acting like Mister Negativity since the shooting.

"The way we were using it, yes. Now it's time to borrow a page from the playbook the Egyptians used when they were protesting in Tahir Square. We aren't going to use it just to disseminate information—we're going to use it to organize and act."

"Act how exactly?" Brian queries, knowing that anything we do for social media effort falls on him.

"By arranging rallies and demonstrations in every city in America."

"That's a little ambitious, isn't it?" Amanda responds.

"I'm not so sure it is. You've all been watching the news. Vigils and protests have already been popping up everywhere. We just need to make them bigger and focus them on our goal."

"You think that will translate into getting the Republicans and Democrats in the House to support an independent for Speaker?" Vanessa retorts.

"No, not by itself. What the rallies do offer is the members of the House some political cover. Convincing them to cast that ballot during the roll call is part two. We need to reach out to the chief of staff of every Republicrat in the House and convince them that this is in their boss' best interests."

"Why not just reach out to the members directly? They make the final decision. Wouldn't that be easier?"

"Not in this case. Staff will be easier to convince. Once we win them over, we'll have advocates to help plead our case to their principals."

In Washington, our elected representatives defer to their trusted staff members more than most Americans realize. Politicians keep ridiculous schedules on the Hill. It's so bad that many members of Congress can't be bothered to even read the bills they vote on. They listen to their inner circle and trust their judgment. If we can convince them, we'll have a shot to get Congressman Bennit elected as Speaker of the House.

"This is a fool's errand, Chels," Vanessa finally opines after taking a long moment to think about it. "Regardless of how they feel about him after the shooting, there is no way the members of either party will be allowed to vote for him. No amount of social media pressure or deal-making you do on the Hill is going to change that."

"Remember the story of Joan of Arc?" I say, channeling my mentor.

"Really? You've been hanging out with Mister B too long," Vince blurts out. He's right. I have.

"Okay, I'll play your game. Go for it, Chels. Let's have today's history lesson," Brian muses, almost enjoying me fulfilling the role of our beloved former teacher.

"Nineteen-year-old Saint Joan of Arc claimed God told her to free her homeland from English domination towards the end of the Hundred Years' War. She gained prominence when she lifted the siege of Orleans in only nine days, despite the hostile attitude of her commanders. As thanks, she was tried and executed for heresy for her beliefs. The judgment was invalidated by the Pope. She was declared a martyr a quarter-century later. Now she's the national heroine of France."

"Wasn't she burned at the stake?" Brian asks with a wink.

"I like it hot," I respond with a wink of my own.

"So, you think you're Joan of Arc now?" Vince says with a derisive snort.

"No, but I know how she felt. What's the matter, Vince? Not up for a fight? Are you afraid to finish your 'revolución' now that it's gotten a little too 'calor en la cocina'?"

Thank God Congressman Reyes is not around to hear me butcher his language, but it has the desired effect. Vince has always been the most combative amongst us—he has never shied away from wanting to mix it up with whoever is in our way. I'm not sure why he is balking this time, but my challenge hits the mark.

"Hell no, but since I know the congressman doesn't know about this, I feel weird going behind his back." Okay, that explains his reluctance.

Vince has always regarded Mister Bennit as the father he never had, and I'm sure he isn't eager to do anything to disappoint him. I understand the feeling.

"Vince, you know as well as I do that when push comes to shove, this is what good staffs do." He nods.

"All right, I'm in," Emilee says.

"Me too," Amanda adds.

"I guess my project at MIT will have to wait," Brian says with a slight shrug. His agreement was vital. We would be lost without him.

"So, where do we start?" Vanessa wonders.

"Before we get to that, you're acting like Mister Bennit. Now we need our inspirational quote. How about it?"

I think about Amanda's request. Unlike Mister Bennit, I can't pull these things out of thin air, but I think a favorite old quote he's used regularly in Washington will do nicely.

"How wonderful it is that nobody needs to wait a single moment before starting to improve the world," I respond.

"Didn't Hitler say that?" Brian asks in jest.

"No, but one of his victims did."

"Who?"

"Anne Frank. C'mon guys, let's go get some coffee and get warm. I hope you already finished wrapping your Christmas presents because we need to get to work making Congressman Bennit the nation's first iSpeaker."

-TWENTY-

KYLIE

Fort McHenry was built on the site of the former Fort Whetstone, or so the information in the visitor's center pointed out. It was designed to improve the defenses of the increasingly important Port of Baltimore from enemy attack. Constructed in the form of a five-pointed star surrounded by a dry moat that served as an infantry shelter to defend the fort from a land attack, each of the five bastions could provide crossfire from cannons and small arms.

In the early morning hours of September 13, 1814, British warships bombarded the fort for nearly a full day. The poor accuracy of the British weapons at maximum range and the limited reach of the American guns resulted in minimal damage to either side. The British ceased their assault when they ran low on ammunition. With the British naval invasion of Baltimore repulsed, the resulting stalemate paved the way for signing the Treaty of Ghent that December.

In the harbor, a Washington lawyer of all people witnessed the bombardment from a nearby truce ship. He was so moved by the scene that he composed a poem that would later be put to music renamed *The Star-Spangled Banner*. How our national anthem came into being is the kind of thing you learn when dating a patriotic, history-obsessed, former high school history teacher.

After taking a water taxi from Baltimore's Inner Harbor, I enter the legendary fort and make my way to the flagpole, somehow knowing the mysterious Mister Nyguen will find me there. My watch reads ten till noon as I reach the replica of the U.S. flag with fifteen stars and stripes fluttering over Fort McHenry.

"It's beautiful here, isn't it?" Nyguen asks as he comes up alongside me. Dressed in jeans and a North Face jacket to protect against the biting wind, I didn't immediately recognize him under his Oakley sunglasses. Even looking like a badass, Terry still manages to not stand out in a crowd.

"It is. Michael likes to bring me to places like this. Fort Sumter in South Carolina, West Point, Fort Ticonderoga in New York...I have to admit that I have grown fonder of American history since I started dating him."

"I bet."

"What did you—"

"Not here," he interrupts, waving me to follow him.

It will not be a white Christmas, so we don't have to navigate snow-covered paths on our way up to one of the bastions overlooking the harbor. I'm glad the wind isn't blowing hard. Otherwise, I would insist on getting out of the arctic weather and move inside one of the buildings to conduct this clandestine outing.

"This is an interesting place to meet," I comment upon reaching the scenic vista overlooking the harbor.

"I thought it was a symbolic choice. The British threw everything they had at this place, and it never wavered. It reminds me of you guys."

"That's not why you have me freezing my ass off up here instead of spending quality time with my wounded and terribly upset boyfriend. Speaking of which, while I always wanted my own personal Deep Throat, why couldn't we meet at the hospital?"

"I think you may be under surveillance, so I'm taking precautions."

"Surveillance? Okay, let's start this little chat with you coming clean about who you really are," I demand, losing my patience with his lack of transparency.

"I work for a think tank in Washington."

"You're lying. I don't know a single think tank employee who is so well-versed in counter-espionage."

"You know one now, only I perform more of a security function than I let on. It was a job I got when I came out of the military."

"What unit?" I inquire, probing his background. Two years ago, whatever answer he produced would have been alien to me. It's a whole different world for me now. The *Who's Who in the American Armed Forces* is required reading when you are romantically involved with a former Green Beret.

"Dev Group." Well, that figures.

The United States Naval Special Warfare Development Group got a lot of press following the killing of Osama bin Laden and is often referred to by the name of its predecessor, which was officially disbanded in 1987—SEAL Team Six. Dev Group, and its Army counterpart, Delta Force, are the most elite counterterrorism units in the American military. Working with Terry just got more interesting, and I'm sure even Michael will be impressed.

"Okay, who has us under surveillance?" I know better than to bother him with any more questions about his former life.

"I'm not sure you actually are, but what I'm about to tell you is sensitive enough to not want it heard by prying ears, just in case."

"Why the charade if you aren't sure?"

"It's what we do. Now, do you want to hear this, or would you rather play Twenty Questions?"

"Sorry, I'm a reporter, remember? Go ahead."

"I have a source that was close to Viano reach out to me the other day. He told me some interesting things that go a long way in explaining what you guys have been up against."

"What source?" I blurt out, almost cutting him off.

"I'm not going to tell you right now. Did you know Viano was friends with Reed?" Terry asks before I get the chance to hit him with yet another question.

"Yeah, we found out from Blake not long before the shooting."

"Okay, this may surprise you then. Did you know that the two of them were working together to get rid of Bennit last summer?"

"No…I mean, how? Michael's a sitting congressman. Short of causing him to lose the election, they don't have the power to get him removed from office."

"They could if they had someone on the inside that they could leverage to do their bidding. Someone with enough power and status to round up a posse to drive you out of town. Ring any bells?"

"Albright."

Speaker of the House Johnston Albright had it in for Michael from the moment he was sworn in following the special election. After a constant barrage of reprimands and censures failed to get Michael to resign, Albright had pushed forward with a resolution calling for his expulsion after receiving dubious evidence that he had taken a bribe from a lobbyist.

Michael was absolved only because he had followed his instincts and had Brian record the whole encounter. The entire thing was proven as a blatant attempt to frame him, although the elites in Congress weren't about to let that pesky fact stop the effort. Congressman Parker changing his vote at the last moment was the only reason Michael had survived the resolution to kick him out.

"Exactly. James Reed was bullying Speaker Albright into removing Michael so Viano could swoop in and help the icandidates ride to victory. It didn't go as planned because Michael became a national sensation again for flipping a table and telling off a congressional committee. Reed got mired doing damage control after being linked to the false accusations, so Viano cooked up a new idea for the icandidates joining your ranks in Washington. That's where her push for the third party came from."

"And that failed too because my boyfriend is beyond stubborn. Was she responsible for the rules change bill?"

"No, according to my source, that was all Reed."

This rules bill would force the independents to caucus with one of the political parties, negating the main reason they got elected in the first place. Michael had managed to turn the Republicans and Democrats against each other, and the bill was defeated. What happened at the press conference following that vote brought me up here to talk to Terry.

"Okay, this is all interesting, but none of it helps figure out if someone had Jerold Todd Bernard take a shot at Michael or if he did it on his own."

"Bear with me. When the vote was over, Viano joined you guys at the press conference."

"Yeah, so?"

"Why was she there?"

I think about that for a moment because I don't really know. Michael and Marilyn were barely on speaking terms, much less allies at that point. Why would she be standing right there with us?

"Let me answer that for you. Viano was *told* to be there," Nyguen adamantly professes. "We viewed her as collateral damage in the attack against Bennit. I believe she was as much of a target as he was."

"You're speculating. There's no proof of that."

"No, but I trust my instincts. If I wanted them both gone, that's how I would set it up. It was only a matter of convincing her to be there. There's one more thing, though," Terry continues. "The police learned that Jerold Todd Bernard got a call on his cell phone moments before he walked up to you guys and opened fire. It was made from a disposable, untraceable cell phone."

"A burner phone?" I mumble under my breath.

"I see you share Michael's love affair with spy novels."

"Not really, but you pick up things like that when you live with him. How did the police find that piece of information?"

"They have Bernard's phone."

"Yeah, duh, but how did they know where the call to it originated from?"

"The NSA told them."

"Of course they did."

The NSA's domestic spying program was implemented by President George W. Bush in the wake of the terror attacks on September 11, 2001, and has been rumored to have expanded under every administration since. The government considers the program officially classified, but that hasn't stopped whistleblowers, public statements, and newspaper investigations from leaking the details.

"The police think it's a coincidence, but I think the call was a go order made right before the press conference."

"Where was the call made from?"

"Inside the Capitol Building."

I'm floored. In addition to monitoring real-time Internet and phone traffic, along with the call history of every American, the NSA must have a few capabilities that haven't leaked.

During murder investigations, police can track the cellular tower a phone pings off to get the device's approximate location. To isolate the origin of a call to a building, say the U.S. Capitol, requires a whole different subset of technology. It's a capability the National Security Agency is more than eager to develop and deploy.

More important than the violation of our privacy, the implication of what Terry is saying is astounding. Michael may be right, as much as I hate to admit it. Investigating this could get extremely dangerous.

"Are you saying it could have been a member of Congress?"

"Or a staff member, government employee, or someone who was watching the proceedings in the House. But I have my money on one man who we know was on the premises, wanted Michael out of the picture, knew Marilyn Viano, and could convince her to be out there standing with him. I also believe he possesses the means to convince an assassin to take a shot."

I exhale deeply at the thought. I know who Terry is referring to, and if it can be proven, the shockwave will resonate for generations in this country. People already detest how lobbyists, special interest groups, and corporations co-opt the political process because of the money they dump into it. If it ever got out that the nation's most prolific and well-respected lobbyist made this call from the Capitol...

"You know what you're saying, right?"

"Yeah, assuming my analysis is correct, James Reed didn't just try to get Michael removed from office. He tried to have him executed."

-TWENTY-ONE-

JAMES

"Merry Christmas, James."

"And a Merry Christmas to you as well, Senator. I'm glad y'all were able to attend my little Christmas Eve soirée this evening."

"Well, with a son graduating from Georgetown and a daughter attending Johns Hopkins, it just made sense to celebrate the holidays here instead of schlepping back to Arizona."

"I understand the desire not wanting to travel this time of year," I say with a hearty laugh. "Delays, crowded airports, cranky people…it's a recipe for misery, even for an important member of the government. Speaking of which, I'm sincerely glad we will be able to continue working together once Congress reconvenes next month."

"Yes, in no small part because of your support of my campaign. It made an enormous difference down the stretch." The remark makes me smile.

Congressional candidates are prohibited from accepting more than five thousand dollars in direct donations from any political action committee, but that never stopped my industry from devising some more ingenious funding channels. In this instance, my support for the senator came in the form of voter registration. We organized a drive in his state that specifically targeted signing up those apathetic souls likely to pull the lever for him on Election Day. I also sidestepped the law by making a generous contribution to his personal political committee. It's shady but perfectly legal. God bless America.

Seeking public office, and getting reelected to it, has historically come at a high cost. Critics are correct when they argue that fundraising distracts elected representatives from lawmaking, but that's the system. Politicians need the contributions I provide to finance their expensive campaigns. My firm is rewarded for its support with a sense of obligation, unfettered access, and an incredible amount of influence over them.

"Excuse me, Senator. Can I borrow James for a moment?"

I hate being interrupted in the middle of a conversation. That's especially true when it's some lowly House staffer while I'm talking to an increasingly powerful senator whose legislative help I'll need.

"Of course," the senator says, much more diplomatic in handling the intrusion than I am. "We will talk again after the holidays, James. Thank you again for the invitation this evening."

"You're welcome, Senator. We'll talk again real soon," I say before he walks off.

I turn my attention to Joshua Dudek, chief of staff for one of the more extreme left-wing members of the U.S. House of Representatives.

"What the hell is so important that you needed to interrupt me like that?" I bark at the slight, mousy, but professionally dressed man.

"Michael Bennit."

"What about him? Last I heard, he's still convalescing in the hospital," I relay, wishing I could go a day without having to think or talk about this guy.

"You haven't been on social media, have you?"

"Joshua, do I look like the type of guy who spends a lot of time on Facebook?" I grumble.

"No, but considering Michael Bennit is your mortal enemy and goes by the moniker 'the iCongressman,' I figured you would pay a little more attention. I know my party is, and I'm sure the other side of the aisle is equally interested."

Bennit's infatuation with social media, specifically his ability to motivate large numbers of voters with it, is why I was so determined to get him removed from Congress before the election. It didn't work out due to Albright's ineptitude and Viano's duplicity, and the result was Bennit's reelection and the rise of seventy-six of his icandidates.

"All right, what about him?"

"It's all over social media and is going viral pretty quickly."

"What is?"

"A movement that is calling on Congress to make Bennit the next Speaker of the House."

"What?" I practically shout, getting the unwanted attention of some of my guests standing closest to me. If Bennit being in the House is a bad dream, his getting elected Speaker would be a nightmare.

"Yeah, I said the same thing. Even though it's Christmas Eve, it seems to be gaining a lot of traction," Joshua says before taking a sip of his drink.

"It will never happen. People can talk all they want on the Internet, but it's not going to change anyone's mind here," I say, knowing there's plenty of evidence to the contrary.

"The only problem with that thought is that it's not just on social media. The vigils that popped up for Bennit turned into demonstrations, and now those demonstrations are going to turn into rallies of support after Christmas. Bennit's staff is organizing a big one on the National Mall right before Congress reconvenes."

Damn that man. He is using social media to organize the masses to rally in support of him. Keeping the lid on something going viral is an impossible proposition these days. Once it's out there, the game is over.

No media outlet in the country will be able to ignore large gatherings across the nation any easier than they could avoid covering the Occupy Wall Street movement when it hit its peak. Visuals are compelling, and the public pressure politicians will be under to select him as Speaker will be almost irresistible.

"You shouldn't overestimate Bennit's abilities," I say, continuing to try to dismiss Joshua's concerns as deftly as I can. "He may be a social media idol, but I don't think he will be able to translate that into any meaningful action. The election is over, and Americans will go back to their usual apathetic attitudes once they start nursing Christmas hangovers."

"Don't be so sure, James. Bennit is extremely popular right now," Joshua argues, not buying into my weak assurance.

"He's always been pretty popular."

"Yeah, but someone tried to make him a martyr," he says, causing me to grimace at the remark. "Now he's being regarded as the bright, shining light here in D.C., and the people are turning to him to restore sanity to government."

"You don't believe that crap, do you?"

"Hell no, but the American public increasingly believes it. That's enough to make my boss as nervous as a Kardashian without room service."

"Bennit doesn't have the experience to be elected Speaker, so I don't—"

"That won't stop him from winning," Joshua states with the adamant eyes of a man who has preordained the outcome. "I spoke to my boss earlier this evening. He's considering supporting him if the balloting stays deadlocked too long."

"You have to be kidding me! A staunchly liberal congressman would support a moderate, independent...whatever he is?"

"If they can't agree on a leader before that, yes, he will."

Appealing to the logical mind of any political operative is a fool's errand at best. You can get through to them, but it is increasingly rare. Fortunately, I can fall back to the tried and true tactics of blackmail.

"Do y'all like the money my firm brings to your campaign, Joshua?"

"You aren't really going to hold that over our heads, are you, James?" he questions, annoyed at the audacity I am displaying with my lack of subtlety.

"I will if it means stopping you from sinking the country by electing a maverick independent to lead the lower chamber." And I mean it. I would blackmail God Himself to keep that man away from any position of influence.

"What would you have us do, vote for a Republican instead?" That's precisely what I plan on having you do.

"If need be, yes."

"Okay, you've had a little too much scotch tonight."

"I'm serious. I think you need to consider supporting a Republican over Bennit if it comes to that." In fact, I insist on it, but I can't tell him that yet.

"If you are looking to form a consensus candidate between the two parties to stop Bennit, why not convince the Republicans to support one of our guys?"

"For the same reason that Bennit cannot be allowed to be Speaker— nobody in your party is strong enough politically to lead the chamber."

"The president-elect thinks otherwise," he argues.

"And his chief of staff is coming around to my line of thinking. Diane will convince him of the political upside of my argument." At least I hope she will.

Joshua looks around the crowded room, his face transforming as he flies through the stages of grief from anger to acceptance.

"Who do you have in mind?" he finally asks, realizing that with the defeat of the entire Democratic leadership in the chamber back in November, I am right.

"Stepanik."

"No way in hell. He's a fascist who falls to the right of Benito Mussolini." Harsh words, but truthful ones.

"Normally, I would agree with that...colorful...analysis, but what if I could guarantee that Harvey would play ball with you guys in the spirit of, say, bipartisan cooperation?"

"James, you have the most reach and wield the most influence of anyone in this town, but even you can't make—"

"What if I could?" I implore, cutting him off mid-sentence. "Would your boss consider it?"

"It's a hard sell."

"I agree, but the world is changing, and he needs to understand that. If the threat of losing my financial support isn't enough to sway him, imagine a world where independents run the House of Representatives and a sizable number join the Senate in two years. Then envision life with Michael Bennit third in line for the presidency leading them. If you and your boss don't get past your partisan ways, that's the reality y'all are going to face in the not-too-distant future."

PART II

GUARDS FOR THEIR FUTURE SECURITY

-TWENTY-TWO-
MICHAEL

"Santa Claus couldn't find this place," Kylie observes, taking turns between looking out of her window and the windshield as she gingerly pilots our rental car down the quiet street.

"At least he gets an aerial view," Chelsea comments from the backseat. "Are we sure he has a driveway? He could just have a helipad in his backyard or something."

"It should be another few hundred feet ahead on the left," I say from the passenger seat, the GPS on my iPhone working hard enough to make it burn my hand.

"That's what you said the first two times we went down this street," Kylie observes.

As much as I hope Kylie is here for the same reasons I am, I know she isn't. She's on a mission, and her meeting with Nyguen only managed to further steel her resolve. I want answers from Johnston Albright too, but we will be asking different questions.

I was discharged from George Washington Medical Center against my doctor's recommendation. Chelsea flew back down to Washington the day after Christmas just in time to help wheel me out of the hospital. Cisco pleaded with me not to go, but I was not about to indulge his "misery loves company" shtick. Both Kylie and Chelsea weren't thrilled with my insistence on being released, and neither was surprised when I handed them plane tickets to come to South Carolina.

"It should be right here," I say, still bewildered as to why I cannot find this man's house. The military could take lessons from his landscapers on the art of effectively camouflaging a building.

"Kylie, are we sure the congressman passed land navigation when he went into Special Forces?"

"I'm beginning to think he lied about his rank and is actually a second lieutenant," she remarks, alluding to the reputations junior officers have for getting lost in the woods.

"You guys are real funny. There it is! We just passed it."

"What are the odds?" Chelsea ponders as Kylie starts a K-turn in the street.

"Better than the odds of you getting more than a few dozen people assembled on the National Mall for a rally," I fire back.

"We'll see," she responds. "Brian, Emilee, and the gang have managed to stir social media into an uproar about you being Speaker during Christmas, of all holidays. If they can create a viral sensation this time of year, I can do this."

"You realize that it's a long shot," I add as Kylie slows enough not to miss the impossible-to-find driveway again.

"Yeah, but I can always cancel the event. Until then, it will scare the crap out of anyone without an 'i' in front of their title."

Chelsea is growing up. She set this up on her own and didn't wilt when I expressed my displeasure at the plan. Despite confronting her with the possibility of failure, she hasn't backed off one bit. Forget being the proud former teacher. I feel like the proud parent.

Kylie parks and we pile out of the car and stretch before walking up onto the large wraparound front porch that dominates the front of Johnston Albright's massive house. A petite older woman answers the door a few moments after we ring the bell.

"Hello, may I help you?" she asks in the unmistakable drawl of someone native to this part of the country.

"Good afternoon, ma'am. Is Speaker Albright available?" I ask in as pleasant a southern voice as a yankee like myself can muster. I haven't used that since my days at the Special Warfare Center, located not far north of here at Fort Bragg, North Carolina.

"I'm sorry, he's not accepting guests today," she coldly advises. After noticing the sling securing my left arm, she reconsiders. "Although, he may be willing to make an exception for you, Congressman Bennit. Please come in, and I'll fetch him."

Founded in 1670 as Charles Towne in honor of King Charles II of England, Charleston adopted its present name in 1783 and is the oldest and second-largest city in South Carolina. Located in the state's southeastern corner, its harbor was vital throughout much of our nation's existence. Known for its stunning architecture, rich yet controversial history, and friendly people, it's a wonderful place to live or visit. Too bad this is a business trip.

We wait quietly in the foyer until she returns and then follow her down the hall until we reach a large oak door. "He agreed to see you in his library," his wife gingerly warns, "but he's in a foul mood. You may wish you had picked a different day to come."

I give her a quick nod and enter the spacious study with Kylie and Chelsea in tow. The room is stunning in a nerdy, man cave kind of way. Bookcases are built on every wall in the room and filled with enough expensive cloth-bound books to make a small-town library envious. Albright offers us seats on faded red leather couches and sits in one of a pair of obscenely expensive-looking chairs.

"This is a magnificent room, Mister Speaker. I'm jealous," I say to break the ice. I mean it, though. This is the type of room I could see myself kicking back and relaxing in someday.

"Why are you here, Bennit? Do you want to gloat about the end of my political career?" The ice has refrozen quickly.

"If you thought I was here for that, you would have turned us away at the front door and never had your lovely wife show us in."

Albright snorts derisively and then gets back up out of his high-backed wing chair and moves to the small wet bar near his desk. He wastes no time in making his selection. After filling three tumblers with amber liquid from a crystal decanter, he returns to us in the small seating area.

Albright resembles your typical D.C. politician, complete with hair that's more salt than pepper and a generous waistline. The swagger and arrogance he exhibited throughout my first year in Congress are gone. The anxiety over his political future is taking its toll.

"I'm sorry, Miss Stanton, I don't have a Shirley Temple to offer you," he goads in the most disparaging remark I have ever heard directed at Chelsea.

I am about to say something when she saunters up to him, snatches his own tumbler of scotch out of his hand just as he was about to take a sip, and downs every drop of it. She turns the glass upside down and places it on the small table across from the couch as I gawk in awe. Where did that come from?

"You need a refill, Mister Speaker," she observes before taking her place beside Kylie and me. "It's very smooth with a slightly smoky flavor. Drink up," she advises us.

Okay, now I'm really impressed. Kylie is equally amazed at her brash display and snarky yet brilliant response. I turn back to Albright, who I expect to fly into a rage. He just smiles.

"Well played, Miss Stanton. There's a future for you in politics, after all." Albright moves back to the bar to refill his glass before continuing. "Why aren't you here to gloat, Michael? I would be."

"Gloating is bad karma, and I don't need any more of that."

"We need information, Mister Speaker," Kylie says with a tinge of impatience and dispensing with the small talk.

"The high today is going to be around fifty-seven, the Panthers should make the playoffs, and retailers are reporting one of their best holiday sales seasons in years. Any more information you're looking for?"

His wife was right. He is cranky.

"Yes, and thanks for recapping *USA Today*. It will cut down on my reading during the flight back," I retort, letting him know that two can play this game.

He tilts his glass in my direction before taking an impressively long pull on his scotch.

"You know what informa—"

"How's the shoulder, Michael?" Albright asks, cutting an increasingly agitated Kylie off mid-sentence.

"Almost as painful as sitting here and playing this game with you," I respond.

"The door is right over there. Feel free to let yourselves out if you don't like my company."

"This is a waste of time," Kylie says.

She knows Albright is under no obligation to give us any information and swallows her own scotch as she rises to leave. I start to follow, but Chelsea doesn't move a muscle.

"You coming, Chels?" I ask.

"No, not until I get what we came here for. You see, I don't think Mister Albright is acting this way because he's in a bad mood. He's acting this way because he's nervous."

"Nervous? About what?" Albright snaps at Chelsea.

"That you're being visited by a former Green Beret, a jaded journalist, and a pissed-off redhead. That, and you have no idea how much we already know."

Where is this coming from? I always knew Chelsea had it in her to be a bit of a badass, but it's still a little weird. Johnston is taken aback, too. Instead of the angry tirade I again expected to see him launch into, he just renders her with another amused smile. Kylie sees the opening and pounces before I get the chance.

"So, how about it, Mister Speaker? Will you let us ask the questions we came here to ask?"

"I already know the one question you want answered most, Miss Roberts. You want to know who put out an order to have Michael assassinated."

-TWENTY-THREE-
KYLIE

"So, you know?" I ask, more to see his reaction than blindly believing he just implicated himself in a murder and numerous counts of attempted murder.

"Of course not!" he barks in irritation. "I'm the former Speaker of the House, Miss Roberts. Do you really think I would have that kind of information?"

"Our sources are under the impression you would," Chelsea fires back, managing to keep a level of cool that I'm not.

"Which sources are those, Miss Stanton?"

"The ones we don't plan on divulging to you in case you decide to have them killed also."

Redheads are stereotypically known for their fiery tempers and sass. Outside of the occasional outburst, Chelsea has tamped down those attributes in the time I have known her. Now she summons them at will. Whatever self-discovery she has done since the shooting has had a profound impact on her attitude.

"How dare you, you insolent little—"

"Do you deny working with Reed to throw me out of office?" Michael asks, trying to prevent Albright from uttering something to Chelsea he would come to regret.

Johnston Albright's face contorts into a look of surprise. For a seasoned politician, I would have expected him to hide his reactions better. I want to play a couple of hands of Texas Hold 'Em with this guy. He has a lot of tells.

"No, I don't deny it," Speaker Albright says as he again uncaps the decanter and pours another drink while we awkwardly stand in the middle of his study. "It doesn't seem like there's much of a point in doing so, even if I wanted to. There were a lot of people last summer who wanted you gone, Michael. He was just one of them."

"Yes, there were a lot of people. Like Marilyn Viano, for instance. Did you know she was working with Reed, too?"

"What?" he reacts reflexively, in astonishment. I guess he didn't see that one coming.

"Reed was using you to push me out so Viano could step in and lead the icandidates. If she could help carry them to victory in November with me out of the picture, they would have virtual control of a sizable chunk of the House of Representatives."

"Are you telling me that bastard Reed wanted to create his own private legislative army?" Albright asks in disbelief.

"Yep."

"And the rules bill I proposed?"

"It would have forced the freshman independents to choose sides. If we formed a third party, he would have an organized group he could weasel his way in control of."

"And if they chose to caucus with the Republicans or Democrats, he could coax the genie back into the bottle and maintain the status quo until he found another way to reach his goal," Chelsea finishes for Michael. Now it's my turn.

"And we all know how lucrative the current system is for the nation's largest, richest, and most influential lobby. So, do you want to tell us what you know about the assassination attempt now?"

"I don't know *anything*, Miss Roberts. You're fishing in the wrong crick. If Reed was involved, I would be the last to know. It wouldn't surprise me, though. You were an obstacle to him," he says, turning to Michael, "and James Reed does not like adversity. He's used to getting his own way."

"Is that why you went along with him for the ride?"

"Michael, you have no idea how much pressure I was under. My party was screaming at me to do something about you before the election. The Dems even promised not to make waves during your ethics hearing. It was why it went to the Floor even after it was clear you were framed."

"And why I had to flip a table."

"Everyone overestimates the power of the Speaker of the House. The public is led to believe I control what gets voted on and what doesn't, but nothing could be further from the truth. The real power lies with the people who lurk in the shadows of power. I was doing everyone else's bidding but my own when it came to forcing you out. Had it been left up to me, I would have left you alone, isolated, and powerless. You would have lost last November on your own, but I was overruled."

Unfortunately, he's right. Michael would have been beaten badly had he been left alone. The candidates that ran against him were good, while Michael, as an incumbent, had no substantive accomplishments to his name. He had lost a sizable portion of his social media following and had no money to even try running a traditional campaign.

"You find it hard to make the tough choices, don't you, Johnston?" Michael challenges.

"It's so easy to judge when you're not standing on the rostrum. Sit in my chair and see how easy it is. I heard you may be looking to take it anyway."

Our nation's leaders don't have an easy job. They deal with a fickle electorate, disinterested constituents, shady colleagues, opinionated special interests, partisan ideologues, and a national media that feeds the divisive atmosphere that exists today. Unfortunately, the constant scandals, underhanded dealings, and entitlement attitude give us every reason not to feel sorry for them. Or trust them.

"I think you're a liar, *Mister Speaker*," I say, getting menacingly close enough to his face to smell the alcohol on his breath. "And once a liar, always one. I've been a journalist long enough to tell that you know more than you're saying. When your name surfaces, and it will surface, I'm going to ensure they bury you in the deepest hole I can find. Even if, for some reason, you manage to avoid prison, I promise, I will end your political career."

"No, you won't," Michael says, causing me to whir around to face him.

-TWENTY-FOUR-
CHELSEA

"What? What do you mean?" Kylie stammers.

She's not used to being undermined by the congressman. Even I'm curious as to where he's going with this. He's not one for pulling punches himself, as Blake found out quite literally last spring in Arlington National Cemetery.

"He's already burying himself, at least politically, aren't you, Mister Speaker?"

Albright doesn't say anything. Kylie, still seeing red, is directing her anger between the Speaker and her boyfriend like a ball at a tennis match. Since nobody is eager to say anything, I restate the question.

"They're forcing you out, aren't they?"

"Not 'they,' Miss Stanton, 'he.' One man always had designs on my office and has dedicated his whole career to positioning himself as the heir apparent when I decided to leave it. I guess that wasn't happening fast enough, so he chose to cozy up to the RNC and build enough support to force me out."

"Who has that kind of power?" Kylie prods, suddenly seeing another target.

"Harvey Stepanik," Michael guesses. Albright nods a confirmation.

"How is that supposed to work?" Kylie demands.

"I have been strongly encouraged to cite health reasons for withdrawing my name from the running for Speaker when the caucus meets in January. Then a few months later, resign my seat for the same reasons."

"The Republican Party isn't showing you the same loyalty you did them," Mister B concludes.

"Yeah, well, they need a scapegoat for this debacle. The setup job was embarrassing to the party, and losing the rules bill only made that worse."

"You reap what you sow, Mister Speaker."

"Yes, Miss Roberts, you do."

"Why did you get into politics?" the congressman asks unexpectedly. Kylie shoots him another harsh glance. It dawns on me that it will be a long and awkward plane ride back to Reagan National.

"What?"

"You heard me. You were a successful prosecutor after law school and an even more successful corporate attorney once you got your trial experience. Why did you decide to run for the House?"

"Do you remember Watergate, Michael?"

"Only what I read in books and have watched in documentaries. How old do you think I am?" That causes the Speaker to smile. It's the same question we pose to the congressman all the time in the office.

"I was barely a teenager when Nixon resigned. I didn't understand what I was watching on my parents' television until I reached college. Then I watched as a parade of scandals desensitized us to them. Iran-Contra, the House banking scandal, dozens of congressmen being indicted for everything from bribery to campaign fraud.

"It made me sick. I was sworn in as a freshman congressman in the House just in time to see Bill Clinton impeached for perjury and lying under oath about his relationship with Monica Lewinsky. I wanted to be different. I wanted to do it right. Twenty or so years later, look where it got me."

The congressman looks moved by his story. He ran for the same reasons Speaker Albright claims to have. I feel a little sorry for him too, but Kylie doesn't share our opinions. Standing with her arms crossed, I'm not sure who she's more pissed at, Albright or the congressman.

"It's all a moot point now, Michael. My political career is over, and your girlfriend wants to put me in solitary."

The comment elicits a short laugh from the congressman and an angry nod from Kylie. The tension rises in the room until Mister B drops a bomb of his own.

"You can quit if you want, Mister Speaker. It's the best thing that could happen, given everything you've done, but I have a better idea."

-TWENTY-FIVE-
MICHAEL

"Michael, she tried to destroy your political career. Did you think I would be thrilled about going to her memorial service?"

"No, but she got herself killed in the process of trying. Regardless of how we feel about her, she didn't deserve that." Reading her facial expressions, I'm not sure Kylie agrees with that. "I was hoping you were just worn out from our day trip to Charleston yesterday."

"I'm not, but I don't think you really want to talk about that right now. I might get the idea in my head that I need to measure you up for a coffin." That's an inappropriate touch of macabre humor, considering I was almost killed a week ago.

I think she's only playing around, but I'm not going to press the issue. We barely spoke on the drive to the airport following the meeting with Speaker Albright and said nothing on the plane ride home. In fact, the uneasy feeling in the pit of my stomach has only grown worse since we left Charleston. It's been a long twenty-four hours.

Attendees to the service pay their final respects to Marilyn Viano near the altar at the front of the church. Her injuries precluded the possibility of an open casket, so a large floral arrangement of white roses adorns the lid. A poster-sized picture of her as a senator stands vigil on an easel surrounded by bouquets of flowers.

The service was graced with elegance and sophistication that characterized her personality. It was also very sterile, devoid of any raw emotion and remorse typical of most services. Marilyn Viano came across as a cold, calculating woman. Her memorial service had the same feeling.

Attendees are beginning to make for the exits, but Kylie remains standing next to where we were seated. She's looking around, and I don't know if it's to take mental notes of who attended or because she's looking for someone.

"Is it me, or did her husband not seem that torn up about this?" she asks, still scanning the sanctuary.

"They were the typical wealthy Washington power couple. I don't think they had what most Americans would consider a loving marriage."

A quiet grunt is all I get in response. I'm beginning to wonder if that is a consequence of living in that town.

"Are you done looking for...whoever...so we can get out of here?"

"When I'm satisfied that he's not here. You owe me that much."

"What do you mean?" I regret the question as soon as I ask. It's like taunting a lion with a steak before deciding to put your head in its mouth.

"You cut me off at the knees with Albright. He knows more about the shooting than he's telling us, but instead of pressuring him to get to the truth, you go and strike a political deal with him," she summarizes, making no effort to hide the anger in her tone.

"You're still pissed about that?" She just gives me a look. Dumb question number two. "Okay, what can I do to make it up to you?"

"A trip to Turks and Cacaos would be nice, but right now, I'll settle for Door Number Two."

"What's behind that door?" I ask, beginning to realize I may have earned the stupid question hat trick.

"Him," she says, pointing to the large man standing at the back of the church and chatting amicably with Marilyn's widower. Without another word, she stomps off in his direction. I follow, wondering whether I'm up for a confrontation right now with one of the most powerful men in Washington.

* * *

"Good morning, Mister Reed. I see you are hard at work finding ways to line more politicians' pockets. Nothing like the memorial service of an old colleague to provide you with a target-rich environment to ply your trade,"

Kylie fires as she approaches Reed, Viano's widower and a current ranking member of the Senate Banking Committee.

The latter two men quickly excuse themselves, recognizing Kylie as a journalist and not wanting to be around for whatever fight she is about to pick with Reed. He stares hard at her for a moment before turning his attention to me. The people around us are trying hard not to make it evident that they're watching our interaction and failing miserably.

"How's the shoulder, Congressman? You seem to be recovering well from the *tragic* shooting."

There isn't an ounce of sympathy in his voice. He even drew out the word "tragic" to mock me. It's a callous remark even for him, considering we're at the memorial service of one of the victims.

"Spare me your platitudes, Mister Reed. We both know what 'crocodile tears' are," I respond, equaling the cold tone of his voice. Two can play this game.

"So how about it, Mister Reed?" Kylie questions, wrestling the conversation away from the shooting and onto whatever she plans to catechize him about. "Have you made any purchases while you've been here? I mean, look around. There are so many elected officials here ripe to be bought."

"Miss Roberts, I'm not sure if y'all were born yet, but the Supreme Court ruled in 1976 that money is free speech in *Buckley v. Valeo*. They upheld limits on direct contributions to campaigns to curtail the appearance of corruption but held that spending money in other ways to influence elections is protected as 'free speech.' I would think that, as a journalist, you might know something about that."

"As a journalist, she also knows that you didn't answer the question," I chime in before Kylie can.

"I'm sorry if you find my methods distasteful, Congressman Bennit, but you can't argue with the results."

That depends on what results he's referring to. He didn't manage to force me out, which is what I want to say but don't.

"If by results, you mean every election since the ruling serving as a constant demonstration of how the corruption problem isn't solved by siphoning campaign contributions through political action committees, then you're right, I wouldn't argue." I smile just to annoy him.

"The problem is, Mister Reed, that your idea of exercising free speech is giving the wealthy and elites a megaphone that drowns out ordinary Americans," Kylie says, taking up the argument. I am not entirely sure why she chose this tactic, but I have known her long enough to tell she is setting him up for something.

"I am helping them exercise their *constitutional* right," he explains.

"A constitutional right to free speech for all Americans is worthless if the only voices that can be heard belong to members of the one percent."

Reed smirks, and I have a burning desire to erase the condescending smile from his face with my fists. Setting aside my urge to give him an old-fashioned military-style beating, I can only wait to see what little gem comes out of his mouth next. I don't have to wait long.

-TWENTY-SIX-
JAMES

"I didn't set up the system. I just operate within it," I tell Bennit. "If you don't like the fact that money is free speech and corporations are not people, then get a constitutional amendment passed that says otherwise. You are a congressman, after all."

Good luck with that. In 2002, Congress amended the Federal Election Campaign Act of 1971 in the Bipartisan Campaign Reform Act, colloquially known as "McCain-Feingold." Fortunately for my firm and me, significant portions of the new law were struck down by the Supreme Court in a series of landmark cases.

The result was a complete failure to reduce the growing power of special interest money. Coupled with a loophole that permitted candidates to raise campaign funds from political action committees, lobbyists like me were free to deposit vast amounts of money into candidates' war chests.

"Is that why you're so scared of the icongressmen? You're afraid that they could garner enough support to do precisely that?"

"Please, Miss Roberts, don't overestimate the abilities of a small minority of the House or my opinion of the threat they may pose."

"We're not," Michael responds in this tag team match. "You know we are the greatest threat to the system you set up. Up until last November, elections were paid for by corporations and the über-wealthy. Those politicians did what the people who paid them wanted. The social media candidates were leased by the voters in their districts, and we do what *they* want. Are you telling me, with a straight face, that you don't find that threatening at all?"

I smile at the audacity of the question. Yes, I wanted Bennit removed, but not because I thought he was a threat. If things had gone a little different, I would be controlling his legion of followers right now.

"Y'all flatter yourselves if you think you're anything more than a minor annoyance in my world."

"A minor annoyance you went through all the trouble to frame to get removed from the House?" There it is.

"Yes, that was an unfortunate decision by an overzealous employee looking to make a name for himself," I assert with the same collective calm as I did when I told the story to the F.B.I. Of course, the feds were easier to convince that Logan Tyler was operating on his own accord than these two are.

"Is that lame excuse the same one you use to explain away how it was your idea to try to get the independents to caucus with the other parties?" Damn, they've been talking to Albright, although he could not have known the rules bill was ever meant as anything other than a means to manipulate him.

"I think you are confusing me with the former Speaker of the House," I say with a smirk, "but I understand why you are so adamant about implicating me. Y'all resent what I do."

"What exactly is it you think you do, Mister Reed?" Kylie asks without any attempt to hide her disdain.

"I exercise the right 'to petition the Government for a redress of grievances.' Americans have families and kids and jobs…I perform a service on their behalf, so they do not spend their precious free time wandering the corridors of power in Washington. Our First Amendment rights are sacred in this country, and my job is to help protect a free people against the overbearing and tyrannical government for whom you work, Mister Bennit.

"To hear the way members of Congress tell it, lobbying is held in the same esteem as waterboarding and practiced by voodoo witch doctors on behalf of the wealthy elite to plague the poor middle classes. The truth of it is quite the opposite, and I find it unfortunate that a reputable journalist and a distinguished lawmaker have failed to achieve that level of understanding."

Kylie is about to explode, which is the exact reaction I was going for. Michael, on the other hand, is a rock. His face is impassive, and I can see why people who try to get under his skin are met with spectacular failure. I've heard rumors that he has a temper and have even seen it firsthand. Flipping the table during the hearing was a spontaneous act and not for show. Regardless, he isn't as overt in displaying the level of rage as his girlfriend is.

"That is a well-crafted response, and surprisingly accurate considering you're a professional liar," Michael says with an inexpressive tone. Kylie is about to chime in when he continues. "I agree that lobbying is constitutionally protected and almost universally despised."

"This may be the first thing we have agreed on, Congressman."

"True, but you left out an important distinction. There are two types of lobbying. One is the actual redress of a legitimate grievance, like protecting teachers from drastic cuts in personnel and pay. Teachers are busy educating our kids and cannot fight the battles in the halls of legislatures without assistance. Unfortunately, that's not the lobbying activity you engage in."

"Since you are presumptuous enough to know my job better than I do, why don't y'all explain to me what activity you think I do engage in?"

"You don't advance an agenda based on the merits of an actual argument against a policy. You leverage the ability to influence elections with infusions of cash. As a result, the candidates you back owe a debt of gratitude they repay by propagating a system that can only be characterized as legalized bribery."

"I resent the impli—"

"That system," Michael continues, cutting me off, "threatens the 'one man, one vote' principle our democratic government is based on. If the sum of a candidate's financial resources predetermines success in elections, then average voters who trust their elected representatives with political power will have their voices drowned out by special interest donors. The result is a situation where the principle of equality, fundamental to the health of any democratic government, is egregiously violated."

Bennit is an idealistic fool. He has bought into the mythology of the Founding Fathers that is perpetuated in our schools to indoctrinate our young children starting in the first grade. These men were not saints. They were merchants, plantation owners, slaveholders, and opportunists. They convinced the other colonists to support their cause by using European thinkers like John Locke, but their real motives were selfish and self-serving. They weren't heroes or brilliant thinkers. They were master manipulators, just like me.

"I hear you like giving history lessons, Congressman, so let me tell you one of my own. When the Republicans got shellacked in the 2012 election, they sought ways to avoid a similar embarrassment in the future. Do you know what their top proposal was for how to win? Dismantle the nation's campaign finance laws to allow even more influence over politics and politicians.

"And if you think the Democrats are any different, you'd be surprised to learn they concluded to allow the wealthiest Americans to subjugate the political system years before. Your colleagues in Congress may publicly decry money in the system, but the political parties secretly work behind the scenes to increase it. They encourage laws changing how much campaigns may receive from rich donors, repeal the limits on contributions, and undermine support for a public financing system that could supplant their power."

"All of which benefits you most of all," Kylie interjects, having recovered from her repressed temper tantrum.

"It does, and y'all will never be able to change those laws so long as the political parties embrace that system and refuse to reform it. There's nothing illegal or unethical about operating within the confines of the law," I say, flashing the biggest smile I can muster.

"We'll just see about that," is all she can respond with. My smile disappears.

"Is that what this is about? Y'all are trying to get me to implicate myself in the commission of some sort of crime?" I ask in feigned surprise. It's time to end this ridiculous conversation. "Congressman, I would have thought you knew better than to accompany a second-rate journalist on a fishing expedition like this one. Good day."

-TWENTY-SEVEN-
KYLIE

The last time I was called a "second-rate journalist" was by my sister Madison at a trendy bistro in Manhattan when I confronted her about Beaumont getting me fired from the *New York Times*. I didn't appreciate it then and still don't now. Not from her and certainly not from this guy.

"Mister Reed, can you comment on allegations surfacing that you were involved in the attempted assassination of Michael Bennit and the *murder* of Marilyn Viano?" I announce, loud enough for everyone remaining in the church to hear.

He stops, looking around the chapel in embarrassment. Every person remaining in the house of worship, including Marilyn's widower and several prominent politicians, is staring back at him. I sneak a glance at Michael. He closes his eyes briefly, wishing he was anyplace but here. I'm sure I will hear about this antic later tonight, assuming we are talking by then.

"This is not the time or the place, Miss Roberts," Reed replies in an adamant whisper once he turns around and makes his way back to us.

"Should I take that as a 'no comment'?" I respond, holding the recorder I dug out of my purse in front of him for dramatic effect. I'm not even sure I switched it on.

One of the best things about being a journalist is having the ability to make people uncomfortable just with our presence. Reporters cause people to get nervous, unseasoned politicians anxious, and political operatives either defensive or aloof. Reed has thus far been immune to my intimidation, so I hope this rattles his cage and forces him to step out of his comfort zone long enough to make a mistake and say something stupid.

"I have nothing more to say. This conversation is over."

I'm not going to let him bury his head in the sand that easily.

"Mister Reed, you lectured us just moments ago about how we could never remove money from the political process and how your undue influence on it benefits the democratic principles of the country. Are you telling me now that you have nothing to say when I ask you if you were responsible for the death of such a close friend?"

"I am warning you, Miss Roberts!"

"Warning me about what? Are you going to have me killed too?"

At this point, we have the undivided attention of everyone in the church. I know Michael is fuming because this is not how he likes to handle things. Of course, his dealing with Speaker Albright wasn't how I do them, so I consider us even. This is my version of flipping a table, but I doubt he'll see it that way.

"I was in no way involved in the shooting, and anything printed to the contrary will result in me suing y'all for slander," Reed barks, using an adamant tone for the benefit of those in the church listening in.

"It's called libel when it's in print. R-e-e-d. The spelling is easy enough. Is there a middle name you'd like me to include in the article?" I ask in my best professional voice.

The question evokes anger and then a creepy smile from the large man. He decides to start ignoring me and focusing on Michael.

"You know, when I was growing up in Kentucky, I had this crazy uncle who had a mean old coon dog that was always biting people. One day, he bit Buster Jenkins right on the leg. Buster told my uncle that if he ever heard anything about that dog biting anyone again, he'd put him down himself. It wasn't an idle threat since he walked around with this big 'ol silver Smith and Wesson revolver. Anyway, do you want to know what my uncle did?"

"I don't really care, but we've come this far," Michael says for me.

"He put the dog on a very short leash." Reed looks at me and then back at Michael, the implication of his ridiculous story very evident. "You should think about doing the same."

I have been with Michael long enough to know when he gets angry. I'm not sure if it was the gun metaphor and some latent sensitivity to being shot, or if it was the veiled threat against us Reed leveled. Either way, if it weren't for having his left arm in a sling, he would be choking the life out of the big man in his swanky Italian suit right now.

"Buster was used to having his way in town, wasn't he? I bet he was always making threats and issuing ultimatums to get whatever it was he wanted."

Michael lets the statement hang in the air for a couple of beats. He does a remarkable job building tension usually reserved for theater and cinema for a guy who is not into drama. I wonder if he even realizes he does it.

"There are two problems with your story as it relates to us," he continues. "I'm not your crazy uncle. I'm not scared of Buster Jenkins and his hand cannon. The second is that Kylie isn't some out-of-control coon dog. She's a disciplined military canine. Do you know what happens when the bad guys run and one of those fine animals chase them down? They only die tired."

"Please, start running," I beg James, not overly thrilled with being compared to a dog but more than happy to indulge the metaphor. "This chase is only beginning."

-TWENTY-EIGHT-
MICHAEL

My office is not the most spacious on Capitol Hill by any stretch of the imagination. However, I have grown fond of my 958-square-foot room with a Capitol view and consider myself fortunate I didn't end up with one of the non-coveted spots up on the fifth floor. The space I occupy was vacated by a colleague who snagged Beaumont's old office when he resigned. I could have traded up after the last election, but I like this view and have no interest in moving.

Before the start of each Congress, incoming members of the House enter a drawing to determine who gets to choose first from the available office space. The lottery is held after the veteran members of the House get to move to the most plum offices if they desire. I was late to the party, so I never had the privilege of suffering through the office assignment process.

In truth, there are no winners in the freshman House lottery. None of the incoming icongressmen can even dream about landing in the coveted Rayburn House Office Building or any other prime real estate on the Hill. Some of them desire to occupy my building, turning it into a bastion of independent, social media candidates. We'll see if that happens.

An overeager producer is micromanaging staff busy setting up tonight's live interview. I wasn't even at the hospital when the first media requests for interviews began pouring into my office following the shooting. In the week since, reporters, news anchors, distinguished journalists, and even late-night television personalities have been clamoring to entice us into selecting them for the first big interview. Some took to trying to bribe my junior staffers to put in a good word for them.

I left Vince to make the final decision of who to pick while I recovered. I have had a lot on my plate these past seven days, from flying to South Carolina to confront Johnston Albright to keeping Kylie from strangling James Reed this morning at Viano's memorial service. While knowing an interview is inevitable, it wasn't my priority.

He settled on a live interview with *Capitol Beat*, a newer political program run by one of the twenty-four-hour cable networks. It is hosted by the venerable Wilson Newman, who anchored the show's predecessor for a decade before it moved time slots and was rebranded into its current incarnation.

None of my staff was about to miss this prime-time interview. My inner circle is small and limited to the students who ran my campaign. Vince, Vanessa, and Chelsea may have the bragging rights about being with me from the beginning, but the other members of my fourteen-person staff are equally dedicated. They have been hard at work every day since the shooting, some even choosing to come in on Christmas to catch up.

Of my former students, only the members of my staff are here today. I know the others will be watching from home, and all except Xavier will be coming to Washington on New Year's Day for the rally we are putting together.

When eight o'clock hits, Wilson gets the hour-long live interview rolling. Considering my social media pedigree, I've had limited experience dealing with the media during any of my three campaigns. Even while in office, the major parties succeeded in keeping me isolated and irrelevant.

The first three segments get spent discussing the shooting and the immediate aftermath. That is what most Americans have tuned in to hear about. None of his questions are unexpected, and I answer them as honestly as I can manage. I can tell he isn't used to that level of candor given the years he's spent in this town.

"Let's spend a few minutes talking about social media, Congressman," Wilson says after we return from commercial break. "Politicians have been using it since Facebook and Twitter first became household names, but you have brought it to a whole new level. You ran your entire first campaign on it. Why did you choose to do that?"

"Lack of finances was the primary reason. Running a traditional campaign costs an enormous sum of money. It is the reason why so many of my colleagues spend an inordinate amount of time fundraising instead of serving their constituents. Social media provided a platform that allowed me to communicate with people and share a message without incurring the costs of advertising on traditional media."

"And it worked, although you did get a lot of free airtime during both campaigns."

"Yes, we did, and that media attention was important in raising awareness at the time. The last election cycle was a turning point, though. A hundred more 'icandidates' used the same model, yet they did not benefit from the overwhelming and almost suffocating media exposure," I say with a smile. "Seventy-six of them will be joining us here in a few days, so I believe there has been a meaningful change in how Americans view candidates."

"Not everyone thinks that change is for the better, Congressman. They claim this reliance on social media makes you distant and unapproachable. Do you feel you lose touch with your constituents?" I am getting the feeling "they" means him in this context. Wilson is old-school, so I know he is not one of my biggest fans.

"Actually, I feel it brings me closer to them. Do you know how I passed the time recovering in the hospital from my wounds?" I ask, nodding toward my left arm, which is still supported in a sling to take the pressure off my shoulder. "By interacting with my constituents and countrymen via social media. I can have those interactions with people electronically far more frequently than without it."

"There is an important aspect missing — a voter being able to look their representative in the eye and shake his or her hand."

"You are assuming that my use of social media means an absence of personal contact. The part of this job I enjoy most is getting out and meeting with the residents of my district. Social media is simply another tool to help me do my job. Constant communication of ideas, issues, thoughts, and explanations about why I vote the way I do all helps my constituents understand the type of representative I am trying to be. The best forums I know of to do that are social media sites, but as I said at the end of my first campaign, they should never be used exclusively, especially once you're in office."

"There are a lot of rumors circulating around Washington that you are seeking to replace Johnston Albright as Speaker of the House. Is that true?" Where did that question come from?

Wilson Newman is a competent political journalist and friendly guy, but I must remember he is not in my corner. I got spoiled meeting someone like Kylie during my first campaign, who, despite her desire to remain impartial, really wasn't. Wilson has been waiting to try to catch me off guard with that question, and he succeeded.

"No, I am not pursuing it," I offer as a terse reply.

"Will you accept the position if you are elected to it by your peers?"

"I'll cross that bridge when I get to it, but I wouldn't bet on it happening, though."

"The president-elect is working hard to find allies in the House. He wants to get right to work once he gets inaugurated and already has the Democrat-controlled Senate on board with his agenda. Are you planning on having your caucus work with the new president, or will you be looking to generate your own political agenda?"

As the clock on this interview winds down, Wilson is stepping behind the arc and lobbing three-pointers. He gave Americans what they wanted in terms of how we are dealing with the effects of getting shot at. Now, he is creating sparks for the media to dump fuel on to keep their ratings up heading into the new Congress and the presidential inauguration.

Nothing serves the media apparatus better than conflict and tragedy. With both come viewers, ratings, and at the end of the day, advertising revenue. They got their tragedy on the Capitol steps, so now Wilson is stoking the fire to generate conflict.

"We are going to discuss the issues Americans are asking us to, whether it coincides with what the president wants or not." Yeah, I think I just gave it to him.

"Does that agenda include campaign finance reform?" he asks.

I shoot a quick glance over at Chelsea, who returns a warning with her eyes. The party elites think this is going to be our issue du jour since we eschewed the typical cash-intensive methods for winning elections. How right or wrong they will prove to be is still yet to be determined.

"Wilson, Americans have waited a long time for a Congress that was willing to address the issues that face our nation every day. Money in politics may be one of them or may not be. I can promise you, though, we are going to do everything in our power to be the Congress that people want."

-TWENTY-NINE-

JAMES

"Well, you won a hard-fought race, no doubt in part because of the money we funneled through the Super PAC to y'all," I comment to the Democrat as a means of taking his temperature. Like the several meetings and calls before this one, I find myself trying to get my footing following the uproar over Bennit's assassination attempt and the reality of a house of Congress with a sizable independent presence.

"I'm sure it helped. I consider myself fortunate that I did not have an icandidate running against me," Congressman Peter Dowd responds. The fact he was so quick to evoke the icandidates is not a good sign.

"I don't think that would have mattered. From what I saw, y'all ran a smart campaign by highlighting your strong family roots in the community and everything you've done as their representative over three terms. Do you really think some yahoo with no political experience would have bested you in a district you've represented for six years?"

"I do."

I take a moment to survey the ambiance of the restaurant. Located off D.C.'s bustling M Street, Vidalia is a four-star restaurant boasting flavorful Southern dishes and a killer wine list. The place with crowded with bureaucrats, staffers, and even a few high-ranking executive branch members. I hope their discussions are proving more fruitful than mine are. This conversation is not going well at all.

My firm rakes in big dollars to lobby members of Congress and government officials. All the millions that corporations, industry, and labor unions pour into lobbying efforts pale in comparison to the potential rewards when we are successful. To facilitate that success, a lobbyist needs to have personal connections to make the magic happen. Once they take our money, although there is no explicit quid pro quo, it is only human nature for the receiver to do their best to repay that debt and secure future...donations. Unfortunately, the popularity of Michael Bennit is testing the strength of these personal and financial relationships.

"I guess we'll see in a couple of years whether the icandidates can repeat that performance. I'm betting that once they realize that compromise is nearly impossible in this town anymore, their caucus will collapse faster than Enron did."

Dowd smiles and takes a sip of his wine. "I hope not. I plan on joining it," he mutters before taking another long drink.

"What?"

"You heard me, James. I'm joining Bennit's caucus."

Representative Dowd has always been a guy I could count on to help advance my clients' agendas. He is popular in his district and a well-respected member of his party. Despite being a little more moderate than many of the other powerful Democrats, he has garnered a lot of favor within the party apparatus by toeing the line.

"Why the hell would you do that?"

"Simple. If Bennit delivers what he's pledging to, I want to be a part of it. I've played the political game. You know better than most that it's the same story year in and year out. It doesn't matter which party is in charge—the gridlock is asphyxiating our country as the problems become more daunting."

"Congressman, I—"

"Let me finish," he snaps, clear that he's in no mood to hear how I plan to spin this. "I may have my disagreements with Republicans, and they have theirs with me, but it's my constituents that are paying the price. If there is any small chance that I can be a lawmaker and pass meaningful legislation to the benefit of the citizens in my district, then I'm going to take it."

"That's a big mistake. You're not going to want to be associated with that debacle when the bottom drops out of it. I thought you were more sensible than that."

"I will be in the same position as many of my colleagues on both sides of the aisle. I'm not the only one who plans on caucusing with the icongressmen."

"Who else is?" I demand, feeling myself begin to lose control of my temper. I loathe the moments when I realize one of my contacts has more information than I do. This is one of those moments.

"A couple of dozen representatives that I know of from both parties have mentioned it. Do your own homework if you want names."

I recover from the shock in time to play the only card I have left. "Then y'all have lost your collective minds. I'm pleading with you, Peter, don't do this. It will be hard for me to support you in the future if you do."

"I never realized the support you gave me came with strings attached. Thank you for making that clear to me."

He dabs his mouth using the napkin in his lap. Instead of replacing it and waiting for our dinners to arrive, he abruptly gets out of his chair. I guess our meal is over before it even begins.

"You'll have to excuse me. I've lost my appetite."

"Peter, you're overreacting. Sit back down and—"

"It's Congressman Dowd, not Peter. Have a good evening, *Mister Reed.*" He turns to leave and takes a step before stopping and turning back. "You resent what Bennit was able to do in November. I understand because I did too. Now I'm beginning to think his method for finally getting the money out of politics is the best thing that can happen after all."

* * *

When you're one of the most powerful lobbyists in the country, you are never really alone. Peter Dowd may have left me to dine solo, but there has been a parade of other patrons stopping by to say hello during my meal. Outside of the interruptions, the lack of a dinner guest has given me time to think.

Michael Bennit has been the bane of my existence since he got to Washington. At first, he was simply an obstacle in the way of me getting what I wanted. Now his popularity is turning into a problem for me on several fronts. The first is what I experienced here tonight. He is undoing the decades of work I, and many others in my industry, have spent to create a system we can work with.

Politicians pay lip service to campaign finance reform every two years. Of all the talking points they spew out on the American people, serious candidates and incumbents understand it is a crowd favorite and happily oblige the masses by talking about it at length. Some of them might now be serious about it.

We have rigged the process against anyone dreaming of serious change. With the recent Supreme Court decisions and a virtual phalanx of lawmakers having no incentive to change the system that protects them, the constitutional amendment that would be required to foster substantive reform is nothing more than a distant dream.

That leads to a second problem. Bennit has found a workaround to our roadblocks by circumventing Washington altogether. Tapping into the will of a frustrated citizenry eager to shake up the "business as usual" approach, Bennit is forcing change. With a small army of supporters joining his ranks in a few days, the iCongressman is enticing even loyal party lawmakers to sit at his table.

Much of the credit for this new era of cooperation belongs to his staff. Who would have thought a couple of years ago that a group of high school students could accomplish so much and give me ulcers in the process? They came within a hundred votes of beating a popular, longtime incumbent in Winston Beaumont. Four months later, they trounced their competition in the second election. Then, instead of going out drinking every night in college, they came together again to make more Michael Bennits. Amazing. I should start treating my interns better.

"More wine, sir?" the pleasant waitress asks after seeing my dinner is complete and my wine glass edging closer to empty.

"No, thank you, but I will have some cognac."

"Certainly, sir. I will bring it right over to you."

The waitress departs, and I realize she is not much older than Bennit's staff is. I will never understand this generation and their infatuation with social media. It's scary to watch them win elections using it and how it enables Bennit to communicate with vast numbers of Americans.

If they pull off this rally that his chief of staff is running around planning, it could be a game-changer. Social media in America has meant nothing more than providing people with a digital voice and a forum for exercising it. If she finds the ability to mobilize citizens into actual action and create change like Egypt and Ukraine did, it could result in a fundamental shift in the political process.

Chelsea Stanton and those students may just help vault Bennit to become the most powerful legislator in Washington. He will become even more popular with the electorate, and if he ends up as Speaker of the House, it would be catastrophic to the lobbying industry. Under his leadership, incumbents could become successful enough to run on their records. They won't need large sums of money to convince people to vote for them. Instead, they will have the gold ring of politics that has remained elusive for decades — achievement.

Bennit was dead-on with what he said at Viano's service. The peasants in this country have been drowned out by the wealthy elite who pay extraordinary sums to ensure their voices are the loudest. Michael Bennit has given the nation the hope it has long yearned for.

Obama won the White House in 2008 using the "hope and change" mantra, but it never really materialized because Congress, his own failings, and people like me never let it. Washington is a hard place to change, especially in a brief period. Bennit and his students are on the precipice of having unparalleled success if they can pull it off.

If the system is to be preserved, Bennit must be defeated fair and square. No setups to force him out, bills to silence him, or even assassination will stop his influence as effectively as some high-profile defeats.

The waitress returns with my snifter of cognac, and I take a sip of the luxurious liquid. The warming sensation seeps through me. It is a heavyweight title fight in the nation's capital, and the American people will have ringside seats. If the iCongressman needs to be handed a defeat, I'll make damned sure that's exactly what he gets.

-THIRTY-
CHELSEA

Six months ago, I would not have had the guts to walk into this office. I didn't consciously avoid the people working for many of the congressman's colleagues, but I did not go out of my way to talk to them either. The Three Amigos even implied once that my introverted ways contributed to my ineffectiveness.

These guys always regarded me as an amateur because I looked like one and, as I realize now, acted like one. The world seems like a much different place after the shooting. I'm not sure if it is changing, I am, or a mix of the two.

I stride into Amigo One's office and am not surprised to see the other two there. I recently found out they are all named Chris, which can become confusing since the three of them spend every waking moment together on Capitol Hill. Despite knowing their names now, I still call them the Three Amigos and assigned each a number to keep them straight.

"How are you, Chelsea?" Amigo One asks, rising from his chair as I enter the cramped room.

"I'm okay, thanks, Chris," I say, with the same level of pleasantness. "The headaches are finally starting to go away."

"How's your boss?"

"He's tired of taking bullets for his country, at least in the literal sense."

"I don't think anybody could blame him for that," Amigo Two says, from his perch in the corner.

The Three Amigos are the chiefs of staff for three prominent moderate New York Democrats. Vertically challenged in height and aging despite being in their late thirties, they're not wholly unattractive men. Their boss's proclivity to work together on issues meant constant proximity to each other and the start of solid friendships.

"Yeah, I wouldn't blame him either, but there's no quit in him. Other than wearing a sling, you wouldn't know anything had ever happened." That's not entirely true because I've noticed a change, but they don't need to know that.

"And Blake Peoni?"

"They still have him in a coma. He's had the surgeries he needs, but they need to be certain that the damage done was properly fixed before waking him. I manage to get over to G.W. most days to see him."

The three guys all nod their heads at the same time, making me wonder again if they were separated at birth.

"What brings you over to our digs in the Rayburn Building?"

"You are the closest thing I have to friends on the Hill, outside of the members of my own staff. I was looking for some information."

"What makes you think we have the answers you're looking for?" Amigo Three asks with a bemused smirk.

"C'mon, you guys have your fingers on the pulse of everything that happens on the Hill. Hopefully, I'll develop the relationships to do the same for myself. Right now, I need your help to fill in the blanks for me. I need to know what the members are thinking."

The three men look at each other in that "we don't need to speak to communicate" way that annoys the crap out of me. It wouldn't be the first time they've managed to bring the redhead in me out.

"Guys, I'm done playing politics around here. We are an open book, and I'm hoping you're along for the ride. There is no hidden agenda, so if you have a question, ask."

"Okay, I'll bite," Amigo Two offers. "Is Bennit using this rally of yours in two days to announce he wants to be Speaker of the House?"

"No."

"No? That's all we get?" Amigo One presses.

"That's the answer. I could fluff it up with some really impressive SAT vocabulary and put some neat spin on it to make it even more ambiguous like everyone around here does, but the answer is still the same. If

Congressman Bennit ends up running the House, it isn't going to be because he begged for the job."

"Would he take it if he won?" Could these guys already be thinking of talking to their bosses about supporting him? Have their bosses approached them? If so, how many others are considering it?

"I don't know, honestly. We haven't talked about it. Congressman Bennit is focused on the caucus."

"Fight Club," Amigo One offers with a smile from behind the desk.

The congressman made an offhanded comment about our fledgling caucus being like the fight club in the Brad Pitt movie of the same name. The first rule is the same: nobody is to discuss what happens there. The moniker stuck, and people in Washington and around the country have been calling it that ever since.

"Rumor has it the first item of business is campaign finance reform. True or false?"

"I heard the rumor too, although we didn't start it. Do you want to know why?"

"Because the first rule of Fight Club is nobody talks about Fight Club?"

"You got it," I praise, rewarding Amigo Three with a wink. "Tell your bosses to come to the first caucus meeting if they want to know what's being discussed. They can find out for themselves."

"But some could have leaked—"

"Now, it's my turn," I demand, cutting a surprised Amigo Two off before he finishes. I don't want to talk about the caucus. That's the congressman's baby, and I'm here for mine.

"The Speaker of the House is not going to be decided on the first ballot, is it?"

"We'd be surprised if it's settled on the first day. Why are you asking?"

"What would it take for me to persuade you to convince your bosses to support Bennit?"

The three men exchange glances like I just announced to the room that I'm pregnant and that one of them is the father.

"I thought he wasn't asking for votes to get the job," Amigo One finally answers when it was clear neither of his colleagues would.

"He isn't asking for them, Chris. I am."

-THIRTY-ONE-

MICHAEL

"Do you make it a habit to rummage through your staff's desks when none of them are around?" the voice of Johnston Albright bellows from the door with amusement.

"Only when I'm looking for the keys to the supply closet that she keeps in here somewhere," I respond, continuing to search in her junk drawer without looking up. "I need to replace the toner in the printer."

"Printer maintenance is a little beneath a sitting congressman, don't you think?"

"Actually, no," I say, finding what I was looking for and closing my youngest staffer's desk drawer. "Not being willing to change it is beneath me."

The Speaker shoots me a smile, walks in, and looks around at my completely vacant outer office. I know it's rare to ever see anyone's office on Capitol Hill this quiet or empty, even when Congress isn't in session.

"Did you fire all your staff or something?"

"Are you kidding? They wouldn't leave even if I did. No, they're all keeping busy helping Chelsea plan this rally of hers, so I'm holding down the fort."

"Alone?"

"Even the last soldier on a post has responsibilities," I answer, knowing he won't get my point.

"Oh yeah, like what?" I was hoping he'd ask that.

"How many trucks are there on an army post, Mister Speaker?"

"I have no idea. I suppose it varies by post. Why? And call me Johnston."

"It's an old 'Soldier of the Year' competition board question I used to hear while I was on active duty. The answer is there's only one, and it is at the top of the post flagpole."

"I get the feeling I'm about to be treated to one of your history lessons."

"In fact, you are," I say with a smile, motioning him into the small room that houses the laser printers. "At the top of the post flagpole is a finial called a 'truck.' In the military, the flag is the embodiment of everything we pledge to defend—our land, people, and principles. It defines our territory, can be a symbol of resistance, raised as a declaration of victory, and captured as a harbinger of defeat.

"Legend holds that three items are hidden at the top of the flagpole to honor the flag in the case a post is ever overrun. Those items vary from one interpretation to the next. One item, like a match or razor, is provided to destroy the flag. A second item, like a revolver, serves to arm the defender, and the third item is a patriotic symbol like a key, penny, or grain of rice."

"So, this applies to you how, exactly?" Johnston asks.

"I'm getting to it. There is a secondary theme in the folklore of the 'truck.' It is the notion that the flag must be destroyed by one of its last defenders, and the somewhat more romantic image that the last man standing must not be taken alive."

"Your history lessons are becoming something of a legacy around here, but I'm sorry, I still don't see your point."

"Even alone, an individual can still make a difference, even if it's a symbolic one," Michael says. "That imagery of a lone man standing before a horde of invaders and performing his last duties can still inspire a nation."

"I know that firsthand after dealing with you last summer," Johnston proclaims with no hint of the snarky tone I'm used to from him.

"I suppose you do, but right now, I'm alone, and my mission is to change the toner in the printer," I say, unlocking the cabinet that holds the supplies.

"I didn't realize so many of you were in this building," he observes, changing the subject and making small talk while he avoids getting to the point of his visit. At least, that's how I'm interpreting it.

The incoming icongressmen did end up making the Cannon House Office Building our stronghold in Washington. The one-hundred-plus-year-old Beaux-Arts architectural styled behemoth was completed in 1908 and looks like a fortress among the other congressional office structures. Now it is our bastion because all of us ended up here, either through luck or by trading with other representatives. Even the half dozen rumored to be defecting to the two major parties procured space here.

The Republicrats, a term of derision Vanessa uses to besmirch both groups simultaneously, has managed to erode our ranks. They promised the sun and moon to get the independents to pledge their allegiance to them. The riches were too enticing for some to refuse.

"I know you didn't stop by to talk about office space. What brings you here, Mister Spea...Johnston?" I ask, correcting myself at his request.

I am listening, but my attention is divided between focusing on him and ripping open the toner cartridge package. I'm thwarted even by simple packaging while wearing this cursed sling. To paraphrase Shakespeare, my kingdom for a pair of damn scissors.

"I wanted to talk to you alone."

"Destiny obliged that request. What's up?"

"Why did you invite me to join you guys back in South Carolina?"

I visibly wince at the memory of the aftermath of that meeting. Kylie wanted to rip his throat out and was prepared to do that, at least verbally. When I deviated from the game plan and extended the proverbial olive branch, she was too stunned to react. That changed during the car ride back to the airport. And at the airport, on the plane, and later at home that evening.

"What do you mean?" I ask, stalling for time. I am rewarded with a look from the former Speaker of the House that lets me know he knows I'm doing just that.

"You know exactly what I mean. We have a short, tumultuous history together. I censured you, tried to expel you, and even abetted a lobbyist to set you up for embezzlement. Most politicians would have helped throw dirt on the coffin my political career has found itself in. Instead, you're offering to work with me. Trust me when I tell you that you are the only one. I just want to know why."

"You are my Japan."

My former antagonist Robinson Howell, Millfield High School's principal, is Nazi Germany.

"I'm sorry?"

"The Japanese attacked our forces at Pearl Harbor and marked our official entrance into World War II," I explain, finally winning my battle to free the toner from its hermetically sealed tomb. I open the printer door and remove the spent cartridge holding the black toner.

"We locked horns in deadly naval battles and vicious jungle fighting for almost four years. The war ended with the incineration of two hundred thousand people with atomic bombs. Our two countries should hate each other for eternity, but instead, they are one of our closest allies and trading partners. The American people and the Japanese people changed. Maybe we can too."

"Is there anything you *can't* place in historical context?"

"No," I respond with a sideways smirk. "History does not repeat itself, but the themes in history do. Once you understand that, its study has a practical application to the modern world."

"You must have been one hell of a teacher," Albright says, a hint of admiration in his voice. "I'm not going to be much of a help to you now, Michael. I am persona non-grata in my own party. Stepanik is going to make sure I'm dragged into daily hearings for months. The House Republicans will push for an ethics investigation, and I'll have the option of spending hundreds of thousands of dollars on legal counsel or resign my seat and spare myself the cost and humiliation."

"No, they won't be doing any of that. Stepanik is posturing. Neither he nor your fellow Republicans will want the negative press for the party that would accompany that course of action."

"Regardless, I won't be the Speaker of the House and don't have any contacts or allies that can help you achieve your goals."

I close the printer up and turn the power back on to let it cycle through its pre-operation checks. I toss the residue in the trash next to the recycle bin before finding a response to Johnston's warning.

"A man's usefulness is not measured only by who he knows, but also by what he does. What will you do?"

"I don't have a course anymore, Michael."

"Maybe you do now. We're going to get attacked from every direction the moment the House convenes. Republicans, Democrats, lobbyists… Anyone interested in seeing us fail is coming to get us and anyone brazen enough to join our caucus."

"You think it will be that bad?"

"It'll probably be worse. The question I have for you, Johnston, is if I raise the flag, will you defend her?"

Yeah, I quoted Bon Jovi. "Raise Your Hands," off their *Slippery When Wet* album, is a personal anthem for me.

"Maybe I have one more good fight in me. If you get a chance, stop by my office later today so we can talk some more." He starts to walk out before stopping again before the door to the hallway. "As grateful as I am, I hope you don't regret including me."

"I won't so long as you don't give me a reason to."

I lean against the doorjamb of my small printer room and study him as he uncomfortably stands in the doorway to my office. He's conflicted, and I can only presume to know why.

"Michael, if you give me a chance to do what I was elected to so many years ago, I will stand with you even if we are the last two," he says, looking over his shoulder at me.

"Let's hope it doesn't come to that, Johnston. I don't want to have to find out what actually is in the 'truck.'"

-THIRTY-TWO-
JAMES

"What the hell is going on?" Harvey Stepanik yells as he comes crashing into the office with my secretary hot on his heels, trying to stop him.

"I'll have to call you back," I murmur into the phone receiver pressed to my head before hanging up.

"I'm so sorry, Mister Reed, I tried to stop him," one of my secretaries says, worried about her job.

"It's okay," I reassure her, knowing a platoon of marines would have had difficulty keeping the House majority leader out. "Have a seat, Congressman Stepanik."

He doesn't accept my offer of a chair. Stepanik is a politician's politician. With looks, intelligence, and a chess master's aptitude for the game here in D.C., I am surprised to see him so ragged and on edge. It's out of character for him.

My junior secretary leaves after another volley of apologies. The doors aren't closed for more than a second before Harvey launches his verbal assault.

"Do you have anything to do with this? Are you double-crossing me?" he barks.

"I have no idea what you're talking about," I rejoin, fighting back my anger at the interruption and his attitude.

"Do you think I'm a fool? I am not Johnston Albright. You aren't going to play me like you did him and expect to get away with it."

"Congressman, you've lost your mind if you think you can barge in here and start throwing your weight around without any explanation. Now, you'd better tell me what on God's green earth you're talking about, or I will throw you out of here myself." I lost the fight with my anger.

"Bennit."

"What about him?"

"There are rumors up and down the Hill that he's getting support from both parties for Speaker."

"Is that so?" I play dumb. I am well informed about those rumors.

"Yeah, it is, and you know it. You're the only person in this town capable of swaying that many politicians. I thought we had a deal."

"We do," I snap back at this insolent bastard. "I have nothing to do with this."

"I don't believe you."

"You'd better. I'm the best ally you have. I have been talking to the key players in both parties nonstop about supporting you. Do you have any idea how hard it is to sell Democrats on the idea of supporting a Republican for anything in this political climate?"

"You're doing a crappy job at it."

I am not the type of man who likes getting dressed down, especially by a politician. They think they are all so smart. All they ever have managed to accomplish is to win an election or two. Congratulations and big deal. I tolerate Stepanik because he is my best hope at keeping my influence in the face of all these independents, but he needs to understand a simple truth: I run this town.

"Why, because I'm not countering every move that Chelsea Stanton makes?"

"What are you talking about?" he retorts.

"Chelsea Stanton. Bennit's chief of staff. She's turned into quite the political operative since she almost got gunned down. She and the rest of Bennit's staff have talked to every member of the House to build support for him." Confusion marches across his usually stoic face. He didn't know that.

"And you are sitting here doing nothing?"

I'm tired of this conversation already. I get up and peer out my office window down at Franklin Square below. I should not have to explain this to the heir apparent to the Speaker of the House. Even someone like Michael Bennit could understand this.

"You ever read Sun Tzu, Harvey? The *Art of War*, chapter twelve, verse seventeen: 'Move not unless you see an advantage; use not your troops unless there is something to be gained; fight not unless the position is critical.'"

"I don't need to hear your whimsical precepts. This position is critical! This is about becoming the third most powerful man in the United States government!"

"You are smarter than this, Harvey. You are single-handedly responsible for the fall of the man you are trying to replace."

"Yeah, so what? He won't be Speaker. He won't even be a representative in a few short months."

"Are you so sure about the second part of that?"

I'm not sure if my comment or the knowing look on my face is giving him pause. He takes a moment to review what he knows wants to *believe* is true. If my sources are correct, Johnston Albright's days in Washington may not be as numbered as Stepanik hopes they are.

"Yeah, it's a done deal," he finally surmises. "The party is forcing him out to make room for me to ascend to the leader of the caucus and the nomination for Speaker."

"You should head back to the Capitol and visit his office. You may be interested in what you find there. Once you do, come back, and I will explain to you exactly what I'm doing on your behalf."

-THIRTY-THREE-
KYLIE

It's a week removed from my Christmas Eve meeting with Terry in Baltimore, and my investigation is going nowhere fast. We've collectively moved not one inch forward in uncovering who was behind the shooting. It's not the first time I have been stymied in searching for the truth, but this has been the most frustrating.

Terry and I are both getting stonewalled by everyone we talk to. We're convinced James Reed was somehow involved in the shooting, but nothing connects him to it. Employees at Ibram & Reed who might know aren't talking. Terry's sources in the Capitol Police haven't relayed any helpful information either. The police investigation is a black hole no light is escaping from.

Their silence isn't all that surprising. In the nine days since the shooting, investigators at the federal and local levels haven't made any more progress than we have. Of course, they aren't taking the same outside-the-box approach we are. They are content with the lone gunman theory. Every indication is that they are getting ready to close the case, in practice if not officially.

The Capitol Police are responsible for protecting the legislative branch of the government and providing security details for members of Congress, much like the Secret Service does for the president. They have exclusive jurisdiction on the grounds of the United States Capitol and, much like any municipal police force, are charged with ensuring the safety of lawmakers, their families, the buildings they occupy, visitors to the area, and public spaces on Capitol Hill.

I stopped in at their headquarters located in a boxy, seven-story structure on D Street to meet with the chief. She politely refused my request for an appointment, leading me to implement my plan B. I have been waiting outside the main entrance of the building for a couple of hours now.

"You don't take no for an answer, do you, Kylie?" the chief says, spotting me as she emerges from the building. Tall at six feet and impressively fit, she commands respect even without the four gold stars on the collar of her white shirt. Recruited away from the Chicago Police Department while working in some of the city's roughest areas, Deana Hayes is as fierce as they come. She must be clad in plate armor to manage an agency with eighteen hundred mostly male personnel.

"I wouldn't be much of an investigative journalist if I did," I reply to her observation.

"I have nothing to say to you. We update the media at our afternoon press conf—"

"At which you have offered next to no additional information in days."

I am tired of everyone in this department offering me the same response to my questions. Chief Hayes is the unlucky individual that won't get away with brushing me off.

"There hasn't been much to uncover."

She begins walking towards the Capitol, presumably for the meeting I am happily making her late for. After a couple of hours standing around and lurking at the entrance, it feels good to stretch my legs as I match her hurried gait. Cops are not unlike soldiers in that they have very little tolerance for media types. As Michael can attest, their reticence doesn't faze me at all.

"My sources say otherwise."

"Your sources are wrong," she responds, using a condescendence that I've come to expect from everyone associated with this incident.

"Or possibly the chief of the Capitol Police isn't being candid about what her detectives have learned so far." That gets her attention.

"We don't discuss details of an ongoing investigation, Kylie, you know that."

"Oh, so you are still investigating? I wasn't sure since I have talked to more people around here than your investigators have."

I've had the opportunity to interact with Deana on a couple of occasions over the past two years as I chased down stories for the *Washington Post.* Our relationship is a cordial one, and although we'll never be BFFs, I'd prefer to keep it on good terms. If this conversation continues like this, I'm not sure that will be possible, but I'm going to get answers to my questions one way or another.

"Yes, I've heard people whispering that you're turning this town upside down to prove some sort of conspiracy."

"I'm exploring theories you aren't even considering," I say, trying to change her outlook. Conspiracy is such a negative connotation in this context.

"I took my tin foil hat off long ago."

"If you were wearing it, you may have intercepted the call made from the Capitol Building to the shooter moments before he tried to kill my boyfriend."

Deana stops dead in her tracks. Terry will be pissed that I tipped her off that we know that, but I need to get through to this woman. Chief Hayes glares at me through the piercing green eyes that were once soft and pretty but now have the hard edge of someone having fought many battles and seen her share of horrible things.

"Fortunately, the NSA caught it," I say, pressing my advantage while avoiding a staring contest with her that I have no prayer of winning. "Have you bothered asking them about it, or does that not fit into your narrative?"

"Kylie, we've known each other for a while now. I have nothing but respect for you as a journalist, and I admire your boyfriend more than you will ever know." She gets a little too close to my face for comfort. "So, please, listen to me when I tell you that you're getting dangerously close to interfering with an investigation."

"Funny, I thought I was getting closer to lighting a fire under it."

Suddenly this confrontation reminds me of running into my sister Madison in the parking lot following Michael's first debate. She was a member of Winston Beaumont's staff and more than a smidge upset that her boss was trounced on television in front of a live national audience. She made her threats using the same aggressive tone Deana Hayes is now. I didn't back down an inch back then either.

"If you print information we have not released—"

"I don't plan on printing anything," I interrupt.

"We will embarrass your paper and seek criminal charges against you for obstruction of justice," she finishes, intent on finishing her statement.

"If unreleased information surfaces, it won't be broken by the *Post*, but probably will be initiated by some crazy blogger. You know how they like to poke around on the fringes of investigations and don't follow the same journalistic principles we do. They'll print anything they think has a chance of going viral, but that never works, right?"

My thinly veiled threat is received loud and clear. One tip to the blogosphere and the story is out without having any possibility of it being traced back to me. Well, no trace leading back to me other than my telling the chief of the Capitol Police Department that I would do it. Good luck proving that in court, though.

"What do you want from me, Kylie?" Like any good field marshal, she knows when the enemy has the high ground. Great, now I'm beginning to think like Michael.

"I want to make damn sure you do your job. That you aren't going to take the path of least resistance."

"Are you challenging my integrity and that of my organization?" she snaps.

"No, quite the opposite, but I am putting you on notice. I'm not going to stop until I find the answers I'm looking for. When I do, I will print them for the entire world to see. If your investigation concludes something different, then you're going to have a lot of explaining to do on the Hill. Don't let that happen, Deana."

"Your warning is noted," she says with contempt more than understanding. Cops really do hate reporters.

"Good," is all I say in response.

"Now, let me give you a piece of advice of my own. Contrary to what you might believe, I respect First Amendment rights. I mean that. However, if anything leaks to the media about this investigation, I'm going to blame you. Then I will instruct the officers in this building to ensure you follow every law ever passed to the absolute letter. If you forget to separate your recyclables or step one foot outside a crosswalk, I will slap the cuffs on you myself. You'll be in and out of my holding cell so often you'll need to claim it as a second address when you do your taxes. Do you understand what I'm saying?"

Crap. So much for holding the high ground. This woman just informed me I would be held responsible for anything *anyone* prints. Not only did this ambush of mine backfire, I just got owned.

"Yes, I think I get the picture," I say as calmly as I can.

"Good. Then we have nothing more to discuss," Deana says with a smile as she walks off into the long shadows cast by the Capitol's surroundings. Dusk is approaching, marking the end of another short December day, and I get the eerie feeling the inevitable darkness serves as an omen for my career.

-THIRTY-FOUR-

CHELSEA

With Christmas now in the rearview mirror and a mere two days before the New Year's Day rallies, it made sense to bring all the chiefs of staff for the incoming icongressmen together before the fireworks really begin. Vince and Vanessa did a fantastic job finding a hole on everyone's calendar before the new Congress convenes so they could attend.

It's been hard to focus on work with Blake still in the hospital in a medically induced coma. They tell me he's improving, but I can't understand how they know that without him being conscious. I spend as much time at his bedside as I can, but preparation for the rallies and the upcoming congressional session is eating up a ton of my time.

At least Congressman Reyes is on the mend. After the stunt Mister Bennit pulled by escaping the hospital on Christmas Eve, the hospital watches the sole remaining congressman in their charge like hawks. Part of me is surprised they stopped short of handcuffing him to the bed. He is driving them crazy in defiance, and I'm sure both he and the hospital staff will be thrilled when he gets discharged.

I'm glad I showed up to the room early. I planned to take a few minutes to organize my thoughts, but that notion went out the door when Amanda and Peyton arrived. I should have known they wouldn't miss this meeting, even though we didn't expect them to come to Washington until tomorrow.

Amanda and Peyton worked closely last fall with many of the men and women in the room. It's counterintuitive to think that grown adults would reach out to college-aged students for help running for a national office. We're the only ones with experience running social media campaigns. I suppose being on the front covers of major magazines also helped with our street cred.

The room we reserved in the bowels of the Cannon Building fills quickly. It's the first time the chiefs of staff and some key staff members have all been together, and I expected it to be...I don't know. I didn't expect it to start this way, though.

"What are *they* doing here?" one of my colleagues asks, firing the open salvo of the verbal assault on two of our numbers.

"They switched sides and shouldn't be here," another chief acidly chimes in.

The room descends into a chaotic cacophony of back and forth accusations. The top advisors for two of the icandidates who we've heard are planning to defect are in the audience. The Republicrats have spent a ridiculous amount of time and energy trying to recruit members out of our ranks. The chiefs of staff for two icandidates entertaining their overtures are being called everything from traitors to things that would have gotten my mouth washed out with soap by my father.

"You ever get that feeling sometimes that we're back in high school every time we attend a meeting in this town?" I ask Amanda, Peyton, Vince, and Vanessa.

"Just think, Chels, we couldn't wait to graduate and get into the real world to escape this petty gossip and adolescent behavior," Vanessa responds.

"College isn't much of an improvement over this," Amanda observes. "This sounds a little like my business law lecture."

"The other turncoats that didn't attend aren't going to regret that decision if we don't get a handle on this," Vanessa concludes.

"Vince, can you—"

"Everybody shut the hell up!" he bellows loud enough to shake the rafters. He's had enough of the BS, too.

The decibel level in the room decreases to a whisper. It won't last long. It's time for me to intervene.

"I know the rumors of what's going on are bothering everyone, but let's give them a chance to explain themselves," I offer to pacify the room. I hope their excuse is a good one.

For the next few minutes, they explain that their bosses were accepting offers from the Republicrats because they wanted to get on committees. They thought that joining the ranks of one of the parties would guarantee them the coveted positions on standing committees we were denied when Congressman Bennit got here.

Republicans and Democrats historically have known the number of seats they will receive in each committee before Congress convenes. When a third-party candidate or an independent gets elected, they have been assigned to committees through either party. Since the congressman was denied the opportunity to caucus with either party after being sworn in, we were frozen out.

Within each party, legislators pick committee assignments based on their position in an order determined by a drawing. Unlike the business world, their choices have nothing to do with competency, knowledge, or experience. Most of the decisions are purely political.

After committee assignments are chosen, each party approves its slate of appointees. The whole roster is voted on by the full House of Representatives. Like many things that happen in that building, approvals are only window dressing. The entire process is borderline ridiculous.

"You didn't think your bosses might want to wait to see how it shakes out? There are over seventy-five of us here now, and both parties know they will never keep that number off committees."

"We're here because we tried to talk them out of it. Our principals are stubbornly dedicated to the people back home."

If this room is a powder keg, that comment just struck a match. Every one of the other chiefs of staff doesn't appreciate the insinuation, because they know their icandidates share the same dedication. Quick to jump on the comment, the ensuing verbal berating is merciless. Vince has no chance of bringing this under control with only one "shut up." He needs three and a hard slap on the table to get the fracas back under control.

I understand why some icandidates are leery. The usual way of doing business is turned upside down because there is no majority party. Republicans only have a plurality in the House, meaning if the Democrats and independents wanted to team up to defeat them on something, they collectively have enough votes to do so.

The impending disaster of this new legislative reality is something the media has been reporting on since Election Day. The only respite the American people got from this constant drumbeat of stories was the fallout from the shooting. With Congress about to convene again, and no additional information being released by the Capitol Police regarding Bernard's motives or accomplices, the political fireworks have returned to the front page.

Vince and Vanessa push to get the mob to back off a bit. There is a lot of tension in the room. I don't want to make my pitch under such a black cloud. Leave it to Peyton to provide the perfect distraction to get us back on course.

"How was orientation?" she asks the group, flipping her long, swooping blonde curls to the side of her head. Immediately, she has the undivided attention of every man in the room, and even some of the women.

"Long," one of braver among them chimes in from the back.

"You guys could have warned us there was so much to do," another says, not willing to let the opportunity of chatting up the beauty in the room slip by.

"That's the price of winning," Amanda says with her own disarming smile. Even she can crank up the charm a notch or two when the situation calls for it. They set about soliciting various short anecdotes from the chiefs, eliciting everything from snickers to belly-laughs. The mood in the room begins to lighten as the group shares their stories.

Freshman orientation is an integrated, bipartisan program for incoming representatives. The curriculum offers invaluable resources and a wealth of knowledge for new members, including seminars on public policy issues and workshops on how to get stuff done in Washington. They are all led by current and former senior legislative and executive branch officials, federal officials, and the national media. None have any experience dealing with a sizable force of independents in Congress.

"They spent a lot of the time talking about raising money during orientation," a woman comments from the third row to near-universal agreement. "It sounds like that's all they do here."

"That's because it is," Vanessa responds. "Representatives spend countless hours each day on the phone soliciting donations for the next race."

"No wonder Congress is so dysfunctional," someone adds.

"It's worse if you belong to a party," I elaborate.

When you win a seat, you get about a week to savor the victories before the harsh reality of Washington sets in. Many new representatives have grand plans to change the toxic atmosphere on Capitol Hill but are rewarded with the only mantra that matters to either party—raise money, then raise more money, and make sure you win.

"Some representatives spend four hours a day fundraising," Vince finishes. "That's over twice the time they dedicate to committee hearings and floor votes and double what constituents get in terms of access."

"That's ridiculous!" a chorus of voices shout in unison.

"Welcome to American politics," I lament.

"Will campaign finance be one of the topics the caucus addresses once Congress convenes?"

The question was directed at me, but I'm not ready to answer it. Congressman Bennit has the beginnings of an agenda but doesn't want anything leaked. I don't want to be the first to test the golden rule that earned his caucus its name.

"You'll have to show up to Fight Club to find out," I say with a pleasant smile. "Remember the first rule."

"New subject," the cute guy a few rows back interrupts. "Chelsea, why is Bennit telling our bosses that he isn't running for Speaker of the House?"

"Because he isn't."

There is a loud grumbling in the room. That wasn't what these representatives wanted to hear. Unlike most parliaments and our own Senate, the Speaker of the House is the primary legislative leader of the body. Typically, he or she is the leader of the majority and sets the agenda based on that party's wishes.

Of course, with no majority party, the rules have changed. The Speaker's duties are not prescribed by the Constitution, so the position is defined by over two hundred years of traditions and customs. The power wielded has evolved, from enormous in the nineteenth century to all but stripped in the early twentieth century. The pendulum swung back in the 1970s, and now the top dog in the chamber wields more than ever.

"Why not?"

"Because he doesn't think he'll win and wants to spend his time getting the caucus set up, not lobbying for votes. He wants to ensure you fulfill the promises you made to your constituents back home. He thinks if he divides his efforts, he'll be setting all of us up for failure."

"He said that?"

"Have you ever heard a twenty-year-old girl not enlisted in the military use the phrase 'set up for failure'?"

"What are we doing here if he isn't running?" A smile etches across my lips. We have finally gotten around to the point of my setting up this meeting.

"Just because he says he isn't running doesn't mean your bosses can't vote for him."

-THIRTY-FIVE-

JAMES

"Has the shooting had any effect on the American people?" the moderator asks his panel of pundits.

"I don't think it has as much as the media is portraying," one of the liberal women in the upper right quadrant of the split-screen says. "As much as people hate Congress, nobody wants to see them shot by a gunman, despite the rhetoric we sometimes hear. The vigils are an expression of that and nothing more."

"I think you've tumbled down the rabbit hole into Wonderland if you really believe that," the conservative voice opines from the lower left. "The leadership of both political parties is terrified of Michael Bennit, and with good reason. He is a martyr for the cause of the independents now. Like it or not, many of these social media candidates are now members of Congress and are here to stay. Their leader is going to get a lot of attention during the election for Speaker of the House."

This is not how I pictured this afternoon going. The president-elect had his staff contact my office and set up a meeting at his temporary residence at Blair House, the place established at the beginning of the Second World War as a home away from home for foreign dignitaries visiting the United States.

The moniker itself is a misnomer. Blair House is a complex of four connected townhouses comprising some hundred plus rooms and an impressive combined footprint that spans seventy thousand square feet. All in, the diplomatic refuge now playing host to the incoming president is larger than the White House itself.

"The political parties are not going to allow any of their members to support an independent for a position that puts him third in line for the presidency," the final panelist argues.

All three guests on the show begin to talk over each other until the moderator regains control. The split-screen format this cable news show utilizes is distracting to the point of being annoying.

"The voters may not give them a choice. If large numbers of Americans from across the country show up at these planned New Year's Day rallies, it could convince representatives that it is in their political best interest to—"

"Not going to happen!"

"You can't say that—"

"Seen enough?" the incoming White House chief of staff asks as she mercifully mutes the television.

"You know, Diane, I expected to be sitting in the Truman Study having a chat with the president-elect, not ushered into a conference room to listen to these idiotic experts pretend they know anything about what is going on in this town."

"He's running late. He'll be here shortly," she replies curtly. Like most political handlers, she will make any excuse she can for her boss.

"So, you decided to show me a movie instead? Are you taking me to dinner too? We can follow that up with a nice romantic stroll down the National Mall and call this a date."

"This is serious, James."

"No one knows that more than I do." Part of me is glad she ignored my comment about dinner. She may have taken me up on it.

"And?"

"And what? Y'all really need to stop panicking around here. Michael Bennit is not going to be Speaker of the House."

"And you plan on stopping that how? The guy is Captain America, Thor, and the rest of the Avengers all rolled into one. The American people want him in a leadership position, and from what I've heard, there are representatives on both sides of the aisle considering it. Some of the 'idiot, so-called experts' seem to back that up."

"You underestimate lawmakers' allegiance to their parties. They'll talk a good game, but in the end, they'll do what they're told."

"Not if they think supporting Bennit protects them from an onslaught of marauding social media candidates two years from now."

"It's a fad, Diane, like the Atkins Diet or Tebowing. It won't last." I could have picked zoot suits and pet rocks, but I already feel old enough.

"That may be true, but icandidates didn't just win national elections. Social media candidates ran across the country at every possible level of municipal and state governments. They were winners of everything from local school boards to town mayors to state assemblymen races. With all that success at federal and state levels, the movement is not a fad that is going to go away in the next two years when the president is going to have midterm elections to worry about."

"Once Stepanik gets elected Speaker, he can help work with you to tamp that down. Y'all need to stop tormenting yourselves over Bennit and focus on putting together a good cabinet and setting a solid legislative agenda," I say, shaking my head. "The president hasn't even taken the oath of office, and he's worried about the next midterms."

"Did you slip and hit your head and forget how Washington works?" Diane responds, her snide retort punctuated with a cock of the head and face contorted in disbelief.

There is no foresight in America anymore, at least coming from its politicians. From Manifest Destiny through to the New Deal, many of our leaders were men of extraordinary vision. Nowadays, politicians can't see past the next election.

Such limited prescience can be bad business for lobbyists like me who need bills passed for our clients, although gridlock does have its merits. Some of my biggest clients also pay me to ensure that bills on key issues never get undesirable traction. Since both parties need a majority in both houses and the presidency to get anything done in modern politics, achieving a legislative standstill is a piece of cake.

"No, I know exactly how it works, and Michael Bennit can have his young chief of staff talk to whomever she wants. They can hold daily rallies on the White House lawn for all I care. Hell, they can even let reporters stick their fingers in the hole in his arm. Do you know why none of it matters one iota?"

"Enlighten me."

"Because, in the end, the members will recognize the dangers of electing Bennit and the consequences they'll face for supporting him." I don't bother to explain further.

"You'd better be right, James. The president has a very ambitious agenda he is planning to unveil, both at his inauguration and at his State of the Union address. Trust me when I say he is going to have enough problems with a Democrat-controlled Senate, but he won't get anything done if an independent is running the House."

-THIRTY-SIX-
MICHAEL

"It's official. We've lost three," Chelsea assaults me in a verbal ambush as I walk into my office. She is joined by Vince, Vanessa, Peyton, and Amanda. I can only assume Brian and Emilee will be here soon. Xavier is unable to make it due to his basketball schedule. Syracuse is having a good season, and he's a rising star on the team.

"It's New Year's Eve, Chels. Can we at least start with the good news?"

"That was the good news, Congressman," Vince explains. "It could have been seven. We managed to bring four of them back into the fold after meeting with the chiefs of staff yesterday."

"At least for now," Vanessa laments.

"Who defected?"

Peyton tells me the names, but none of them sound familiar. Despite being the anointed leader of this crew of misfit toys, I have only met a handful of the incoming icongressmen in person. Only two of us have relationships with any of them.

"Amanda, I'm surprised you're not freaking out about this. You too, Peyton." Those are the two.

"They'll get theirs eventually," Peyton offers in an innocent voice that tells me she is already plotting their demise.

"Sooner rather than later, if I have my way," Amanda mumbles for good measure. She worked closely with one of those campaigns. There is no doubt that she's taking their defections personally.

"I don't understand why they would leave us," Vanessa offers, either out of genuine confusion or as a nod to the efforts of her former classmates.

"They found out how addictive the dark side of the force is, and now that they're inside the Beltway, they can't resist its pull. That's why the longer politicians stay, the more they look like the emperor in *Return of the Jedi*," Vince muses.

The group laughs, and although I'd never openly admit it, it's a fair observation. Some of my colleagues are scary-looking, but he's missing the point.

"There is one problem with that analogy, Vince. Most of the people here are not malevolent, just misguided."

"All evidence to the contrary," Vince says under his breath.

"I don't understand," Peyton states before turning to me. "What do you mean?"

"The representatives in Washington are not all evil souls leeching off the country like most people think. Some of them are born scoundrels, but even decent politicians get caught up in the corrupt system."

"Is that why you are choosing to work with Albright?" Amanda wonders aloud.

"Yeah, that's one of the reasons. Americans have endured greedy politicians and petty partisan bickering for a long time now. It's the system that has become rotten, not the people serving in it. There's too much money sloshing around politics. It's not only been legalized; it's become institutionalized. If Johnston Albright helps us reform that system into something this country desperately wants to see, I will have only proved that point."

"And taught the country another lesson in the process."

I wink in agreement. I initially set out to teach my students a lesson in civics. When the campaign took off on social media, despite my lack of positions on issues, it became a lesson to the American public about the dangers of unchallenged conformity.

When I got to Washington, I saw the effects of unchecked partisanship. I chose to team up with Cisco and Viano to run a crop of a hundred icandidates to show Americans there was a better way to govern. It was a lesson to our political parties that compromise shouldn't be a dirty word if it's in the people's best interests. Now, I'm going after the "root of all evil."

"Do you think America understands these lessons you're trying to teach them?"

"Some do, Peyton. Others don't. What I do know is they have voted to send a cadre of lawmakers here that can help us make a difference." At least, that's what I've been working toward.

"Now we're going to see if we can bring it to the next level," Chelsea interjects. "We campaigned using social media and helped the congressman keep from getting thrown out of Congress using it. Tomorrow, we're going to see if it gets Americans out of their homes to rally for a cause."

"Do you really expect a big turnout on New Year's Day?" Vanessa asks. She's as skeptical about the prospect of significant numbers showing up on a holiday as I am.

"People will show. There should be a small group there, and they're going to want to meet with you," she replies optimistically after turning to me. She knows how to appeal to me by reminding me about the fun part of this job.

"How small of a group are we talking about?" I ask, hoping the smaller, the better. As a teacher, I am used to being in front of small groups of students and am comfortable with the classroom's intimate setting. Public speaking on a stage to a large crowd is not my strong suit, and not wanting to admit that to my former students, I'm trying to keep the anxiety to myself.

During my campaigns, I was physically nauseous for days over the thought of participating in nationally televised live debates. Arguing with an experienced incumbent or a pair of well-prepared candidates didn't bother me. Doing it in front of an audience did. I was careful not to let my students or Kylie see how nervous I really was. Those feelings are coming back, and I don't even want to think about tomorrow, let alone talk about it anymore. A few hundred is as terrifying to me as a few thousand is.

"I don't know. I've never used social media to organize something like this, and considering it's a holiday...a few hundred people at the D.C. rally, I guess."

"Okay, well, I guess we'll see tomorrow. In the meantime, I'm off to G.W. to see Cisco. He's going stir crazy there. If they don't let him out soon, he'll make a break for it *Shawshank Redemption* style."

"Tell him we said hi," Chelsea says as the staff goes back to work to get everything prepared for what should be a nerve-racking experience.

* * *

"That looks appetizing," I observe, catching Cisco with his fork halfway to his mouth.

"I hope that's sarcasm," he replies, plopping his fork full of...whatever it is back onto his tray.

"Dude, this is inhumane," I say, taking a closer inspection of Cisco's dinner. "You should have told me to pick up something on the way."

"The nurse offered to sneak out to get me Taco Bell."

"Taco Bell? That's a little racist, isn't it?"

"Just a touch, yeah. But I'll tell you, bro, I could really go for some decent yellow rice and beans right now," he says with a smile. I guess that's Cisco's idea of comfort food.

"How's the leg?"

"It's healing up nicely. I should be out of here in time to be there when Congress convenes, but I'm going to miss your rally."

"I'm willing to trade places," I offer.

"Just imagine them all naked," Cisco advises, knowing full well how much I loathe public speaking.

"No, thanks. I don't think that's an advisable course of action unless this speech is being given at the Playboy mansion or something."

"You won't need to imagine it there," Cisco says with a chuckle. "Although I'm sure Kylie would have something to say about that. Speaking of which, how are you and her doing?"

"We've been better."

"She's still running around like Nancy Drew, and you still don't like it," my friend concludes. Yeah, that about sums it up.

"She and Nyguen are turning over every rock in this town trying to pin the shooting on Reed."

"And you're not convinced he was behind it?"

"Who knows? If he was, I don't think we'll ever be able to prove it, and I have better things to spend my time on. We get one shot to make our time here mean something. I don't want to blow it."

"Okay, I get why you aren't playing Sherlock, but why do you care if she does?"

"Manfred Albrecht Freiherr von Richthofen."

"Manfred Allbrok Frey…who? Man, I'm Latino. I can't even pronounce those syllables!" After a moment, he comes to the realization of what's coming next. "Aw, crap. I'm about to be treated to one of your history lessons, aren't I?"

"You're a man of unparalleled wisdom. Richthofen was a famous German fighter pilot during the First World War. Because of the distinctive plane he flew, the world knows him better as the Red Baron. He shot down eighty aircraft and was the most lethal pilot on either side during World War One."

"Kylie will be thrilled to hear that you are comparing her to the guy Snoopy flies his doghouse against."

"Shut up and listen," I reprimand playfully. "In April of 1918, he began chasing a Canadian trying to escape a battle and strayed behind Allied lines. He dove close to the ground and didn't check his six to see another plane coming up behind him to help his comrade."

"For the love of God. How did your students survive your class? Is there a point to this?"

"Yes. The world will never know whether ground fire or that second Canadian pilot took out the Red Baron, but he met his end because he made the mistake of pursuing that plane too long, too far, and too low into enemy territory."

"Again, your point is?"

"We are in enemy territory, Cisco, and the election of the icongressmen is a declaration of war against the political elite. Everyone is going to be gunning for us when Congress convenes on the second of January."

"And you think Kylie is flying too low?"

"She's high enough not to be under anyone's radar but low enough for everyone to take shots at. We don't need more targets on our backs. Or leg and arm, for that matter."

-THIRTY-SEVEN-
KYLIE

Frustrating. That word best sums up my day, my week, and my life since the shooting. I suppose I could wordsmith some alternatives: aggravating, exasperating, infuriating, troubling, and vexatious all come to mind.

Doing follow-up interviews on the heels of investigators is a waste of time. I shouldn't expect anything less, considering I only embarked on this quixotic escapade to placate my editor and mask my true intentions. All I have managed to learn are two things during my exploits. The first is the Capitol Police are checking off boxes and not doing any real investigating. The second, and most infuriating, is that nobody is interested in talking to me after talking to them.

The result is what you would expect—nothing to write about. My editor will lose his patience and take me off this story if I don't produce something. The specter of my imminent reassignment adds to the stress of running a clandestine side investigation with Terry. I desperately need to discover something fast to keep the cover story in place.

The challenge of placating my editor would be a welcome one had I not run into my own obstacles. Terry and I have not enjoyed any success in our own inquiries. Even the smallest leads we manage to develop never amount to anything. With no earth-shattering revelations, it's no wonder investigators are convinced Jerold Todd Bernard worked alone. There is just nothing to lead anyone to believe otherwise. I know better, though.

I finally make my way into our apartment in "NoMa." Local-speak for the area north of Massachusetts Avenue, it's the part of the capital that most reminds me of my East Village roots in NYC. I love this place, and my furniture fits in it perfectly. Michael lobbied to move some of his own stuff in, but that was a non-starter. The man may be a brilliant teacher and decorated soldier, but he has no aptitude for interior design.

"I was beginning to wonder if I would be spending New Year's Eve alone," Michael quips as I drop my stuff on the chair in the living room.

"Sorry, things ran a little later than I had anticipated."

"It's already ten p.m.," he says, adding a bit of melodramatic flair by staring at his watch until he's sure I notice. "It must have been something important to keep you so late on the last day of the year."

The sarcasm in his voice tells me all I need to know about what he's thinking. Things between us have gotten progressively worse in the days since Viano's funeral. He's still pissed off about how I dealt with Reed, and I'm just mad at him in general.

"I doubt you'll think so."

"What is that supposed to mean?"

"You've taken no interest in this investigation, so—"

"I've been a little busy, Kylie," he protests, using the same tired, weak defense I've heard a dozen times. Too busy to find out who was behind the man who tried to kill you is what I want to ask, but don't.

"So you say."

"Chelsea has this rally all set up for tomorrow that I am obliged to make an appearance at. Do you plan on coming?"

There are a dozen rallies she set up with the help of several icongressmen and volunteers from across the country. I'm not sure where she finds the strength or energy, but I see a side of her she's never shown before.

"I don't know yet. It depends on how the morning goes."

"I figured as much."

"This is my job, Michael. I thought you would be the first to support me, given what I'm trying to do."

"And this is mine. I thought the same thing."

We feel differently about what's important right now. Michael and I have shared all the same goals since the day we met, so it was only a matter of time before we got tested when we didn't share the same vision. I can only hope overcoming the obstacle brings us closer together in the end.

"I'm trying to help you!" I scream, venting some pent-up frustration. If we grow closer because of this, it won't be today.

"By running around D.C. and harassing everyone in the hope that they have information that may or may not even exist? That's helping me how?"

"Sometimes, you need to shake a few trees to get the fruit to fall."

"And you're making my job exceedingly more difficult in the process."

"Oh, I'm so sorry to inconvenience you, Your Majesty," I reply with an awful attempt at a curtsy.

"Whatever," he mutters, shaking his head.

No couple wants to fight during a holiday, but this conversation is long overdue. We need to talk this out or beat the crap out of each other. Whatever it takes to get past the spot that our relationship is stuck in. I figure tonight is as good a night as any until he gets off the couch and heads towards the bedroom.

"Where are you going?"

"To bed. I have a long day tomorrow."

"You aren't going to watch the ball drop with me?" I don't know why I asked. I already know the answer.

"No. I don't feel much like celebrating anything these days."

I need to say something. I *have* to say something. We are never going to solve anything if we don't communicate. The problem is, neither of us wants to listen.

"Happy New Year, Kylie," Michael says before disappearing down the hall.

-THIRTY-EIGHT-
CHELSEA

"A few hundred people, huh?" the congressman asks me after surveying the crowd from behind our hastily constructed makeshift stage.

"Okay, so maybe a few groups got bused in." We expected a couple of thousand here when we were doing our planning, and that was optimistic. I look out on the mass of humanity and know that you can increase that by a factor of one hundred.

Which location on the National Mall to hold this rally was the subject of intense debate. We decided that the best spot was in the shadow of the Capitol itself and set up at the bottom of the stairs on the west side of the building. Everyone was supposed to fit in the triangular wedge of grass formed by connecting the Capitol, James Garfield Memorial, and Civil War Sailors Statue. Yeah, not so much.

Overflow crowds spill out around the Ulysses Grant Memorial and Capitol Reflecting Pool all the way to the other side of Third Street and the grass of the Mall. Laterally, the crowd extends all the way from where we stand to Independence and Constitution Avenues.

I'm sure the unseasonably warm low fifties temperatures haven't hurt the turnout. It is a beautiful day to be outside for January in this part of the country, and many people took the opportunity to show up just because they wanted to enjoy their day off from work outdoors. How's that for a lucky break?

"A few groups got bused in? Are you kidding me? This is unbelievable. I'm glad I decided to dress up."

Mister Bennit has never been known for his excessive style. He is most comfortable in denim and wore jeans to school every day back in Millfield.

Today is no different, except the suit jacket has even been replaced by a windbreaker. He looks like the common man because, deep down, he is the common man.

"Considering we didn't think there would be much of a turnout, I'm surprised we bothered to rent a sound system."

The guest speakers I handpicked for their patriotic orations have been getting the crowd all riled up, but the congressman is the main event. Since I have been dividing my attention between organizing the rallies and getting support for the Speaker of the House vote, I had to rely on a combination of staff, interns, and volunteers to do a lot of work. Trusting people has never been a strong suit of mine, but I had no time to micromanage. It reminded me a little of old times.

When Mister Bennit ran his first race, we had volunteers from all over the district help with the campaign. Being a senior in high school with grades to maintain, I had to rely on others to do much of the heavy lifting. This was no different, and I can only be forever grateful they pulled it off.

"Well, this rally would make the hippies proud. I probably should have planned some remarks."

"No way, Congressman. I would have ripped them up if you did. You work better without a net," I tell him.

"How would you know? How many speeches have you ever seen me give?" I don't have to think about it. He's never given one, at least officially.

"I've heard how many history lessons you have given us?" I argue, not conceding his point.

"This is different, and you know it."

"Okay, I saw you at the debates. That counts."

He humiliated Winston Beaumont and Richard Johnson in the debate during our first campaign. In the second and third for the special election and the race last fall, he dismantled both sets of opponents. It's the same thing, right?

"Arguing with people is what I'm good at. Speeches are something entirely different."

"You'll be fine." I hope.

"Easy for you to say, Chels, you aren't going up there," the congressman argues as I hear the last speaker finish his speech to applause from the massive crowd.

"Oh yeah, watch this."

I walk up the steps to the platform and stop in front of the microphone stand. The crowd enthusiastically cheers, and now I really wish I had thought this through. I have no idea what to say. Thank God they're in no rush to stop cheering.

The last time I was this nervous was at the press conference Mister Bennit set up for us at the end of the first election. At least we had time to write down what we wanted to say for that event. I glance over at Vince, who is looking at me in awe, before turning back to the raucous crowd.

"Please, everyone, save your applause for the man it really matters for because he's climbing up on this stage in a matter of minutes," I shout into the microphone, causing the crowd to go crazy again.

I'm nervous yet exhilarated. I'm standing on Capitol Hill, addressing an enormous horde of people. I think back to the first days of my senior year when my old friends Stephanie and Cassandra shunned me for not hanging out with them that summer. I felt guilty at the time, but standing here, I don't feel a tinge of regret about what I did back then. Had I never worked on the campaign, I may never have felt this alive. Did I almost give this up for college?

-THIRTY-NINE-
MICHAEL

"Do you remember when she was the shy one?" Vanessa asks me as Chelsea launches into her introduction.

"I do. I think Chels needs another CT scan. She must have bumped her head hard on those steps."

The crowd calms as Chelsea tells the story about the day when the class made a bet with me. She was one of the most persuasive voices goading me into accepting the terms. I thought she had lost her mind and thought I had lost mine when I agreed. I had never done that before and wouldn't ever have thought we would come this far.

"Without further ado, let me introduce a man who is my most esteemed mentor, cherished employer, and closest friend. He is a second father to me and has become a beacon of hope for a beleaguered country."

"She's laying it on thick," Emilee comments.

"Congressman, whatever you say had better be epic, or she's going to upstage you," Amanda warns.

"Amanda, you guys have been upstaging me since the day we started this whole thing. I'm used to it," I say, meaning it.

"No pressure, but Brian is going to have this on YouTube seconds after you finish," Vince says, having fun trying to rattle me.

"Don't listen to him, Mister B. He's just having fun at your expense. You already know the media is broadcasting this live," Vanessa piles on. These two are something else.

"He's been battered in the press, punished in the House, and shot on the steps, but he's far from broken. Ladies and gentlemen, it is my distinct pleasure to introduce to you the iCongressman, Michael Bennit."

The crowd erupts as I walk up the shaky stairs to the stage. Chelsea waits for me with some applause of her own. I give her a short embrace.

"Thank you," I whisper in her ear.

"Knock 'em dead," she replies and walks off the way I came. How far we've come indeed. I hope I do half as good a job bringing up my child someday as Bruce did raising her.

I look out over the tens of thousands of people cheering wildly and wait for absolute silence. The butterflies doing the Harlem Shake in my stomach before I came up here now feel like pterodactyls doing gymnastic floor routines. I have been to war, but the nerves of going out on a mission you could be killed on are nothing compared to this.

"Take a minute and look around you," I begin, more to calm my nerves by saying something than for any other reason. "You don't see this every day. We exercise our First Amendment right to gather in protest of many things. At the other end of this Mall, Martin Luther King, Jr. pursued equality. This same patch of earth has witnessed the Million Man March and the Million Mom March. We've seen rallies against income inequality, over-taxation, governmental intrusion, and the social issues that define our era. We've come together to pledge our support for wars and to protest them.

"We are here for none of those reasons today. We are not here to advocate for one side or another on the issues that divide us. We are not here to widen the rift between us that others have perpetuated. We're here because we refuse to be divided any longer."

The crowd gives me another thunderous applause, and the knot in my stomach eases a little. I wait for the din to subside, finally realizing what I think I want to say.

"Look around you. Do you see the Gadson Flag of the Tea Party being waved only a few dozen yards from Guy Fawkes masks of the Occupy movement? Do you see the white-collar executives that run America's most respected companies standing shoulder to shoulder with the blue-collar union workers who helped build this nation? Do you see people of all colors, creeds, genders, and religions gathered peacefully in one location? We are assembled together today for one singular purpose—to reclaim the government we feel has forsaken us.

"It seems strange that it should come to this," I say when the latest applause subsides. "Thomas Jefferson once said, 'I know no safe depository of the ultimate powers of the society but the people themselves; and if we think them not enlightened enough to exercise their control with a wholesome discretion, the remedy is not to take it from them but to inform their discretion by education. This is the true corrective of abuses of constitutional power.'

"That is not the world we currently live in. That is not what the leaders of our country preach. That is not what those who abuse our system want you to know. Our government is designed to work with the consent of the people. For too long, your voices have not been heard. Our elected representatives have misinterpreted your silence as consent, and you have been powerless to change that.

"Now, we stand on the precipice of change in this country. It is a change that you began in November when you decided that money should be the currency of our economic prosperity but not our politics. That change will not be nurtured and fostered in the marble halls of the building behind me. It comes from the hearts and minds of the citizens that send their representatives here. True, lasting change begins and ends with every American standing up and exclaiming in one unified voice, we will be heard! Our votes will matter, and you will ignore us at your peril!"

I stop only because I am drowned out by thunderous applause and cheers. I wait until the crowd noise gradually dissipates to a level where they can hear me. I'm starting to enjoy this a little, but it's time to wrap this up. This time, no matter how loud they get, I am not stopping. Let's see how loud this group can get.

"Look around again, and let me tell you what I see. I see America in all her glory and with all her flaws. I see people with a long lineage of overcoming great obstacles on a path to greatness. I see my fellow citizens who, despite their differences, still forge ahead to make this nation better today than it was yesterday. I see men and women who believe Abraham Lincoln's words when he said this nation was 'conceived in liberty and dedicated to the proposition that all men are created equal.'

"I see a nation of my countrymen tired of the bickering and partisanship that has defined our political process for generations. I see many people but hear one voice that screams, 'This is the land of the free! This is the home of the brave!' The time has come to remind everyone in this city, this country, and this world exactly what that means!"

-FORTY-

KYLIE

Although protests and rallies are nothing new in the United States, one that receives this level of coverage is not commonplace. Like Tea Party gatherings and the Occupy movement, most of the noteworthy ones were covered as video clips at the bottom of the nightly news. This one is being carried live on every cable news network.

"You just don't see that every day," one of my colleagues opines as we watch Michael finish his speech to a delirious audience on one of the televisions in the newsroom. She's right.

I watched from my office cubicle as Michael gave the speech of a lifetime. Millions saw it live, and I'm sure millions more will hear about it on the news and over social media. Twitter is already erupting with comments about the speech, and my Facebook news feed is blowing up with new posts. I give it another five minutes before countless people start posting the whole thing on YouTube.

The small flock of my fellow reporters gathered around the large flat-screen television mounted on the wall is watching the crowd at the rally go completely nuts. Michael's speech may be over, but the legion of people who descended on the Capitol to watch him speak don't look like they're going anywhere soon. I've seen college football pep rallies less enthusiastic than this.

"That's the most inspirational speech I have heard in my twenty years in Washington," another of my colleague says.

"And downright presidential. Politicians don't have that kind of vision of national unity anymore," another colleague chimes in.

"Hell, I'd vote for him," opines a fourth.

This is precisely why I didn't choose to watch the speech with them. The first question the reporters would ask me is if he has presidential ambitions. We've never talked about it, and since things between us aren't good right now, I wouldn't dare ask.

I watch as Michael jumps off the makeshift stage into the crowd, using his working arm for balance. He begins shaking people's hands and giving hugs. The Capitol Police must be going crazy right now. They're charged with keeping him safe, so what does he do? Jumps into a crowd without any thought of himself.

I don't know what goes through his head sometimes. His closest political ally is still in the hospital, his chief of staff's boyfriend is still in intensive care, and Marilyn Viano is dead at the hands of an assassin who walked right up to them. There could be all sorts of crazies in the crowd right now looking for the same notoriety Jerome Todd Bernard has received. Stupid. Forget getting shot again. Any loon with a shiv could end it all right now.

"Your boyfriend loves his job," my editor says, standing at the entrance to my tiny cubicle. "At least the part of it we hope all politicians really enjoy."

"It's the only part he enjoys."

"I know that tone, Kylie. Why are you pissed? He'll be in the news cycle for weeks because of this. Wasn't that the point?"

"I don't know what the point was, Carl," I snap back.

Michael is poking the bear with a stick. He relishes taking on the political elite and was subjected to an anthrax scare and shot for his troubles. Does he think the danger isn't real just because the white powder in the envelopes was inert and Jerold Todd Bernard can't aim? He's the most significant threat the establishment has faced in generations and is out gallivanting in a crowd instead of taking sensible precautions.

"I'm surprised you aren't attending the rally. You're never one to miss—"

"I have work to do, okay?"

"Okay, okay," Carl retreats, his hands held up at shoulder level in surrender. "It's not a criticism. I just wanted to stop by and tell you that I'm looking for an update on your investigations. Swing by my office before you leave today."

"I will," is my curt reply before he moves on to friendlier conversations.

I don't mean to take it out on my editor, but he doesn't understand. The guilt I feel over not being at the rally is overwhelming. I know I should be there. I once criticized Jessica for her lack of interest in such an amazing man during his first campaign. Now I wonder if I'm doing the same thing.

In my heart, I know I'm not there to support Michael because I need to be here doing this. He is blind to the danger he's putting himself in, and if he isn't going to open his eyes, I'll protect him myself. Whoever was responsible for the assassination attempt will try it again unless I get to him first.

Michael needs to realize what I'm doing is just as important as what he is. Carl is right – the media is going to go crazy over the rally. Washington has lost its mind in the past month. If I want to get anything accomplished, I need to stay on the outskirts to avoid getting sucked into the frenzy. Michael will reach out to me if he needs me. At least I hope he will.

-FORTY-ONE-
CHELSEA

The congressman killed it at the rally. After he finished speaking, he jumped off the stage and spent the next three hours shaking hands, giving out hugs, and meeting people in the crowd to pose for pictures with them. While he was off fraternizing with his supporters, we were busy checking out what people were posting on social media sites like Instagram in real-time. #PeoplesRally trended quickly on Twitter, and word spread at light speed that he was out mingling with his supporters.

Once we finally left the rally and got to the office, he dove into social media himself and left us to help manage the mainstream media. Vanessa and I handled the phones in the losing effort of dealing with all the requests for interviews pouring in. Vince was busy with reporters who wanted answers for stories destined for the morning newspapers and television news shows.

The congressman was still at it after a couple of hours and, despite our protests, ordered us to go to dinner to catch up with each other. We were all willing to order pizzas at the office, but he was insistent. We haven't been out as a group of friends just to enjoy each other's company in a long time.

Going out to dinner in the District of Columbia can be an expensive proposition, especially in the touristy areas around the National Mall and Capitol Hill. Considering most of us are in college, a hundred-dollar steak dinner was out of the question. Fortunately, I knew a great burger joint in Georgetown that fit our limited budget, and so we all filed onto the Metro and headed over there.

Our serious post-rally buzz was a level of excitement we hadn't experienced since the first election when the result came down to the last hundred or so votes cast. The first half-hour of dinner conversation revolved around the afternoon's spectacle, and it didn't stop even when our burgers were brought to the table, and we dug in.

"When did you grow a set, Chels?" Brian asks after swallowing a substantial chunk of his bacon cheeseburger.

"What do you mean?"

My friends look at each other and share smiles. Oh, not this again. I hate it when they do this.

"He means you got up on that stage like a champ. Where did that come from?" Emilee clarifies.

"Honestly, I don't know. I thought it was a good idea at the time, and then I got in front of those people and was terrified."

"It didn't show one bit. You looked comfortable up there," Peyton professes.

"Yeah, like you had been speaking in public for years."

"I just went with what I know and tried not to make a complete fool of myself."

"You sound more like Mister B every day."

"I'll take that compliment, Vince."

"Seriously, you are amazing. Vince and Vanessa, you guys are too. I have no idea how you do this day in and day out," Emilee beams with sincere admiration.

"Necessity," Vanessa says, grinning.

"I'm surprised you didn't get up there, Vince. I figured that was more your speed."

"I would have, Peyton, but she stole my thunder," he answers, with a nod toward me.

"It's not that big of a deal, guys," I retort. I really don't think it is.

"Are you kidding me? The Chelsea I knew even a few months ago would never have done that."

"Emilee's right. You've changed a lot, Chels," Peyton agrees.

"Is that a good thing?" I ask suspiciously. I'm half expecting to get ambushed by them again.

"I think it is," Amanda continues. "Look at everything you've accomplished and how much you've grown."

"You make it sound like you guys haven't accomplished anything. You're all going to be college graduates in a couple of years. The three of us won't have that."

"Yeah, big whoop," Brian dismisses. "We'll have a piece of paper, yippee."

"He's right. You'll have already experienced more than most college grads ever will."

"You sound jealous, Amanda."

"Damn straight."

"So am I," Emilee declares. "If we're lucky, next year we'll get good internships or something like that. Maybe we'll go on to find decent jobs when we graduate. We've spent all our time preparing ourselves for the world, but you guys are actually in it."

I find their words invigorating. I have spent so much time doubting every decision I've made that it feels good to hear someone validating what I have done. What Amanda told me in Blake's hospital room wasn't a feint to make me feel better, nor was it exclusive to just her. She meant it, and the others feel the same way.

"You guys have experienced stuff, too," Vanessa consoles, trying to make sure they continue to understand they're the valued team members in this endeavor that they genuinely are. "You've helped us every step of the way since high school."

"And you got shot at just as we were. Not too many college kids can say that," Vince says, providing this evening's most poignant foot-in-mouth moment so far.

Amanda winces and drops her eyes to the table. She's still sensitive about not being on the steps with us that day, and it's a wound that just got ripped open. Vince notices it before I can correct him.

"I'm sorry, Amanda, I didn't mean it like that." She waves a dismissive hand.

"We could have done without that excitement, Vince. I don't want to ever be in a position of getting ushered inside a building by a bossy cop and forced to wait to hear if my friends are alive or dead," Peyton decrees.

"Being right there in the line of fire wasn't all it was cracked up to be, Peyton. Trust me," Vince consoles, attempting to redeem himself from his last insensitive comment.

Part of me believes he has some guilt over not being shot or injured. We are all in need of therapy, I guess. Everyone looks at me just as I shove some french fries in my mouth. I manage to swallow most of them before talking.

"Don't look at me. I was unconscious."

Everyone laughs, and I realize we are once again in a group therapy session. The first time was during our lunches in the high school cafeteria after losing our first election. Now, it's over cheeseburgers in Georgetown, coming to grips with the actions of one Jerold Todd Bernard. It's just another thing that will bind us all together for the rest of our lives.

-FORTY-TWO-

JAMES

It's the first of January, and the steps of the Lincoln Memorial are cold and dirty. I've been on my feet all afternoon. I want to sit down following my long constitutional up the National Mall but opt against it to avoid ruining my expensive suit.

Dedicated back in the Roaring Twenties, the Lincoln Memorial is one of several monuments erected to honor an American president. It resembles a Greek temple and houses a large seated sculpture of Abraham Lincoln with inscriptions of his two iconic speeches: *The Gettysburg Address* and *Second Inaugural Address*.

It is one of our capital's most recognizable landmarks, made famous partly by being the site of iconic addresses, including Martin Luther King's "I Have a Dream" speech. As I stare across the National Mall, I wonder if the speech Michael Bennit gave earlier today will someday be remembered with similar reverence.

I glance back at Honest Abe, illuminated under the taxpayer-funded floodlights bathing the majestic marble monument in a warm glow. Only a couple of weeks removed from the winter solstice, the days are short, and the nights are cold, long, and dark. The sunset was hours ago, but fortunately, the temperature hasn't plummeted. With the air still mild, I continue to wander around and let the effects of Bennit's gathering set in.

"Did you see coverage of the rally?" Harvey Stepanik says, coming up next to me. Dressed in a long wool overcoat inappropriate for the moderate temperature, he looks like a representative from Florida instead of a congressman from Ohio.

"I was there."

"There had to be two hundred thousand people that showed up to hear him. Presidents don't draw crowds like that. How did some two-bit congressman from the backwoods of Connecticut manage to pull that off?"

"I don't know, but I think it was closer to three hundred thousand people. It was awe-inspiring."

So impressive, I couldn't even get close to the stage. I was hoping to unnerve Bennit by standing front and center, but no such luck. I felt like I was a mile away.

"I'm glad you think so. You wouldn't be so glib if you've heard what the media is saying."

"I have heard some of it. I have a smartphone too, Harvey." I get alerts the same as everyone else does. I would have said that if he was still listening.

"They are calling the speech presidential! Presidential! One said he wouldn't be surprised if he ran for the White House in two years with his popularity."

"He's not running for president."

"Could you imagine anything more terrifying than Michael Bennit in the Oval Office?"

"Harvey—"

"And the media is buying into this! They are calling him 'The Great Uniter' when they aren't using that stupid 'iCongressman' name."

"Harvey, you need to—"

"I think most of them were waiting for him to walk on water, right across the Capitol reflecting pool."

"Are you done?" I finally bark to end his rant. Is this guy off his leash, or what? I'm sure if I hadn't stopped him, his diarrhea of the mouth would have continued.

"Good, now take a deep breath. It doesn't matter how many people show up, what the media are calling him, or even what the polls say," I try explaining to him.

"The Marist Poll has seventy-three percent of the American public supporting him for Speaker of the House. ABC/News Washington Post has it closer to seventy-eight percent. Those numbers are huge, considering

Congress has a single-digit approval rating. Are you honestly telling me that it doesn't matter? Wake up, James!"

"People's opinions don't matter because it's money that controls Congress, not voter will." He shakes his head but doesn't say anything. He won't admit it because he sees the coverage of the Bennit lovefest and is scared, but he knows I'm right.

"He has to be stopped. You need to stop him," Harvey utters, probably in the same manner and tone that he used with Albright last summer.

"Congressman, you are the majority leader of the Republican Party and the leading choice to become Speaker of the United States House of Representatives. You'd be best served to start acting like a leader and not a five-year-old throwing a temper tantrum simply because another kid on the playground is trying to become captain of the kickball team."

There is an irony to meeting here. Behind me, the sixteenth president of the United States is immortalized in stone because he displayed strength and wisdom. Harvey Stepanik may have delusions of grandeur, but he exhibits neither of those two qualities.

"You said you would handle this."

"I swear, between you and the president-elect, y'all are going to drive me to drink. I am handling it."

"It doesn't look like it," Harvey harangues.

This guy has some nerve. I am tired of being put in a position of needing to defend myself. Do any politicians exhibit anything resembling leadership anymore? I mean, anyone other than Michael Bennit?

"I can help you ascend to lead the House, but I can't do all the work for you. Tomorrow is a big day, and I suggest you spend this evening working toward getting as much support as you can. I'll guarantee that Bennit won't be Speaker, but unless you start showing people why you should be, you might not be either."

With that, I walk away and leave Stepanik to wallow in his own self-pity. There is nothing more to be gained by continuing that worthless discussion. I almost wonder if it would be worth having him in my pocket if I need to deal with him every day.

Michael Bennit. Now there's a leader. As much as I despise his naïve approach to government, I can't help but admire how he handles himself. If only I could find a way to corrupt him, what a prized ally he could be.

-FORTY-THREE-
CHELSEA

"Hi, sweetie," I say, posting myself at my usual side of his bed and giving him a kiss on the forehead. It's a ritual I am looking forward to coming to a quick end. I miss him and want him back.

"You're looking better. Some color is returning to your face," I continue, knowing that Blake can't respond or even hear me. I hope he can.

I run my fingers through his black hair. He's always been handsome with his Italian features and strong jaw. He needs a shave, although the stubble on his face is growing on me. It gives him a rugged, manly appearance.

"We had our rallies today. Groups gathered in cities all over the country. Many of the incoming icongressmen held them in their districts, and some bigger ones were hosted in New York City, Los Angeles, Chicago, and Houston. You would have loved seeing so many people coming together. Remember when I told you I didn't think there would be a good turnout? Well, I was wrong."

He would have argued with me had he not been in a medically induced coma when I initially told him that. He would have been adamant that the crowd there would have resembled the outside of a Wal-Mart on Black Friday.

"There were hundreds of thousands of people at the Washington rally, and let me tell you, the congressman rocked. You would have been impressed. The media is. It's all they're talking about tonight on every station. Even the programs that criticize us every chance they get are cashing in on Bennitmania all over again."

"Bennitmania" was a term the media coined to refer to the national sensation our first campaign had become. We didn't refer to it that way very often, but it was an accurate description in hindsight. Eager to recapture the ratings our campaign brought them, the mainstream media have dusted off the nickname and are putting it to use again.

"I really wish you were going to be with us tomorrow. I've worked so hard to get the congressman positioned to be elected Speaker. I don't know if it will be enough, and I could use your advice. I bet you never thought you'd ever hear me say that," I utter with a short laugh.

"Chelsea?" I hear from the doorway as one of the ICU nurses comes into the room. "I'm so sorry to interrupt, but visiting hours are almost over."

I have a newfound respect for the nursing profession. The men and women who work in this hospital are angels and saints, and I don't know how they manage to keep it together enough to do their jobs. With all the pain and suffering they must see, I would lose it if I did their job for even an hour.

"Okay, thanks, Maddie. I'll only be a few more minutes. I need to get back to work anyway. Have you heard anything from the doctors about how he's doing?"

"Nothing official, but I do know they're pleased with his progress. I think they're hoping to wake him up in the next few days, but don't hold me to that."

"I won't, but that's good news."

It's also dreadful news. Nobody can say with any certainty how much damage has been done. Will he walk again? Is there any nerve damage? There are questions only Blake will answer, and part of me is scared to find out.

"I saw your rally today. We had it on at the nurse's station," Maddie says. "It was amazing. You were amazing."

"Thanks, but I think the congressman deserves all the credit."

I find it hard to consider anything I do impressive compared to what she faces every day. Politicians think of themselves as the most important people on the planet, but it is people like Maddie who really make the world a special place. No wonder the congressman never takes himself too seriously.

"It must have been fun having him as a teacher."

"It was, at least until exam time came around. Mister Bennit's tests were so hard you wanted to curl into a ball and cry."

I mean that. His exams were brutal. If they had been easy, he never would have taken the bet to run for Congress, and we wouldn't be here.

"It sure seems like you learned a lot, though," Maddie says, almost sounding like she wishes she had been one of his students.

"We all did, and we still are. The lessons never end when the congressman is around."

"Is there any thought of him running for president?" she asks innocently. God, I hope not. I already have enough stress in my life.

"I think he's focused on the start of the session tomorrow and electing a Speaker of the House."

That politically correct response is a byproduct of having been in this town for too long. Everybody here qualifies everything that they say, whether it be to other politicians or to the media. It's why so many of our representatives struggle while interacting with ordinary people. Her question only required a simple yes or no answer.

"Well, if it were up to me, he'd be a shoo-in. It would be nice to get some good leadership in this country for a change. I think a lot of people think that way."

"Let's hope the people they elect do too. I guess we'll find out tomorrow."

-FORTY-FOUR-

MICHAEL

Now I know what rock stars feel like, only the applause isn't for me. At least most of it isn't. Minutes away from Congress getting gaveled into session, our entrance is greeted with an enthusiastic standing ovation directed primarily towards the man I'm wheeling down the center aisle. I was *only* shot in the shoulder.

Nothing was going to keep Congressman Francisco Reyes from making his triumphant return to this chamber on the first day. There is no assigned seating, but many of the new icongressmen took seats along the center aisle in a show of symbolism. Every House member joins the ovation to avoid looking spiteful on C-SPAN. Regardless, the energy is palpable along the aisle where my caucus members set up shop.

"They won't be clapping so hard once I start feeling the ill-effects of that breakfast burrito," Cisco turns in his chair and says with an evil grin.

"You let one rip without warning me, that leg will be the least of your problems," I tell him in response. I'm kidding, or not.

"Whatever you say, *Mister Speaker*."

I had some colleagues reserve two spots for us, and with little more fanfare, Congress is gaveled into session. The Constitution mandates that we convene at noon on January 3rd unless the preceding Congress designates a different day. In this case, we're coming together on January 2nd to set in motion the ceremonial process leading to the first and most important order of business. The election of the Speaker of the House is a formality at the start of a typical Congress. With this unique blend of Democrats, Republicans, and independents, it is anything but typical.

The possibility of needing multiple ballots to select our leader only exists when party discipline breaks down, or a third party has sufficient strength to force them. Rare in the modern era, it is not unprecedented. In 1923, the Progressive Party forced nine ballots before finally electing Republican Frederick Gillett as Speaker. In this case, it's not a party but a group of independents beholden only to their constituents back home who are forcing the issue.

The House follows a well-established first-day routine that includes a prayer led by the chaplain and the Pledge of Allegiance led by the Clerk of the House. After the quorum call, the Clerk gets the show started.

"Pursuant to law and precedent, the next order of business is the election of the Speaker of the House of Representatives for this session of Congress. Nominations are now in order," he decrees from the rostrum. "The Clerk now recognizes the gentleman from Iowa."

"It is with utmost optimism that, as chair of the Republican Conference, and upon a unanimous vote of that conference, I present for election to the Office of the Speaker of the House of Representatives the name of the Honorable Harvey Stepanik of Ohio."

"The Clerk now recognizes the gentlewoman from California," he continues as the previous nominator leaves the podium.

"It is my privilege to be tasked, as chair of the Democratic Caucus, through the vote of that caucus, to present for election to the Office of Speaker of the House of Representatives Honorable Brian Lockwood, a duly elected representative from the Commonwealth of Virginia."

"The names of the Honorable Harvey Stepanik of Ohio and Brian Lockwood of Virginia have been placed in nomination. Are there further nominations?"

The chamber collectively waits for what happens next. I did not lobby for the nomination, nor did I make backroom deals to try to entice members to vote for me. Regardless, the icongressmen insisted I get nominated, and it was decided by the independents that Cisco should have the honor. He wheels himself down to the Well of the House, where the microphone is removed by a staffer and handed to him.

"We are not men and women of words, but actions. So, without any ado whatsoever, I nominate Michael Bennit from the great State of Connecticut to the position of Speaker of the House for this Congress." I am thrilled he did not embarrass me by embellishing any further. He was more than capable of making that nomination last five minutes.

I shake his hand when he returns as the Clerk goes through the motions of readying the vote. Debate on the nomination of candidates for Speaker is allowed but not customary. I half expect one of the parties to initiate a debate on my inclusion, but no such motion is forwarded.

"There being no further nominations, the roll will now be called, and those responding to their names will indicate by surname the nominee of their choosing. The Reading Clerk will now call the roll."

A viva voce roll call is a vote in which the members respond orally to the calling of their names instead of using voting cards as we usually do. In this vote, representatives shout out the last name of their choice for Speaker when their names are called.

"Are you nervous?" Cisco whispers as the names start being read for the vote.

"I don't think there is anything to be nervous about in this ballot. I will be shocked if this isn't a party-line vote."

The majority party assures the election of its candidate because the vote is almost exclusively along party lines. If no candidate receives a majority vote, the election process repeats until a Speaker of the House of Representatives is elected.

The attention of every member in the chamber turns to me when they realize I am next. The candidates for Speaker often vote "present" or do not vote in their election. Since this is no ordinary vote, they can hang their customs.

"Michael Bennit," the Clerk announces. The chamber takes on an eerie silence as they await my response. All eyes are on me. Cameras record every movement for posterity. I take a deep breath, puff my chest out, and stand as erect as I can make myself.

"Bennit," I call out, causing an audible murmur in the chamber.

-FORTY-FIVE-
KYLIE

I do not like to live with regrets. Not going to Michael's rally yesterday has been wearing on my conscience, so I was not about to miss this first ballot. I know his winning is a long shot, but I'm so incredibly proud he has made it this far. I wish I could tell him that, but I'm still so angry at the same time.

The House Visitor's Gallery is full of Washington's power brokers. There is a lot at stake with this vote, so I knew some of the people I need to talk to would be here. Well, one person for sure.

Being an investigative journalist covering one of the most traumatic events the capital has seen since Hinckley shot at Reagan in the 1980s means people avoid me like I have an infectious disease. When I manage to confront people of interest, their reactions vary, but most are not happy to see me. James Reed is one of those people when I take the seat beside him.

"This is the same seat you were sitting in when you watched the rules vote last November, isn't it?"

Reed doesn't respond. He knows that I'm aware it's the same. I take a deep breath and exhale loudly for theatrical effect.

"And that means I'm sitting in the same seat Marilyn Viano was that day. Wow."

"I didn't realize you held her in such high esteem, Miss Roberts."

"I didn't like her at all. But I wonder if Viano ever could have realized that she would be dead twenty minutes after sitting here with you that day? Nah, she probably didn't know."

I watch him clam up. Yup, that's definitely one of the fun parts of being a journalist. He can avoid me at his residence or office, but it's so much harder to escape the media in public.

"No, probably not," he mumbles. I bet he would pay any amount of money to make me go away.

"I'll bet you knew."

Michael loves Brad Thor's books, so I decided to read a couple of them. His main character, Scot Harvath, was trained as a Secret Service agent to read micro-expressions to identify threats. I thought it was complete hooey until now. Reed just had one of them. It flashed by so fast I would have missed it if I blinked, but I got the confirmation I was looking for. He knew what I was talking about.

"Miss Roberts, I know you have a job to do. I appreciate all the fine work you do to uncover the dirt in this town that the American people have a right to know," he lectures. "But if going around making false accusations is accepted as the new way of journalism, I weep for our republic."

"Those are strong words coming from the man who has done everything in his power to destroy our Republic."

"I don't want to destroy anything, Miss Roberts. Quite the opposite. The system works just fine as it is, despite the best efforts of some to 'fix' it. The people below us don't need any help killing off democracy. They seem to be perfectly capable of doing that on their own."

The Clerk of the House is already on the names beginning with 'T.' There isn't much time left before they announce the results. I had better get to the point.

"I understand why you would think that way. I mean, your clients have a lot to lose if it does change, right, Mister Reed? Their money runs the show in this town, which I imagine is why you're here to watch that collapse before your very eyes."

"I have an interest in knowing who I will need to work with to accomplish the goals of my firm during the next Congress, nothing more." Lying bastard.

"Oh, so you weren't running around town threatening lawmakers to vote for Harvey Stepanik?" That got his attention, and he looks at me coldly.

"I made no threats. I simply reminded our esteemed representatives that actions have consequences that are beyond my control."

The clerk steps up to the microphone on the rostrum at the front of the chamber. I timed this conversation to end so I could watch his face as the ballot results are read. I don't expect Michael to win, but it would be one of the greatest moments if he did. No, I want to see his face to see how disappointed he is when the realization dawns on him that his grand plan didn't pan out.

"The tellers agree in their tallies that the total number of votes cast is four hundred thirty-five. Of which, the Honorable Harvey Stepanik of the State of Ohio has received one hundred seventy-seven votes, the Honorable Brian Lockwood of the Commonwealth of Virginia one hundred seventy-two votes, and the Honorable Michael Bennit of the State of Connecticut eighty-five votes. One vote has been recorded as "present.""

There is an audible groan in the chamber, although I'm not sure why anyone is surprised. Michael said the first ballot would go this way. It's the second vote where we'll see the action happen.

"Therefore, no candidate has received a majority of the votes cast. The position of Speaker of the House of Representatives remains vacant until the next ballot," the Clerk announces.

-FORTY-SIX-

JAMES

"Oops. It doesn't look like your bullying helped in this case, now does it?" Kylie mocks with more than a touch of satisfaction in her voice.

"Did you expect anything less than a near-party line vote on the first ballot, Miss Roberts?"

Unfortunately, I did. I can't hide how pissed off I am, and worse, Bennit's in-house pit bull can see it. After all the work I put into this, I expected defections from the Democrats on the first ballot. Maybe not enough to put Stepanik over the top, but enough to show he had the momentum to win.

The problem has to lie with the nominee himself. I don't think Stepanik lifted a finger for his own cause. That's the problem with politicians today—they are lazy. He wanted me to use my influence to do all the leg work instead of cashing in some political favors himself. I thought Stepanik was better than that, but I guess not.

Instead, we're nowhere close to a majority vote. The Constitution dictates that they cannot move on until they elect a Speaker, and the only way that happens is through a compromise. Negotiation is a lost art in Washington, at least between the two main parties. The independents have come to town ready to do precisely that, and this may be their chance. The leverage they could earn would make them extremely dangerous.

"You and Bennit. Y'all think you're so smart, don't you?" I continue after she doesn't respond to my retort. "Your social media candidates ran on a platform of ending gridlock in Washington, but all you've managed to do is mire the simplest vote the House casts in a complete deadlock. It's unfortunate."

"Oh, it's a little early to worry about that, don't you think? But if things get too bad, you can always start knocking people off, right?"

I have enough to worry about right now without indulging in Kylie Roberts's glib comments. Stepanik is underperforming, Bennit is looking strong after the first ballot, and I wonder how seriously the president-elect took my offer as relayed through his chief of staff. I need a lot to go right today. So far, it isn't, including this obnoxious journalist's presence next to me.

"Miss Roberts, I resent your implications. This conversation is bordering on harassment. You're leaving me no choice but to report your behavior to your employer. I am quite certain they wouldn't condone your strong-arm tactics in trying to get me to implicate myself in a crime I had nothing to do with."

"That remains to be seen," Kylie dismisses.

"No, it doesn't. If y'all want to run around D.C. trying to find something to incriminate me, it's your time to waste." I am desperate to regain the upper hand. I do not want to leave a bloodhound like Kylie Roberts with any impression that she has something to hold over me.

"There is no such thing as a perfect crime, Mister Reed. No matter how carefully you think you covered your tracks, you missed something, and I am going to find it."

"Again, Miss Roberts, you're wasting your breath."

"No, Mister Reed, I don't think I am. I guess time will tell which one of us is right."

She flashes me a knowing smile and leaves her seat. I watch her as she walks up the stairs and out of the Visitor's Gallery. Sure, that she is gone and not lurking in the shadows somewhere, I pull out my cell phone. Making a call is out of the question, so I type out a quick text message:

First vote is over. We need to talk.

FORTY-SEVEN

CHELSEA

"Is Congress always this boring?" Emilee leans over and whispers into my ear.

"This is why coverage is shown on C-SPAN and not after *The Voice* on NBC," I respond. I don't tell her that this is one of the more exciting days.

"I don't know. It does have a bit of a *Game of Thrones* feel to it," Brian quips from behind us.

"Without the killing," Peyton absentmindedly interjects.

We all look at her. In fact, there is a body count. She should know because she was there.

"Well...okay, maybe some killing. Sorry."

We're all dealing with the trauma of the shooting in our own way. That includes seeking professional counseling. It's not something that any of us really talk about. Dinner last night was the first time any of us discussed what happened on the Capitol steps.

"My art history class was more interesting than this," Amanda concludes, immediately getting off that painful subject.

"Can we get Congressman Bennit to start flipping chairs down there?" Emilee ponders.

"As cool as it would be, they won't appreciate him turning the House floor into *The Jerry Springer Show*, Em," Vince laments. I have no doubt he would enjoy it the most.

"Mister B almost got expelled for it the last time furniture went flying on Capitol Hill," Vanessa finishes.

"That table flip saved him," Brian argues.

The target of a sloppy frame job by Reed & Ibram, the congressman was hauled in front of a select committee at the bequest of then-Speaker Albright. Despite incontrovertible proof that he was set up, the committee made up their minds to send a recommendation for expulsion from the House to the Floor for a vote.

I had warned him that the video evidence he had Brian record that night was not going to be enough, and I told him he would need to do something drastic. When the committee chairman cut off his microphone, he happily obliged me by flipping a table and giving an impassioned speech that is still a favorite on YouTube.

"Do you deal with this level of boredom every day, guys?" Amanda asks, eliciting a nod from Vince and Vanessa. "I guess I should have had more coffee this morning."

"When we talk about parties in this town, it has a far different meaning than it does at UConn, Amanda," I add.

"How would we know?" Emilee admonishes with a laugh. "We spend all our free time working with you guys. So, when you have real parties here, what are they called?"

"Galas," Vince answers.

"Or balls," Vanessa says, always in concert with Vince. It would be so much easier if they just admit they're dating.

"For a lot of devout pundits and political junkies in this town, this is a party," I add for completion.

"People live for this? That's very sad."

"Says the guy who's addicted to *World of Warcraft*."

"Touché."

"Why do they keep voting if there is going to be no change in the result?" Peyton asks, not wanting to listen to Bri ramble on about his virtual character as he's prone to do.

"They can't do anything else until this is settled."

"No wonder nothing ever gets done in Congress."

* * *

The following six hours didn't get any more exciting for Brian, Peyton, and the gang. I forgot that we have gotten used to this, but for the casual observer, watching Congress do their work is about as exciting as watching paint dry. Less so, since paint drying is real progress.

The first vote this morning was along party lines. Republicans voted for their nominee, the Democrats theirs, and the seventy-six icongressmen who didn't defect voted for Congressman Bennit. It was all very predictable.

We expected the second vote to tell the tale of who was winning the political battles that had happened behind the scenes. I worked tirelessly to drum up support in other parties for the congressman without his knowledge. There is no doubt many players, like James Reed, were doing the same thing to champion their own nominees.

When the Clerk of the House read the results of the second vote just before noon, it was clear who had made the most progress. Congressman Stepanik had increased his total by twenty-five to two hundred two, and Mister Bennit had jumped into triple digits with one hundred and seven. The Democrats have been enticed to choose sides, knowing their nominee was a long shot.

Why they would consider supporting a Republican had everyone scratching their heads. The media was going nuts speculating what backroom deals the GOP and Dems made for that to happen. They will never find out James Reed has his fingerprints all over the process, nor would they want to shatter the American illusion over who is running the government if they did know.

Now approaching late afternoon, I listen to the Clerk as the names get read off for the third ballot. Despite my best efforts, it's clear that I failed to get enough support for the congressman to make a difference. He's playing spoiler in this contest, and if the voting process continues to get dragged out, the icongressmen are going to get the blame.

"Looks like all your hard work is starting to pay off, Chels," Vince observes, noticing there is an uptick in the number of members voting for our boss.

"Yeah, but it's not going to be enough."

"It's a work in progress," Emilee says enthusiastically. Out of all of us, she relishes the role of underdog.

"Yeah, once they call it quits for the day, we can amp up the social media pressure," Brian says, spoiling to use Facebook and Twitter to get the American people engaged in this process.

"A lot of people are paying attention to this because of the rallies. They want the congressman in charge. We need to leverage that advantage," Amanda firmly states.

"Vanessa and I will reach out to the media and see if we can stir them up enough to pressure some fence-sitters to fall our way," Vince informs us.

When the Clerk reads the final tally for the third ballot, the congressman has picked up another eight votes, and the other nominees dropped four each. He would need to almost double his current vote total to win at this point, and I don't see that happening.

My friends are determined to fight the good fight. They all sound like good plans, but the battle lines have been drawn. Vote totals may fluctuate a few here or a few there, but none of the nominees is close to a majority. The crew may be eager to change that, but I have a feeling the congressman has something else in mind.

-FORTY-EIGHT-

MICHAEL

"We'll keep fighting until hell freezes over!" I hear as I slip through the door into the back of the room.

"He's right. I beat an incumbent Democrat who won his previous two elections with eighty percent of the vote. We were all underdogs when we won last November. We can win this too," another icongressman says to rousing cheers.

"We are going to get labeled as obstacles," a third argues. "We were elected to bring the parties together and get things done, not divide them further!"

"We're standing up for—"

"It doesn't matter! That's not how either party will paint it or how the media will report it."

"About time you got here," Chelsea whispers as she slides up next to me along the wall. "This is getting ugly."

"You're letting Vince run the show?"

"He's the only chance of maintaining order, not that it's making a difference right now."

Amanda and Peyton walk over and join us near the doors. Everyone in the room is so caught up in the argument that nobody except Cisco has even realized I'm here. He's sitting in his wheelchair along the far wall, looking at me and shaking his head.

"They're all over the place. Some want to compromise, and some are saying it's either you or they'll spend the next two years voting for Speaker if they have to."

I watch as the room descends into more chaotic shouting. Accusations and insults being exchanged like volleys between two naval fleets in a pitched battle. At least I can't question their passion for the job. Now, if I can only channel it into something useful.

"Jeez, they're all worked up like toddlers who ate too much sugar," Peyton surmises.

"Okay, you guys have had your fun. Now it's my turn."

"Congressman, do you really think you can bring order to this mess?" Amanda asks.

"Absolutely."

"How? Are you going to hit them with a bat or something?"

"Peyton, as Ike once said, 'You don't lead by hitting people over the head—that's assault, not leadership.' Watch this."

I walk down the aisle. I feel like a Caesar entering the Roman Senate, sans the toga. I am hardly a conquering hero, but I am keenly aware many in the room regard me that way. "The greatest leaders mobilize others by coalescing people around a shared vision," Ken Blanchard once said. It's time to exercise a little leadership by sharing my vision.

The crowd hushes by the time I make it to the front of the room. The individuals who were standing and yelling at each other all sit, save one. He's still pretty fired up.

"I admire all your passion," I say, "but yelling at each other isn't going to solve this or any other problem. Please, sir, have a seat."

Like all good noncommissioned officers, I can yell loud enough to command the attention of the most stubborn man. In the classroom, I could silence a room with just a couple of words when the occasion called for it. These are my colleagues, not my students or my soldiers. Instead of barking orders, my words flow in a calm, almost smooth voice. To my surprise, he sits.

"I wanted to take a moment to thank you all for your support today. It's been a long time since balloting in the House has been so contentious, and your loyalty to me is very much appreciated."

I watch smiles cross the faces of many in the room. These new representatives are going to be the lynchpin of the caucus, and I need them to be inspired, not combative with each other.

"I am humbled by your nomination for Speaker of the House. We did not waver after three ballots and made a bold statement about our solidarity. I listened to the comments being made when I walked into the room, and I believe there are merits to both arguments.

"We have made the point that we cannot be bullied. It was important for our colleagues to understand that. It's equally important that we remain strong in the face of adversity moving forward. Thank you for reminding us of our strength," I say to the gentleman who was slow to sit down. He nods in appreciation.

"There are factions in this town drooling over the idea of protracted balloting for Speaker of the House. They'll be quick to point out to the media and the American people that we are no different than they are. They will run to cameras and pronounce that voters only made the government slower to respond to issues by electing us. If we are not measured in our actions, they will be proven correct," I add, soliciting an equivalent nod from one of the other agitators.

"I need you all to remember, our first responsibility is to our constituents, and we will always be dedicated to that simple tenant."

The room breaks out in applause, and I wait for it to die down before continuing. I sneak a look at the back of the room, where my former students watch with keen interest. I think they half expect to hear another history lesson coming.

"Unfortunately, we did not do them any favors today. We need to rise above the petty bickering that has defined Congress for decades. We need to rise above what I saw in this room when I walked in. Passionate disagreement is understandable. Personal attacks and belittling our colleagues is what all of you were elected to end."

"What do you expect us to do, Congressman Bennit?" I get asked from the front row.

"Please, call me Michael."

"Okay, Michael. If we don't convince the GOP or Democrats to vote for you, you'll never be Speaker of the House, and we will have lost."

"The odds of us winning were infinitesimally small despite the Herculean efforts of all of you, my staff, and especially my chief of staff back there. I don't have the experience to lead this chamber, and even members who want to vote for me won't do so based on that fact alone."

"But we are so close," another of my colleagues says, taking up the argument.

"We are as close as we'll ever get. It's far closer than I ever would have imagined. I should stop underestimating what Chelsea and my former students are capable of. Even getting one of the party faithful to vote for me is a coup. The fact is, our victory does not lie in electing me, but what we do to elect anyone under the current circumstances."

"What does that mean?"

"It means it is time to show the nation what we are here for. It is time to compromise."

"You are telling us to vote for someone from one of the parties?"

I look over at Cisco, who gives me a knowing smile. Despite his enthusiasm for nominating me three times on the Floor of the House, he has been much more reserved than usual since the shooting. I guess the effects of that day are taking their toll on all of us differently.

"No," I respond, turning my attention back to the group of assembled icongressmen. "I'm *asking* you to vote for a specific person and hoping you will trust me when I tell you that he's exactly the right man for the job."

-FORTY-NINE-

JAMES

Today is going to be like washing your hair—rinse and repeat. The House will hold three more ballots, and I don't expect the tallies to be vastly different than the last ones. Despite my best efforts last night and this morning, I haven't influenced any of the members to see my line of thinking.

Both parties are looking for political cover to break the stalemate, but nobody can agree on a viable candidate. I managed to convince some Democrats to support Stepanik on the second and third ballots. Unfortunately, he's too much of a partisan for most to vote for. The GOP initially supported him, but seeing the writing on the wall, they're shopping for alternatives.

The Dems know Lockwood couldn't step up into the role. Having lost their minority leader and minority whip in the November elections, they are directionless and only nominated him due to a lack of better options. Part of me is surprised they didn't offer up more nominees, but being at a disadvantage in the House, they wanted to appear to have a unified front. Several members jockeyed for position within the party. He simply emerged as the winner, or loser, depending on one's perspective.

Most members are balking at supporting Bennit for varied reasons. He's the only nominee gaining ground, but the only shot he has at getting the needed majority is to convince the others that he is equal to the task. Not likely, but we are about to find out.

"We will continue the order of business to elect the Speaker of the House of Representatives for this session of Congress. This is the fourth ballot, and nominations are now in order. The Clerk now recognizes the gentleman from Iowa."

"As Republican Conference chair, I once again present the name of the Honorable Harvey Stepanik from Ohio for election to the Office of the Speaker of the House of Representatives." Thankfully, there isn't as much fluffy prose added to the nomination as we heard yesterday.

"The Clerk now recognizes the gentlewoman from California."

"By a vote of the Democratic Caucus, I present for election to the Office of Speaker of the House of Representatives Honorable Brian Lockwood of the Commonwealth of Virginia."

Michael Bennit moves to the podium in the Well of the House. He's sure to be a nominee, so what the hell is he doing? Is he about to nominate himself?

"The Clerk now recognizes the gentleman from Connecticut."

I get the sinking feeling that I'm not going to like whatever Bennit has to say. I try to be optimistic that he isn't offering any nomination, clearing the way for a partisan fight between the Republicans and Democrats with the independents breaking the virtual tie. I doubt it, though. Michael Bennit is the Howard Stern of Congress—he likes to shock people.

"As representatives to Congress in the United States of America, we are beholden to the people who elected us to act as their voice in the deliberations of this great body. For the fourth ballot, it is my distinct honor to offer the name of the Honorable Johnston Albright from South Carolina for election to the Office of the Speaker of the House of Representatives."

-FIFTY-

CHELSEA

As soon as the congressman announces the nomination, a river of staff members streams into the chamber. They pour down the aisles to whisper into the ears of their respective principals. In very un-Washington-like behavior, it appears a shocking few of them gave their bosses any heads-up that this was coming. I see a lot of heads nodding, which is a good sign.

I didn't sleep much last night, nor did Vince and Vanessa. Our other former classmates are equally exhausted as we tracked down as many Republican staff members as we could and gave them our pitch. Peyton, Emilee, Brian, and Amanda should all get an "A" for their Politics 101 course for the effort.

Knowing a sizable majority of Democrats would never support Albright, we approached some of the moderates in that party first, including the Three Amigos. Then we made a list of Republican members, limiting the names to representatives we thought would vote our way who have a staff I could trust. I don't have strong relationships with many of them, so how this didn't get out in a town that leaks more than a BP oil well in the Gulf is beyond me. Things really are changing around here.

For six hours, we ran around to half the bars, restaurants, and gyms in Washington. When midnight approached, we started tracking down places of residence and knocking on doors. We knocked off at one a.m., only to begin again this morning. By the time Congressman Bennit made the nomination, over a hundred staffers knew what was happening and were prepared to brief their bosses.

"They look shocked," Vince observes.

"Why would they keep that a secret?" Peyton asks, curious.

"Because they didn't know if we were trying to pull one over on them," Vanessa replies, beating me to it.

"Huh?"

"If they sounded the alarm about what we told them and informed their principals, they would look like fools if the congressman didn't follow through on it. We gave them enough information to prepare but not enough assurance that it would happen. As a result, most kept quiet and waited to see what happened," I summarize.

"And the chaos you see on the Floor is the result," Vanessa finishes.

"If you pull this off, Chels... Why did you do it? I know you disagree with the congressman's plan."

"I've had to do a lot of things in the past year and a half I don't agree with, Em. I used to resent it. I hated the fact that the congressman never listened to me. Then I realized he does listen, only is still thinking further ahead than I am. My job is to support him in any way I can, even if I don't like it or understand why. I realize that now."

"You never cease to amaze me, Chels," Brian says.

The roll call starts getting called just as it did the three times yesterday. As the Clerk calls through the names beginning with "A," Republican votes are already shifting to Johnston Albright. Everyone is still waiting to see what the icongressmen do.

"Michael Bennit," the Clerk announces from the rostrum.

"Albright."

"Diane Bigler."

"Albright."

"James Blackman."

"Lockwood."

I listen to a few more votes get cast, and a clear pattern is emerging. The Republicans are abandoning Congressman Stepanik and flocking to Albright in the hopes of electing one of their own. The Democrats we spoke to are following suit, understanding that the devil they know is better than the one they don't. Of course, our allies follow the congressman's lead, trusting that he knows what he's doing.

I haven't had a lot of things to feel good about since I came to Washington. Even now, we are so early in the balloting that I have no idea what the result will be. If there is anything that I'm proud of, it's the thought of the Washington insiders, press corps, and the omnipotent lobbyist James Reed had no idea this was coming.

-FIFTY-ONE-

MICHAEL

As I listen to the votes pour in, I can't fight the feeling of pride. It isn't for anything I did, but for what Chelsea and the gang managed to accomplish. My former students have profoundly impacted the election process and government of this country, even though they still are not old enough to legally order drinks at a bar.

High school and college students are often thought to be apathetic slackers. In some cases, I'm sure they are. When I was a teacher, there were always students who did the bare minimum or nothing at all. But if there is a more poignant example of the dangers of stereotyping, Chelsea, Vince, Vanessa, Peyton, Amanda, Brian, Emilee, and even Xavier are Exhibit A.

"Francisco Reyes," the Clerk announces.

"Albright," Cisco sings out with pride. He's enjoying this.

There are a dozen or so more votes to go, and Reed must be going nuts right now. No doubt that Stepanik will be joining him in the loony bin. They got owned, and now they know it.

My students were media darlings and national sensations during my first campaign. How long before that happens again here in Washington? The secret is out about Chelsea for sure. She has proven to everyone in this town that the redheaded firebrand chief of staff for the maverick independent from Connecticut is a force to be reckoned with. So much for people not believing she was up to the task when I appointed her.

The voting ends with the last name being rattled off the list of members. The chamber breaks into a muted applause. The tellers responsible for recording the vote tally move off to the side of the dais to chat with the clerk. All we can do is sit and wait for the result to be read. For the fourth time this session of Congress, the Clerk moves to the rostrum and reads the same dry and formal text from the paper.

"The tellers agree in their tallies. The total number of votes cast is four hundred thirty-five, of which the Honorable Johnston Albright of the State of South Carolina has received two hundred thirty-three votes. The Honorable Brian Lockwood of the Commonwealth of Virginia has received one hundred seventy-six votes, and the Honorable Harvey Stepanik of the State of Ohio has received twenty-two. Four votes were recorded as 'present.'"

The present vote cast the first three times was by a cantankerous old Democrat who must not have liked any of the options. For this ballot, he was joined by three others who couldn't decide.

"Therefore, the Honorable Johnston Albright of the State of South Carolina, having received the majority of the votes cast, is duly elected Speaker of the House of Representatives."

The reaction in the chamber is a mix of applause and consternation. Everyone is happy that we can move on to the remaining orders of business so that the real work can begin. On the other hand, very few of them, Republicans included, are happy with the result.

The Clerk appoints a bipartisan committee to escort the Speaker-elect Albright to his chair on the dais. He is introduced to the chamber by Congressman Lockwood, the presumed minority leader, followed by a short and curt statement from the chair. He is not dealing with his defeat well.

By precedent, the dean of the House, the longest-serving member regardless of party, administers the oath of office to Albright. It's identical to the one I uttered following the special election. Once he's finished, and following another short applause, Speaker Albright addresses the House.

"I wanted to reserve my statement until after the oath in case anyone tries to change their mind," he declares, eliciting some laughs in the chamber. "It is my distinct honor to once again serve as Speaker of this great body. I have had the privilege of overseeing a dramatic change to the way we do business in the past year. Our ranks have been joined by an influx of independents eager to be representative voices of their constituents."

"He's not shy about embellishment, is he?" Cisco asks. "He's making it sound like it's all his idea."

"Welcome to Washington, where the credit gets hoarded, and the blame deflected," I say with a smirk. I'm only smiling because I know what's coming next.

"They have come here to help heal the divide that has been the scourge of this chamber and this Congress for far too long. In the spirit of that dedication, I have decided to join their cause."

The members look around in bewilderment—the few people seated upstairs in the gallery gasp at the recognition of what he is saying. I hope the media have their cameras rolling because his next words are going into American political history books.

"To that end, I am pleased to announce that I'm formally renouncing my affiliation with the Republican Party and will now be regarded as an independent."

The room erupts in chaos. Republicans start yelling at each other, Democrats talk amongst themselves as they try to figure out what just happened. The independents cheer and exchange high fives. Journalists and reporters stream out the doors into the hallway to report what they just heard. The breaking news will circle the globe within the next five minutes. Welcome to the Information Age.

"I've said it before, and I'll say it again: minstrels."

"What?"

"Minstrels," Cisco repeats. "They're going to write and sing songs about you. I mean, who would have thought it?"

"Thought what?"

"That after all this, we would still end up with an iSpeaker."

PART III

UNDER ABSOLUTE DESPOTISM

-FIFTY-TWO-
KYLIE

"I'm assuming since we're here at Union Station that you aren't concerned that I'm under surveillance anymore."

Michael had thought Terry was paranoid when he said the hospital room may be bugged. Despite the apprehension and obligatory questioning of his sanity, I agreed to meet him all the way up in Baltimore on the chance he was right. Since this meeting is in the busy corridor of a landmark that happens to be one of the most monitored transportation hubs in the country, I conclude his fears are assuaged.

"You may still be, but not by anyone that matters." There's the typical vague answer I have come to expect from him. "Your boyfriend pulled off quite the coup this morning."

"Yeah, for a no-nonsense guy, he does have a gift for the dramatic."

"Apparently. He's got the whole town going nuts again."

"Why did you want to meet, Terry?" I ask, quickly changing the subject. The fact that Michael is responsible for elevating Johnston Albright back into the Speaker's chair isn't sitting well with me.

"It is time to introduce you to my source."

"Why here?"

"He insisted the meeting be in a public place. I have no idea why."

"Okay, why are you having him meet me now? All this time and you haven't even told me who it is." This whole thing doesn't smell right.

"He has information he wants to share, but only with you present to hear it."

"Terry, this had better be good. I don't like having my chain jerked. Where is this source?"

"Right behind you."

I don't know what I expected to see when I turned around, but it wasn't him. I wouldn't trust this guy to pick up my dry cleaning, let alone feed us useful information.

"Condrey? You're the source? Terry, you've got to be kidding me."

Gary Condrey is Marilyn Viano's former chief of staff, superhero worshipper, and smartphone aficionado. The man is a walking contradiction, not the least of which is meeting us here dressed in a tracksuit when he hasn't jogged since parachute pants were en vogue.

If Marilyn Viano was our Doctor Evil, he was Mini Me. The two were duplicitous in their dealings to get Michael reelected and our efforts to elect the hundred other icandidates to the House. It's no secret that he knew she was betraying us every step of the way, so why Terry would choose to believe a word he says is beyond me.

"Hello to you too, Kylie."

"Please tell me I'm getting punked," I say. Terry doesn't react at all.

"I agree with Terry. It is quite an accomplishment to get a disgraced Speaker of the House on the ballot and manage to keep the whole thing secret until the nomination is made," Gary continues, despite my best efforts to pretend he's not here. "It's all the media is talking about this morning. They are gushing how Michael is the Great Uniter and doing everything he said he was going to do. It's very clever to cast him as the savior of the modern American political process. How much did you have to do with it?"

"I wish I could take credit, but that was all him."

"Oh. Trouble in paradise?"

"What am I doing here, Gary? What information did you want to share with me?" I don't want to talk about my relationship with Michael right now, especially with Captain Wind Pants here.

"I am here to save you a lot of time and effort."

"How?"

"By telling you to stop investigating James Reed."

"Yeah, that's not going to happen."

"You aren't going to find anything on him by terrorizing the people near his inner circle. Any involvement he may have had in the assassination was echelons removed from the shooter. With five years and an army of people, you would still never find a direct trail back to him, assuming any lead back to him at all."

"Gary, I thought you were here to help."

"I am."

"Then prove it," I bark.

"I'm trying to. You're not giving me much of a chance."

"Why should I? You were doing everything you could to help Viano take Michael out, all behind the scenes and out of sight of your former employer. Pardon me if I'm not in the trusting frame of mind."

Gary unconsciously fiddles with his smartphone while he thinks of how to respond. There is no point in denying it, so I don't know what his problem is. Viano swore he was a political genius. I just see a socially awkward man who could be Sheldon's long-lost father in *The Big Bang Theory*.

"You're right, I was. I was also wrong, and I'm trying to atone for that. 'It's not who I am underneath...but what I do...that defines me.'"

"*Spiderman?*"

"*Batman Begins*, actually."

"Whatever. What you are doing is atoning by telling me to quit without any reason why."

"Not quit... refocus. You believe that Reed ordered the assassination."

"And you don't?"

"I was so convinced of it I tried to record him confessing. Now I'm not so sure. I believe he knows more than he's saying, but I don't know if he's the one who gave the order."

"You're going along with this?" I ask Terry. I can't believe he is buying into this after everything we've been through chasing what little leads we have come across.

"I'm willing to hear him out," Mister Dark and Mysterious says in his calm, unemotional voice.

"Okay, apparently, I'm the crazy one. So, tell me, Gary, what leads you to believe that?" I sneer.

"First, tell me, what are you more interested in, finding the truth or nailing Reed to the wall?"

"I happen to believe those are mutually inclusive."

"What if they aren't?" They are, but I recognize the futility of saying so. I give him the answer he's looking for.

"I want the truth."

He nods and pulls a folded piece of regular copy paper out of his pocket. He takes a moment to open it, revealing a grainy photograph printed on it. He hands it to me, and my jaw drops.

"Does this guy look familiar?"

"Holy crap!" I exclaim, tilting the paper so Nyguen can see it. The man with the Vulcan-like emotional restraint raises an eyebrow in surprise.

"Not exactly the picture the Capitol Police are painting of this guy, is it?"

Jerold Todd Bernard was a scraggly, unshaven mess when he took shots at us on the steps. Standing side by side with a beaming Marilyn Viano, the man in the picture is clean, well-groomed, impeccably dressed, and full of confidence. What happened between then and now?

"Where was this taken?"

"Years ago, at a fundraiser early in the senator's term. She held a few of these events, but not nearly as many as she needed, it turns out," Condrey laments.

"How did you find it?" I ask, suspicious that this photo only now materialized out of thin air.

The police haven't uncovered a single link between Bernard and anybody in Washington. This is a vital piece of the puzzle.

"I thought he looked familiar to me since the moment they released his picture after the shooting. I couldn't put my finger on how or why, so I started going through photographs. After Viano lost her reelection bid, I decided to keep the external hard drives that held thousands of pictures from every event the senator attended. It took me a while to find this one."

"Do you know why he was there?"

"No clue, but they definitely know each other. Determining the how and why they knew each other is the job of an investigative journalist and a...whatever you are," Gary says, with a nod to Terry. "Kylie, I know you don't trust me. I wouldn't trust me either, but I believe that nobody has the right to shoot at a sitting congressman. If the truth is what you are really after, you have to prepare yourself for the possibility that things are not as what you believe."

"Meaning what?"

"Meaning Michael wasn't actually the target the day of the shooting—Viano was."

-FIFTY-THREE-

CHELSEA

I brush aside a phalanx of doctors and nurses as I rush to his bedside. I carefully sit on the edge of the bed, lean over, and give him a kiss. For the first time since before the shooting, it was returned.

"If this is a dream, please don't wake me up," Blake mumbles when our lips part, the smile chiseled on his face.

"How are you feeling?"

"Like someone beat me with a baseball bat."

"How is he?" I ask one of the white-coated doctors standing at the foot of the bed.

"He's doing well, considering. He has full use of his limbs, which is a good sign. The bullets did substantial damage to his organs, but it looks like there won't be any major physical impairment."

"That's great news," I say, fighting to hold back my tears. "Do you remember what happened?"

"Uh, not much of it," he replies. I can tell he's foggy from the drugs dripping into him from his IV, and his voice is hoarse.

I hold his cup of water for him, and he drinks from a straw while I fill him in on what happened. I tell him what everyone explained to me since I was unconscious for all of it myself.

"Damn…thank God you're okay."

"I am, thanks to you."

"Are both of the congressmen all right?

"Congressman Reyes is in a wheelchair until his leg heals, and Congressman Bennit has an arm in a sling, but otherwise they are. They both can't wait to see you."

"And the others?"

"Vince and Vanessa dodged a bullet, literally. Kylie, Peyton, and Emilee were uninjured but pretty shook up afterward."

"Thank God."

"There is something you should know."

"What?"

I don't want to tell him. I remember the panic I felt when I woke up, and I don't want him to feel any emotional pain in addition to his physical. Unfortunately, it's better to come from me than anyone else, and I've already committed myself to say it.

"Your aunt was killed." He looks down at the blanket, staring off into space. All I can do is hold his hand and wait until he says something in return.

"How? I mean, where was she hit?"

"In the head. They did everything they could, but she was pronounced dead shortly after arriving here. I'm so sorry."

He clamps his eyelids down tight. Blake's told me the whole backstory between him and Senator Viano, so I'm not surprised he's taking this hard. They may have been at odds in her last days, but they were very close when he was younger.

"She wasn't one of my favorite people of late for obvious reasons, but she was family, and I don't have much left."

"I know."

"Do we know anything more about the shooter?"

I explain everything I know about Jerold Todd Bernard and what the media has reported. The coverage of the shooting was as comprehensive as it gets in America. It was reminiscent of the media reporting on the tragic shooting at Sandy Hook Elementary, ironically only a few towns away from Millfield. I also tell him about Kylie's investigation and its strain on her relationship with the congressman.

"Do you think she'll find anything?" he grumbles, fighting to keep his eyes open.

"I honestly don't know."

"I'm sorry, Chelsea, but he needs his rest now," Maddie says, touching my arm gently.

I don't want to go. I want to sit and talk to him for hours. I've missed him so much, and now that he is finally awake, I cannot bear to leave him even for a minute. In a million years, I never would have predicted that.

Blake Peoni once tried to destroy my life. Now he's saved it. I used to get sick at the mention of his name and angry whenever he came around me. Now I can't imagine life without him. It could be a reaction to him saving my life. Vince would say so. All I know is our relationship is brand new, yet I have never had stronger feelings for anyone. That's enough for me for now.

"I'm not leaving," I tell her, only now noticing that the rest of the doctors and staff vacated the room sometime during this visit.

"Chelsea, you have to."

"It's okay," Blake says, squeezing my hand. "I'm not going anywhere. I don't ever plan on going anywhere without you."

The softness in his eyes brings tears to mine. I gently cradle his face in my hands and give him a kiss.

"I'll be back later, okay?"

"Promise?"

"Of course. I can't imagine wanting to be anywhere else."

-FIFTY-FOUR-

JAMES

The Smithsonian's National Air and Space Museum is home to the world's largest and most significant aviation and space artifact collection. Operating out of two facilities, it is the most visited museum in the country. Today is a testament to that.

Fleeing the cold temperatures that just seized the area, tourists have flocked indoors to the heart of the Smithsonian complex at the north end of the National Mall. The National Air and Space Museum is the largest of the Smithsonian's nineteen museums. It is hard to believe that their enormous collection began with some kites acquired from the Chinese Imperial Commission over a hundred fifty years ago.

I meander over to the Apollo 11 command module and peer inside at the dummy sitting in the seat. Dummy is an appropriate word. No way you'd ever get me in this thing.

"Why the hell are we meeting here?" Stepanik asks as he steps up beside me.

"What's wrong with politicians these days, Harvey? None of y'all have any appreciation for American history."

"I leave that to Michael Bennit. He has more than enough for all of us." I let the comment go. I had honestly forgotten about Bennit's ability to turn any conversation into a history lesson.

"Can you imagine plummeting back to earth in this thing? I'm getting claustrophobic just looking at it from out here."

"I asked what you wanted," Stepanik decrees, acidly. So much for trying to break the ice between us with some whimsical banter.

"Okay, we'll skip the foreplay. I was wondering if you were planning on following through with your threat."

"Which threat is that?"

"The one you made on behalf of your party against Albright about implicating him in the setup of Bennit last summer?" The look of surprise on his face makes me smile. "I know all about what you told him after the rules vote. How you threatened to make it public that he colluded with my firm to frame Bennit and expel him."

"What makes you think I have the power to do that?"

"You are the House majority leader, are you not?"

"No thanks to you. I should be Speaker." His response gives me all the reason in the world to think he has no reservations about selling me out to embarrass Albright.

"Congressman, despite my sincerest wishes to do so, I cannot control how members of Congress vote, only help influence their decisions."

"Is that why you wanted to meet? To influence me not to have Albright dragged before the Ethics Committee to answer for his unethical behavior?"

"I'm only looking after the best interests of the people in my firm," I lie.

"Yeah, right. You are seriously standing here and telling me you had no knowledge of Logan Tyler's actions whatsoever?"

Logan Tyler is living proof that you should never send a boy to do a man's job. I sent him to Connecticut with the simple task of getting Michael Bennit to accept an envelope under the watchful eye of a camera, so we could put his corruption on display for the world to see. Instead, Logan managed to get himself and the man I sent to record the happenings caught in the act by one of Michael's former students. I've been doing damage control ever since.

"It's the truth. I am just asking if we can spare the young man any further embarrassment and what I'm sure would be ridiculous legal fees."

Is this arrogant bastard pleading ignorance of the whole affair? Stepanik was the one who arranged for Bennit's ethics hearing in the first place. He had to have suspected that the entire thing was ginned up. He turned a blind eye because he knows damn well that Albright agreed to the whole thing. It's what he wanted.

"What do I get in return?" he asks, coming to the same conclusion I did. As before, it's as easy as breathing.

"My continued support."

Harvey laughs. "That doesn't mean as much as it did last election cycle, now does it, James?" This conversation has taken an ugly turn, and I don't like it.

"Money will never be removed from politics. If you think otherwise, you are sadly mistaken," I charge.

"No, but it isn't as important as it once was, and that's what scares you most. As much as I hate to admit it, I learned something from Michael Bennit. I learned what true freedom means. He isn't beholden to you, any other lobbyist, or special interest group. He can do what he feels is best for America, regardless of how misguided that vision might be."

"I don't think that lesson applies to you or any other Republican or Democrat."

"That might be true, and it might not be. I think it's time to find out. If you want to pull your money and support from my party and me, do it."

He turns to leave, and I grab his arm. I cannot let this conversation end with him believing he has me by the balls. I fall back to an old threat.

"You do this, and the next thing you draft in this town is the eulogy for your political career. Without my money and support, you'll never survive the next election."

"Keep playing that tired old card, James. It's not going to work this time," he asserts, prying my hand off his arm. "You're losing your influence on Capitol Hill. Just like this capsule, you're plummeting back to earth. I'm not going to be the one that stands by you waiting to see if the chutes open."

"Congressman..." I say, failing to gain his attention as he gives the capsule an appreciative once-over with his eyes.

"Enjoy the museum, Mister Reed."

-FIFTY-FIVE-
KYLIE

"Is this seat taken?"

"Bill! What are you doing here?"

"I was jonesing for a cup of joe."

"You drove from Manhattan to Washington, D.C., passing about a thousand Starbucks locations along the way because you needed a latte from this particular one? That sounds like something Michael would do."

"Eh, I was in the mood for a road trip," he says with a half-smile.

"You bought another new car, didn't you?" The man goes to the dealership for a trade-in as soon as the new car smell fades.

"Don't mock my love affair with BMWs," he warns, sitting down in the chair across from me facing the counter.

Bill Gibbons is a longtime acquaintance of mine going back to my days when I was a journalist with *The New York Times*. After my firing, I enlisted his help to determine why I got ousted and shunned in journalism circles. The resulting answer led to my crusade against Winston Beaumont and to the campaign of the iCandidate Michael Bennit. That feels like so long ago.

"I need to get down here more often. My, my, my," Bill observes, leering at the three women standing at the register making their order. Despite the temperatures, all three are wearing skirts and high heels.

"Good to see nothing with you has changed much. Now, are you going to tell me what really brings you down here?"

"You do." He looks out the window and squints.

"A cold front just rolled in. It's barely above thirty degrees. We're *not* going for a walk. How did you find me?"

He raises a quizzical eyebrow then shoots me a bemused look. "Really?"

"I know. I forgot that you're the world's best investigative journalist."

He is, or at least one of them.

"I am, but not the most comprehensive or aggressive. From what I'm hearing, a certain former colleague of mine has taken that title from me."

"Heard that up in New York, did you?"

"Kylie, your tactics down here are being whispered about around the newsroom water coolers in Botswana," he says sarcastically.

"You have to play hardball to get results. You know that."

"Are you actually getting results?" I hang my head. "No, I didn't think so. Going after James Reed is a fool's errand."

"You said the same thing about Beaumont," I snap.

"Uh, no, I didn't. The way I remember it, I set you up with Bennit—"

"Okay, fine. Whatever. Get to the point."

"Let's assume for a second that Reed is guilty of anything. Do you really think he would tell *anybody* of his plans, including those in his innermost circle? C'mon, Kylie, he's too smart for that."

"So, you don't think he's involved either?"

"I didn't say that," he snaps back, but I'm not listening. I hear Gary Condrey's similar advice rattling around in my head.

"Because the police don't, and now even Terry Nyguen is questioning it. He wants to work on an alternative theory."

"What theory is that?"

I go on to tell him about the photo of Jerold Todd Bernard with Marilyn Viano. I had to compete with a young, perky congressional staffer who was making goo-goo eyes at him while she was waiting for the barista to make her drink, but I was finally able to finish the story. He even needed to think about it for a time before responding.

"There are two problems I see with that theory. The first is that if Bernard wanted to kill Viano, why do it at a press conference? If he waited until it was over and made his move while she was walking to her car or something, he could have offed her and not gotten lit up by the Capitol Police."

"Yeah, that's been bothering me, too. What's the second thing?"

"The more obvious one—if you're there to kill Viano, why shoot at Bennit first?"

I hadn't thought about that. The police spent an inordinate amount of time piecing together a timeline widely reported on and dissected by the media. When the shooting was over, Jerold Todd Bernard had fired off all ten rounds in his magazine.

The first shot hit Michael, and a second barely missed him. The following two were aimed at Viano, one finding its mark and the other missing her by mere inches and ricocheting off the steps. The fifth struck Congressman Reyes in the leg. The sixth and seventh shots hit Blake in the back as he was pulling Chelsea to the ground.

Police speculate that the eighth round was aimed at either Vince or Vanessa, but it fortunately missed. With two rounds left in his magazine, Bernard was about to shoot at Michael again when the Capitol Police engaged him. Michael pounced and forced him to discharge the remaining two rounds into the air before they collapsed to the ground.

"What about Michael?" Bill asks, pulling me out of my daze. It's one thing when you're just reading an account of a shooting in a newspaper. It's another when you were there to experience it firsthand.

"He's too busy trying to save the country from itself to care," I mutter, not attempting to hide the aggravation I feel over Michael's nonchalant attitude.

"Isn't that ironic?"

"What is?"

"Your quest to destroy Winston Beaumont brought you and Michael together. It's fitting that your quest to destroy James Reed will break you up."

"We're not breaking up."

"Okay, that's fantastic news! Now tell me how great things are in your relationship." This man has the gift of sarcasm.

"We're fine," I lie, not believing the sound of my own voice, much less convincing him.

"You're in denial."

"What do you know about relationships, anyway?" I say, too defensively. It's true, though. Bill hasn't had anything approaching a steady girl since the second grade.

"Enough to know I don't want one, especially with oh, so many options to select from. I mean, how do you expect a man like me to choose one flavor of jelly bean?"

I turn my head to see who he's admiring now. Bill has the focus of a teenager off his Ritalin. Despite that handicap, he does possess this supernatural ability to be aware of everything in his surroundings. A handsome man with a face more suited for television than newspapers, right now he's noticed an attractive brunette in a pantsuit is waiting for her drink. She looks like the FBI to me.

"She's out of your league, buddy, and by the looks of it, armed," I tell him, getting a gruff grunt in return. "I'm so thrilled you traveled all this way to give me unsolicited advice on my love life, so if that's all—"

"Stop being so petulant, Kylie. It's beneath you. Do you want my advice?"

"So long as it doesn't involve a recommendation for a good couple's therapist."

"Ugh. I dated a woman who was one of those once. Horrible experience," he says, shaking the memory out of his head.

"Bill…"

"You are personally connected to this investigation, and it's clouding your judgment."

"It is not!"

"Just listen to me, Kylie. You're an emotional woman…actually, that's redundant…and I don't know if this is how you're dealing with the trauma of the shooting—"

"I'm not dealing with any trauma. I'm fine," I respond reflexively.

"Oh, please. You're all traumatized over the shooting, including Michael. Trust me. In your case, it's manifesting in a witch hunt against a man your mind wants to hold responsible."

"And if I find out he's actually a witch?" A weak response, but all I can manage to think of.

"What are you going to do? Put him on scales and see if he weighs the same as a duck?"

Bill gets bonus points for working a *Monty Python and the Holy Grail* reference in this conversation. I don't remind him that the woman ends up being a witch in that movie.

"You need to take a step back and start looking at this objectively, or you're never going to find the answers you seek," he continues, "and will lose everything else that matters to you in the process."

-FIFTY-SIX-

MICHAEL

I knew there was a reason I decided to call this caucus "Fight Club." With the promise of no cameras, press conferences, or leaks, my colleagues are provided a forum to argue their points without the specter of needing to play politics afterward. While it remains to be seen whether those assurances will hold up, everyone in this room has no reservations about speaking their minds.

"I think we are doing the American people a disservice if we don't draft a constitutional amendment that would require all federal elections to be funded exclusively through public money," a new colleague states.

"Oh, yeah, that's going to be a smash hit. Whenever people first hear the idea of public funding of anything, they all say, 'Gee whiz, I can't wait to give politicians even more of my money.'" That immediate retort precedes a chorus of similar ones.

"We need to explain that the amount of money needed would be less than two billion dollars. That's two-hundredths of one percent of the federal budget."

The debate rages on for a while longer. I weigh each of the pros and cons in my head. I knew this would be the first order of business, and I'm sure it's what the media and members of the parties are expecting us to roll out. It is also the reason why I want to go in a different direction.

"What do you think, Michael?"

The group falls quiet as I get out of my seat. I'm not the leader of this caucus, as we fancy ourselves more like Knights of the Round Table—all with equal voices. However, since I'm the most notable among us, I guess I get some deferential treatment.

"Did you all know that at the time of America's founding, the king of France bestowed expensive gifts to our departing ambassadors after successfully negotiating a treaty? In 1780, Arthur Lee received a portrait of himself set in diamonds, and four years later, Benjamin Franklin received something similar.

"Now imagine a scenario where a neighboring king begins to send the eager legislators of the new republic gifts of wine, money, or even women. They grow accustomed to the tributes and come to recognize that they cannot live as comfortably without them, so they work to protect their gifts. They avoid topics and actions that could offend this foreign king, even if it conflicts with the interests of their own countrymen."

"Is there a point to this, Michael?"

"You are starting to sound like my students," I respond, eliciting a smattering of laughter. "To protect against this, our Framers added to our Constitution Article I, section nine, clause eight. It states 'no Person holding any Office of Profit or Trust under the United States, shall, without the Consent of the Congress, accept whatever, from any King, Prince, or foreign State.' We protected ourselves from undue foreign influence but didn't apply the same logic domestically."

"Now this is our chance!" one of the icongressmen from Alabama decrees to resounding applause.

"I would love to try, but the truth is we can't legislate the money out of politics. Given the recent Supreme Court cases, nothing short of a constitutional amendment will work, and there isn't enough support for that."

"Then how do we do it?" Congressman Parker asks from the back of the room to a chorus of grumbles. He's been listening to the debate the whole time without saying a word until now. In the heat of verbal battle, I get the feeling that everyone forgot he was even here.

"Am I welcome in this meeting?"

"That depends, sir. Have you heard the rules?" I ask, assuming he knows them but checking anyway.

"Yes, and I accept them," he says to an unconvinced room.

"Then you are welcome to participate."

"Michael, are you sure he belongs here? I mean, he's one of the extremists you all ran to unseat. He's not going to want to find solutions, just advocate his right-wing agenda."

"Are you really telling me we won't be hearing plenty about your own liberalism?" I ask my colleague. "This caucus is not about the exclusion of ideas or ideologies. I nicknamed this group Fight Club and not Disneyland. I knew it wouldn't always be the happiest place on earth."

"Congressman Bennit, if I may interject. I will ensure that my conservative beliefs are represented in this room, but I'm an American first and believe, as all of you do, that it's time we begin to work together. I am hoping the road to that cooperation starts here."

Parker's words pacify the room, at least for the time being. Not everyone is thrilled by his inclusion, but in the spirit of the compromise I have hoped to foster, they bite their tongues. I only hope he is true to his word.

"Okay, that seems to be settled," Cisco concludes, "so on to the next order of business. If we cannot pass laws to get money out of the system, we need to start showing Americans how we plan on neutralizing it."

"How will we do that?" one of our members asks.

"By doing what most of us were sent here to do," I respond, taking up the argument where Cisco left off. "Washington is considered nothing more than a charade by most Americans. Many politicians have historically treated what happens here as a game, no offense Congressman Parker."

He gives a dismissive wave of his hand in acceptance.

"People end up frustrated, and participation in the process declines, as evidenced by our low voter turnouts and even lower engagement on issues. The result is policy driven by the extremists at both ends and funded by special interests."

"We need to tackle the issues of our day and find common ground between us," Cisco continues. "The American people aren't going to like every law we pass, but they are going to like the fact we're trying. It's more than we can say has happened here for the last couple of decades. No offense, Congressman Parker."

"None taken. That's why I'm here too," Parker says, flashing an eager smile.

"Where do you want us to start? Gun control? Immigration? Federal spending? What?"

"It doesn't matter. Pick an issue, and let's get to work."

* * *

The next three hours were some of the most exhilarating I have ever experienced. I loved listening to my students passionately debate topics in history class, but this was different. These are serious men and women, and they know what they're talking about. It's no wonder why the incumbents they ran against were terrorized during the last election.

As the caucus members file out of the room and back to their offices, I see Parker lingering and chatting with a couple icongressmen. They all shake hands, and I seize the opportunity to pull him aside.

"I'm surprised you came," I say, ensuring we're out of earshot.

"To be honest with you, so am I, but I did tell you this would be an interesting year," he says with a smile. He did, right before I went outside to the steps of the building and got shot. Interesting is right.

"I am happy you're here but would be lying if I said I wasn't curious as to why you decided to join us."

"I told you. There has been almost no real major bipartisan legislation passed in years. I think that record drought may end thanks to you."

"Congressman, you're one of the most influential members of the Republican Party. You could have done that any time you wanted. Why now?"

"Do you remember when we were on the House Floor, and I tried to trade saving you for a favor?"

"How could I forget? I said no." I had already resigned myself to my fate that day and was not willing to sell my soul for a second chance. It turns out I didn't have to.

"Yes, and after I voted to expel you, I realized you were just the type of representative we needed in Congress. I wanted to see if you would make the difference that I thought you could. When all the icandidates got elected, I knew you would be in a position to do just that."

"I appreciate what you did that day, but it still doesn't explain why you're here."

"I prayed on it. I asked the Lord for his guidance, and he guided me here. I want to play a role in what you are trying to do. I meant what I said, though."

"About being the conservative voice in this room?"

"I am going to be a royal pain in your backside, Michael. I'm going to argue passionately to sway people to my beliefs. Some principles I will not be willing to compromise on. But in the end, I'm willing to find common ground and work with you all. I hope you're okay with that," he promises with a nod.

At least some things won't change. Parker was the bane of my existence my first year in Congress, trumped only by Albright, who was the driving force to have me expelled. Now they could both be allies. Alanis Morissette should have put that in her song, "Ironic."

"I'm sure your viewpoints will be a nice balance to some of our more liberal members who have promised the same thing. It ought to make for some excellent discussions."

"I expect nothing less. It's time for a change in Washington, Michael. I think this caucus just took the first steps down the path to deliver it, and I am going to do whatever I can to help."

-FIFTY-SEVEN-
CHELSEA

Good-byes are rarely ever good. This farewell is the worst because I know it is likely to be the last. Of course, I've thought that before and was wrong, or so I've kept telling myself.

After our meeting of the Fight Club broke camp to get to work on various efforts, the congressman, Vince, Vanessa, and I all headed to Reagan National for a flight back home. This past week was scheduled as a constituent work week where representatives operated out of their respective district offices to spend time with the voters in the district.

I didn't want to leave Blake as he recovers in the hospital, but he insisted that he would be fine so long as I called him at least once a day to hear my voice. It was sweet of him, and I was happy to oblige. He understands how hard the end of this week will be and how important it is for me to be home for it.

Peyton, Brian, Amanda, and Emilee were all eager to join us in Danbury to help coordinate the efforts we were initiating with the caucus staff members. Despite the long hours we put in, they really enjoyed themselves over our week at home. The time with them went by way too fast. By the time Saturday came around, it was time to embrace the inevitable. Vanessa, Vince, and I go back to work on Capitol Hill on Monday, and winter break from college ends for the rest of my friends.

It's fitting we're meeting at the Perkfect Buzz. Among the sound of grinding beans and intense aromas in this shop is where we all became the closest of friends while working tirelessly on Mister Bennit's first and second campaigns. Now it's the spot where we send Emilee, Peyton, Brian, and Amanda back to school. Despite the rigorous basketball schedule that has kept him away over the break, Xavier even drove in from Syracuse to say his goodbyes. I think he knows this is the last time we will all be together, too.

"You know we will still be around when you need us," Amanda says, trying to console me.

"I know," is all I can manage to choke out.

It won't happen, though. There are no more elections. No more massive social media efforts we'll need help with. No more media circuses to generate. They will be seniors and have their eyes on completing their courses and graduating when we hit the next election. None of them will have the time or interest in helping with a fourth campaign.

We will always be bound by the shared experiences in high school, but their participation should have ended there. I was surprised they came back to help once they were in college. In a generation characterized as apathetic, I wonder how many others would have shown that level of dedication. It speaks to just how hard their transition must have been to adjust to just being college students. Like Amanda told me at the hospital, they needed more to be fulfilled.

"Geez, Chels, we're not dying or anything," Brian quips, trying to add some levity to the moment.

"Yeah, you would think we were going off to war or something," Xavier says, draping his arm over my shoulders. It's easy for him to do since I only come up to his chest.

I have bottled up a lot of emotion since the shooting. I haven't released any of it except in Blake's hospital room, and only because he was in a coma and couldn't hear me. If the last month hasn't been emotional enough, the thought of us all taking our separate paths now has sent me into a meltdown.

I am out of things to say to my friends. All I want to do is cry. Vince and Vanessa aren't much of a help either. It's not fair to the rest of the gang because I know they're experiencing pangs of guilt, but luckily the congressman shows up to bail us all out.

"Where's Kylie?" Emilee asks as the congressman joins our gaggle in the corner of Laura's shop.

"I'm sorry, Em, she couldn't make it up here. She sends her love and best wishes." Emilee looks a little wounded. I'm sure she was hoping to see her again.

Kylie has changed a lot since the shooting. She is still determined, but her fixation on finding the mysterious and possibly nonexistent person who ordered Michael's assassination has created a rift between her and us. She has been entirely absent from the office, didn't show up to the rally, and now this is just one more thing.

"It's been a long time since we were all in the same room together," the congressman says, "and I feel like I should have something more profound to say. Unfortunately, I don't. All I can say is that this journey has been a magical one. If I had written a book about what we have faced together, nobody would have believed it."

"This already sounds a little like a commencement address," Peyton says. "All this talk about magical journeys and all."

"If this was a book, Mister B, how would you end it?" Xavier asks.

"I've never been a big believer in happy endings, X. Life is just not that simple. It's filled with complicated relationships and emotional events. Whether they are happy or not is how you interpret them."

"Oh, great. That's going to be a page-turner. Congressman and former students killed in a coffee shop by a meteor."

"There's no way to interpret that as happy, Vince," the congressman scolds with a chuckle.

"Unless you're Winston Beaumont," Amanda adds. We all laugh, knowing that's exactly how he'd want that book to end.

"In all seriousness, I sincerely hope we have the chance to work together again. But if we don't, I want you to know that you guys could not have made me prouder. I will never be able to make you understand just how much I appreciate you all joining me on this journey for as long as you have."

"Do we get any last history lessons?" Amanda requests.

"Yeah, I've missed out on too many of those over the past month," Xavier piles on.

The rest of the group begins to insist on one last lesson. Despite all the assertions to the contrary, everyone feels the same as I do—that this is the actual end of the B-period honors American History class. The congressman thinks for a moment, then unleashes one of his mischievous smiles.

"Does anybody want the honors, or should we make this a group effort?" Vanessa asks. We don't even wait for someone to answer.

"And here comes today's history lesson," we all sing out simultaneously.

"Okay, okay," the congressman says, after taking his spot in the center of the semicircle we unconsciously formed around him. "Did you know one man was regarded by many colonists as the true architect of the American Revolution? He was John Adam's personal doctor, a leader of the Sons of Liberty resistance group, and played a key role in history's most famous tea party. He wrote the blueprint for the first American government and dispatched riders to the Massachusetts countryside to warn of the British approach. You know at least one of them well."

"Paul Revere," I sound out with several of my former classmates. That makes the congressman smile.

"I taught you almost every main figure of the American Revolution, but his name is seldom included on that list. He was one of the first Patriot leaders to risk his life on the battlefield and died fighting the Redcoats at Bunker Hill."

"Who was he?" Vince asks.

"Joseph Warren. His brother would go on to found Harvard Medical School, and more than a dozen states have a county named after him."

"I'm convinced we'll never see the point to one of these without having to ask," Xavier surmises.

"It wouldn't be any fun otherwise," Emilee joins in.

"I wouldn't have it any other way," Vanessa agrees.

"Let's have it, Mister B," Brian demands.

"You always have a point. What does that mean for us?" Emilee asks more politely.

"It means when the history of what we've done over the past two years is written, they may remember me as the first iCandidate, but it was you who created the movement. You are collectively the new Joseph Warren. Everything that we accomplished was because of you. Part of me wants to wax poetically about how you will all go on to do amazing things in this world, but the truth is that you already have."

With that, everybody starts crying, and one by one, we all join in on the group hug in the middle of the quaint coffee shop we will always call our own.

-FIFTY-EIGHT-

JAMES

"Gentlemen, y'all are nothing without me. Y'all should remember that your reelection was because of the money my lobby provided. Don't even pretend to think otherwise."

"That's a bold statement, James."

"Bold or subtle is irrelevant. I could say it in Chinese, and it doesn't make it any less true."

"Even if it is," the two-term congressman from Oregon interjects, "that doesn't give you the right to try to dictate an agenda to us."

"Are y'all blind? Can't you see I'm trying to help y'all out of a horrible situation? Do you not think the first order of business is campaign finance reform with an independent as House Speaker? Bennit, and all of his independent buddies, are going to find a way to level the playing field with the two major parties, and now they have the clout to do it."

This is one of the most frustrating meetings of my life. Sitting in this gaudy Washington bistro, eating subpar food, and dealing with a rude waitstaff put me in a bad mood. Dealing with these three moronic, sorry excuses for human beings is making me crazy.

I used to own meetings like this. All I would have to do is play the money card, and it was like Pavlov ringing his bell—they would start drooling over the prospect of cash. Now, nothing is getting through to them.

"The more you talk, James, the more you sound like you are trying to help yourself more than us." As cool as I am trying to remain, I know I flinched at the remark.

"Where are you getting your information, James?" one of his colleagues asks.

"What do you mean?"

"I have friends who joined Bennit's caucus. They say the exact opposite of what you are. They don't cite specifics, but all of them are telling me they are working on every issue except that one. Now you are here disputing that, so I am wondering where you are getting your information from."

There is an ugly truth in all this I can't reveal—I have no idea what they are discussing in that room. In the old days, you could count on representatives flocking to the nearest camera after a caucus. When I heard Bennit decreed that no one was to discuss the agenda or topics they debated with the media, I thought it was laughable. Politicians love to talk, and precious few secrets stay secrets in Congress.

Unfortunately, none of them are saying a word. They are taking Bennit's threat of kicking them out of the Fight Club for leaking information seriously, and everybody wants to be in that room. I have extensive contacts throughout Congress, but even I'm left to guess their intentions. These guys are calling my bluff.

"How reliable is yours?" I ask defensively. "You know me, gentlemen, and you know I have always had my fingers on the pulse of Capitol Hill. Do you have reason to take their word over mine?"

"I have no reason not to," he replies bluntly. "I was a whisper away from joining them myself when Congress convened. Based on what I think they're working on, I may still."

"Why in God's name would you do that?"

"Because if they're determined to get things done, we don't want to be on the outside looking in," the third congressman interjects. "I don't want to be perceived in the next election as the guy who said 'no' to every proposal they have. I would rather be a part of the solution than the problem."

"James, if they start introducing bills to committee, the parties are going to have a tough time keeping them off the Floor. And now that the Speaker is an independent, there is no Hastert Rule to hide behind. They will come up for a vote, we will have to decide, and we will have to run on that record in the midterm elections."

The Hastert Rule is known as the "majority of the majority" and was a previous tool Speakers of the House used to justify not bringing controversial legislation for an up or down vote on the Floor. With Albright in league with Bennit, they will not be inclined to do anything to provide cover for either party.

"All you gentlemen are doing is providing more reasons as to why you're going to need the money my clients provide more than ever during the next election cycle."

The three men I'm sitting with have been among my most faithful allies. Their vote on pending legislation of interest to my clients could always be counted on. The fact that they are being lured toward the rocks by Bennit's siren song is scaring me to death.

"James, I don't think you fully understand what is going on. There is more pressure to work with the independents than against them. Nobody wants to be the guys who stand in their way. They have too much momentum."

"I think I speak for each of us when I tell you that we appreciate the support you have given us in the past. Unfortunately, the game is changing, and that support you provide just isn't worth the cost anymore."

-FIFTY-NINE-

MICHAEL

After meeting the kids, I should have gone home. I don't get emotional often, but that was much harder than I thought it would be. I know they could be back and would be if I asked them to help with something. But I also know that there is nothing more for them to do, and they won't have a reason to help again. They have their own lives to lead, and it's time for them to move on.

I headed to my district office in Danbury to get some work done after we all said our good-byes at the Buzz but found it impossible to accomplish anything productive. Between my ongoing feud with Kylie, the stress of the new session of Congress, and wondering what the new president will say during the upcoming Inauguration and State of the Union Address, I can't focus.

Giving up, I packed my things and headed to the Black Angus Grill off Exit 8 on Interstate 84. It's one of the premier steakhouses anywhere in the area, and I wanted to treat myself to one of their aged filets. Who cares that I am dining alone?

Kylie hates cooking in the exceedingly small closet that best describes the kitchen in my townhouse. When I bought the place just after taking the job at Millfield High, the kitchen layout ranked low on the list of priorities. As a result, we eat out a lot when I'm back in the district. We love trying new restaurants all around the Connecticut Sixth, but when we stay local and aren't getting takeout from Vera's, the Black Angus is near the top of our list.

I miss her so much. We have drifted apart since the shooting, and the woman I love, the one who has become such a huge part of my life, now feels cold and distant. We've gone from not wanting to spend a moment apart to dreading spending time together at all. If things keep going like they are, our relationship may be one more of Jerold Todd Bernard's victims.

"Hi, Michael," I hear a familiar voice whisper.

I glance up to see who it belongs to. Damn. Sometimes karma is just plain mean.

"Hello, Jessica."

"I…uh…sorry, this is a little awkward," she stammers. Yeah, you could say that.

"What brings you here?"

"I had a…" She trails off, not wanting to finish.

"You had a date?" I finish for her, letting her off the hook.

"Yeah, I did."

It's weird talking to an ex-fiancée about her love life. When we were together, everyone considered us the perfect couple. And we were because the strength of our relationship was never tested. My running for a national office under the hot glare of the media spotlight changed that.

When I lost the bet and decided to follow through on running for Congress, the flaws in our relationship started to emerge. By the time it became a media circus, things between us were already falling apart at an astonishing rate. The alleged affair was the final blow, and the engagement ended with her tossing her diamond ring at me and slamming the door in full view of the national media.

As much as I hate to admit it, and as much as I love Kylie, I will never completely get over her. Jessica Slater has fashion model looks, and with her long, curly blonde locks and style right off the pages of *Cosmopolitan*, she is the most put-together woman I have ever met. And she stepped it up a notch for her date tonight.

Jessica is much more than just arm candy or a trophy wife. She's very bright, well-read, and an excellent English teacher. Considering my atrocious grammar, she took it upon herself to proofread everything I ever wrote. I could have used her expertise during the campaign, as some of my critics pointed out on various occasions. I know the difference between conscious and conscience, but I didn't proofread my posts before I hit send.

"Since you are leaving the restaurant alone, I'm assuming it didn't go all that well."

"It went about as good as the last dozen or so did."

Is it wrong to think I spoiled other men for her? I should be saying, "that's too bad," but the jilted ex-fiancé in me is screaming "good." It's childish to think, but a very guy thing to do. Or at least that's how I'm justifying it.

"Would you like to sit?" I offer, immediately regretting it as she slides into the bench seat opposite me.

"What about you? Where's...uh..."

"You know her name, Jess. Let's not pretend you don't."

"Sorry. Life has been different since we broke it off. I forgot you aren't the game-playing type. So many other men are. What I'm trying to ask is why Kylie didn't join you tonight?"

"She's stuck doing work stuff in D.C.."

The waiter comes over after noticing I have a guest at the table. One thing about the Black Angus, the service is impeccable. The owner runs a tight ship here, so it ought to be.

"Coffee, please," she says.

"Make that two. Thanks."

"I thought about reaching out to you after I saw the shooting on the news."

"Why didn't you?"

"I didn't think it would be appropriate. I mean, I wanted to but talked myself out of it. I wasn't sure it was the right thing to do. How's your shoulder?" Jessica asks, staring at my left arm that's still secured in a sling.

"It's okay. I'm trying to avoid having surgery, but we'll see how physical therapy goes. Regardless of what doctors say about needing an operation, I think that I can rule out a future playing professional basketball."

The waiter returns with the coffees, and Jessica looks more interested in holding it to steady her shaky hands than drinking it. Always the self-assured one, I don't think I have ever seen her this jumpy. Usually, despite my Special Forces pedigree, it was the other way around.

"I was scared for you that day. I was scared for all of you."

"We were lucky, but we came out okay."

"You've had an interesting couple of years," Jessica muses with a half-smile I don't really know how to read.

"Yeah, you could say that. How's school?"

It's time to change the subject. There are already a great many wounds I don't want to reopen. The shooting doesn't rank high on my choices for discussion, either. Those wounds may be of a different kind but are still fresh.

"It's the same. Robinson Howell is as insufferable as ever."

"You figured he would have lightened up once I left."

Robinson Howell was the bane of my existence. The uptight principal of Millfield High School devoted his life to making mine miserable. He stepped up the threats against me during my first campaign, and when the Beaumont camp cooked up the affair with Chelsea, it was all the excuse he needed to ensure my immediate departure.

"No, he got worse. You were one of the only teachers willing to challenge him. Now, the parents run the school. Grades that students deserve get changed when parents complain, disciplinary decisions are overturned, rules aren't enforced, and don't get me going about the curriculum the state has us teaching now."

"And I thought I had it bad in Congress."

"Do you miss it? Teaching, I mean?

"Yeah, I miss it a lot. Having Chelsea, Vince, and Vanessa working with me helps, along with seeing the others when they are home on breaks from college."

"They're a great group of kids."

"Yes, they are."

"It's funny. I was actually thinking about your campaign the other day."

Siren, strobes, klaxons all go off in my mind at once. The robot from *Lost in Space* is screaming, "Danger, Will Robinson, danger!" Not that I'm listening.

"Oh yeah, why?"

"I just got thinking about why I ended our engagement."

Wow, she admitted to it. Jessica has never been one to confess her own faults. I may be a stubborn old soldier, but she brings it to a whole new level.

"I've grown a lot in the last two years," she continues, "and part of that growth was taking a long, hard look at myself in the mirror and coming to terms with the mistakes I've made. Breaking it off with you was one of the hardest to forgive myself for."

I don't say anything because I can't form words. Nothing will come out of my mouth.

"I'm sorry. I really shouldn't even be telling you this. I know you're with Kylie, and I'm not trying to... We never got closure. In the heat of the moment, everything just ended, and it turns out it was the wrong thing to do. It took a couple of years and a lot of bad dates to figure that out."

"I'm sorry you've had a tough time of it. You deserve better." Why the hell did I just say that?

"And I'm happy you're happy," she replies in kind, taking my hand in hers. "Hopefully, someday we can get past the pain of our breakup and find a way to be friends again."

I know what she said, but her eyes are not conveying the same message. Something like ninety percent of communication is nonverbal, and hers is saying scratch "someday" and insert "more than" in front of friends. Oh, boy.

-SIXTY-

KYLIE

"Can I help you?" the woman asks when she opens the door. She'd better be able to. I sacrificed saying goodbye to Michael's students to see her.

"Ms. Schmock?"

"Yes."

"Hi, I'm Kylie Roberts with the *Washington Post*. I was wondering if we could talk to you about your time working for Marilyn Viano."

"You came all the way out here this late at night and in this horrendous weather to talk about a job I had years ago?"

I wish I hadn't and am forever thankful Terry drove. A mix of sleet and freezing rain is falling, giving the roads a thin coat of ice that made travel treacherous. Standing at the threshold of Jennifer Schmock's townhouse, nothing is protecting us from the frigid northwesterly wind driving sleet pellets into our faces.

"Yes, ma'am. It's important." She looks suspiciously at me, then at Terry, who is stoically ignoring the windblown ice tearing at his exposed face.

"Who's Jackie Chan here? Does he work for the paper too?"

A look of annoyance creeps across his face at the reference. Terry doesn't like being stereotyped, as Asians often are, as either a martial arts expert or computer hacking nerd. He has a dozen ways he can kill her where she stands, and I'm afraid he's in the process of selecting one.

"This is Terry Nyguen, and he's with a think tank in Washington. He is helping me with my investigation." I omit his military ties and dubious job description.

"What are you investigating?"

"Can we talk inside, ma'am?" I ask as another gust of wind blows sleet into my face.

She shows us into the living room of the modest Virginia townhouse located less than a mile from Manassas National Battlefield Park. It is elegant, although not an expensively decorated place. Her husband must be a devoted Civil War buff, and the portraits of Generals Lee, Stonewall Jackson, and Stuart tells the tale of which side he rooted for.

The Union and Confederacy fought twice at Manassas, the North calling them the First and Second Battles of Bull Run after the creek that trickled through the field. Both battles were victories for the South, and the crushing defeat they laid on Union forces at the second battle in 1862 sent their tattered army fleeing for the defenses of Washington. The victory opened the way for Lee's first invasion of the North and the bid for foreign intervention Southerners hoped would end the war. I hate the fact that Michael is turning me into a walking version of the History Channel.

"I'm really not sure what this is about, but would you like some tea?"

"No, thank you, Ms. Schmock."

"Please, call me Jennifer," she requests politely.

A plain woman in her late forties, she is average in every identifiable way. Her long, straight hair is tied in a ponytail, and she is dressed in simple blue jeans and a University of Virginia sweatshirt.

"So, what is this about?"

"I was wondering if you could tell me how you met Marilyn Viano."

"Through her husband, about, oh, I don't know, fifteen years ago, I think. He was very wealthy and a big supporter of many of the organizations I worked with. Since he regularly attended many of our functions, she would accompany him, and we became friends."

"And she offered you a job with her campaign during her Senate run?"

"Yes. Viano knew of my experience hosting fundraisers for various nonprofit organizations and thought I could be of assistance during her campaign run. After the election, I stayed on with her to help secure the money she would need for her reelection. Is this about her death?"

"We think it could be related," Terry says in a half-truth.

"I don't see how I can help. I was only a minor staffer working in her finance department."

The finance department coordinates a campaign's fundraising operations to ensure it has the money needed to function and market its message to the voters. The effort's size, the campaign's needs, and the prestige of the position dictate the techniques. Large campaigns include extravagant black-tie dinners, e-mail pleas to prospective donors asking for money, and everything in between.

"Do you recognize this man?"

I pull a copy of the photo Gary Condrey gave us out of my purse, now digitally enhanced using one of Terry's employer's high-tech tools, and hand it to her. She studies it for a moment, cocking her head as if the change in angle will help jar her memory.

"Yes, of course. That's Phillip Bernbaum. I think he was an accountant for a D.C. firm that helped manage our campaign accounts. We saw quite a lot of him during Marilyn's first run for office."

"Did he spend a lot of time with her during the campaign?"

"No, I would have sworn that they never saw each other. I'm surprised to see a picture of Bernbaum and Viano together. He only interacted with my boss. What does this have to do with Marilyn's death?" she asks, handing the paper with the photo back to me.

Terry and I exchange a look. I'm not sure if we should share the real identity of the man she knows as Phillip Bernbaum. This investigation just got a lot more interesting, and it's the first real break since we started it a month ago. He gives me a nod, and I hand the paper back to her.

"Look closer at the picture, Jennifer, and tell me if you have seen that face anywhere else."

"No, I don't think so," she says, staring intently at the image printed on the paper.

"Imagine him unshaven, gaunt, and with longer hair."

"Wait a second, this looks a little like…"

"Jerold Todd Bernard."

"This is the man who killed Marilyn?" she asks, the shock evident in the astonished tone of her voice.

"And shot Michael Bennit, Francisco Reyes, and Blake Peoni."

"This is unbelievable. Is there…I mean… What can I do to help?"

"You can start by telling us everything you know about Phillip Bernbaum and the firm he worked with."

-SIXTY-ONE-

JAMES

"We don't have a meeting scheduled for today, James. What brings you here in this awful weather?"

Diane Herr's words are pleasant enough, but the future White House chief of staff is really asking what the hell I'm doing here. She's about to find out.

"I need to see the president-elect, and I need to see him now."

"He's indisposed," she replies, the terse tone of her voice not hiding her annoyance at my intrusion.

"Indisposed?"

"Yes, James. Tomorrow is the president's Inauguration. It's kind of a big deal in this country, you know, considering it is the peaceful transfer of executive power and all. He is making some last-minute edits to his address."

I know showing up to Blair House uninvited is bad form, but desperate times call for desperate measures. He told me during our last meeting that I have an open invitation to see him, but his top bureaucrat didn't get the memo. Unfortunately, all paths to the president go through his future chief of staff.

"That's what I need to talk to him about."

"It's not going to happen, James."

"Diane, don't screw with me on this. Five minutes to—"

"Try to dictate what the next president of the United States tells the nation during his inauguration? I don't think so. It doesn't work that way."

"How much money did I arrange to get contributed to his Super PAC? How many of my clients donated the funds you needed to beat the Republicans?"

"They donated plenty to the GOP as well. You played both sides, and while we understand your patronage affords you a certain level of access, it's on the terms we alone dictate."

Super PACs are a variant of political action committees created in July 2010 following the *SpeechNow.org v. Federal Election Commission* federal court case. They are independent expenditure-only committees that may raise unlimited sums of money from corporations, unions, associations, and individuals. In turn, they can spend unlimited sums of money to advocate for or against political candidates to exercise their First Amendment rights. God bless America.

"Yes, my clients donated to both sides. They always do. If they didn't and had chosen to support their party over yours, your boy wouldn't have—"

"My boy? You mean your future *president*?"

This is not how I planned on starting this year. I knew Bennit would be a problem, but I never imagined so many would be willing to follow him. The House is turning into a bipartisan lovefest, and now I can't even get an audience with the president I should own, considering how much money I helped funnel to him.

"Diane, listen—"

"No, you listen, James. I went out on a limb with you on the whole Speaker thing, and you didn't deliver. You expect me to ever do it again?"

"I told you after the first vote I needed your help. You didn't respond."

"You sent me a text message like some jilted teenager pleading with his girlfriend to take him back after screwing the head cheerleader. You blew it, James."

I am indignant at her audacity. The president-elect of the United States didn't lift a finger to help my cause, provided she even approached him with my offer. Now she's trying to pin the blame on me? Incredible.

"You need to listen to me for once, Diane! What happens when Bennit and Albright start pushing campaign finance reform? The Democrats in charge of the Senate will do anything to avoid running against another crop of independents emboldened to try their luck against them. They might be desperate enough to go along with them."

"We will handle the Senate if they consent to anything Michael Bennit and his caucus manages to get passed," Diane replies impassively.

"Are you so short-sighted that you're willing to put a new president in the position where he would have to veto a bipartisan law in full view of America? No, he needs to get ahead of this now, and he will need my help to do it."

"James, you are really beginning to bore me. This conversation is over. The president-elect gets sworn in tomorrow, and once the confetti and balloons fall on the last dance of the final ball, he'll get to work advancing his agenda. His agenda, James. Not Congress's and not yours.

"You'd better come to understand that because the next time we have to make you aware of this, it will come from the president and not me. Trust me when I say he's not a man you want to be on the wrong side of. Now, please show yourself out, and don't think about showing up without an appointment once we move down the street."

-SIXTY-TWO-

CHELSEA

"Thank you for dropping these off, Chelsea. I appreciate it," Speaker Albright tells me.

It's weird working with him after everything he has put us through. For most of the congressman's last term, he was our sworn enemy. Now, he's an independent working closely with us to help restore some sanity to national politics. The world is upside down. Now I just need Winston Beaumont to walk through the door to complete my trip down the rabbit hole.

"No problem, sir."

"You didn't have to run this down yourself. We have pages that do that sort of thing."

"I needed to stretch my legs. I spend too much time cooped up in that office as it is."

"How's Blake doing?" he asks with actual, bona fide sincerity in his voice.

"Still in rough shape, but he's improving. He's going to be hospitalized for a while." The Speaker nods his head, assimilating the information before moving to the credenza.

"Can I get you something to drink? Soda, or water, or will you settle for stealing my scotch again after I pour it."

"You should just pour me one of my own if you don't want to find out."

"This scotch is older than you are," he replies with an amused chuckle while wiggling the decanter, "assuming you are even of age to drink it. Are you twenty-one yet?"

"If I tell you the truth about my age, you'll have to admit that the girl behind the man who took you to school twice last year is too young to have a drink with."

"Fair enough. Serving alcohol to a minor wouldn't be the worst thing I've ever done."

He pours me a drink, and I sip it. If the Three Amigos could only see me now. The trio who once accused me of not being effective in this town because I couldn't go out for a drink with high-ranking politicians, special interest groups, and staffers. Now I'm sharing one with the third in line for the presidency. Take that.

"You know, I have a niece only a couple of years younger than you that lives in Jacksonville."

"Oh yeah?" Where is he going with this?

"She asked if she could be one of my interns this summer. When I asked her why she said that it was because she wants to be like you."

"I'm flattered she thinks that way."

"I don't know if you believed me, but I wasn't lying when you, Michael, and Kylie came down to South Carolina. I never wanted to throw him out of the House."

"I didn't believe you," I state honestly. I didn't. I'm still not sure whether I believe it.

"You were pretty fired up that day."

"I'm a redhead. That was nothing."

"I believe you. I never explained to you guys why, though. You see, everybody, and I mean everybody, thought that he was a threat. I just didn't see it. To me, he was just some lightweight who rode the wave of public sentiment into office because some kids were running his campaign."

"So, you went along with the crowd, I know."

"Yeah, I did. But to be honest with you, if I had known then what I know now, I would have led the charge, not just rode along with it. I underestimated Michael from the very beginning. And I underestimated you, Vince, Vanessa, and the rest of his students. Everyone has."

"Well, I think they're starting to figure it out."

I take another sip of the scotch. This stuff is horrible, even though it costs about as much as my car did. Now I understand why you never hear about college kids getting hammered on it during frat parties.

"Yes, they are. When you ran against Beaumont, nobody thought a bunch of high school kids could run a campaign no matter how good the candidate was. Then, when you guys came to Capitol Hill, many of those same people thought you couldn't be a chief of staff, let alone team up with your other classmates to replicate Bennit's success."

"I know I'm young, and I know I've only been in D.C. for a short while, but do you want to know what I've learned in that time? Pundits are wrong more than they are right."

"All true, but not just the talking heads on cable news. Professional politicians, strategists...the list goes on. The entire establishment was wrong."

Speaker Albright leans forward in his chair. He has something he wants to say, and he's taking the scenic route in doing so. Why is it everyone associated with our government takes twenty minutes just to get to the point?

"Americans don't have much respect for your generation, Chelsea. They think you're lazy, entitled, and apathetic. What you have done flies in the face of every preconceived notion everybody holds about Millennials. Everyone except Michael, that is." Okay, enough.

"With all due respect, Mister Speaker, you're buttering me up for something. Just say it."

"Do you trust me?"

"No." Not that my face didn't forecast that answer.

"You share Michael's penchant for brutal honesty. I don't blame you for thinking that. I wouldn't trust me either."

"Sir, the congressman has a saying from back in his time in the military: 'Trust is earned, not issued.' I'm willing to give you the benefit of the doubt, but I won't trust you until you earn it. Now it's my turn for a question. Why does it matter?"

"It matters because Michael listens to you. He trusts your judgment. If I'm ever truly going to earn his trust, I have to start by earning yours."

"Why?"

"A storm is brewing, Chelsea, and it's about to slam into us tomorrow. It will be more turbulent than anything any of us have faced. At the center of it will be the most powerful man in the world—the president of the United States."

-SIXTY-THREE-
MICHAEL

The image of the president getting sworn in on television against the marble backdrop of the Capitol is the usual one for Americans, but that was not always the case. Before my time, inaugurations were held on the east front of the Capitol Building near the very spot Jerold Todd Bernard put a hole in my body that isn't supposed to be there. Ronald Reagan's 1981 Inauguration was the first time the ceremony was held on the west front facing the National Mall, and that has been the official setting ever since.

The tradition of delivering an address on Inauguration Day started with George Washington standing on the balcony of Federal Hall in New York City in April of 1789. He followed it up during his second Inauguration in Philadelphia four years later, setting the record for the shortest Inaugural address in the process. His one hundred thirty-five words should have been a harbinger of those to come for every president forced to speak in bitterly cold January weather. It wasn't.

Presidents use this address to communicate their vision for America and outline the political goals of the next administration. These speeches range from the mundane to some of the most eloquent orations in history. Abraham Lincoln's second address was the "With malice toward none" speech, Franklin D. Roosevelt avowed, "we have nothing to fear but fear itself," and JFK told his countrymen to "ask not what your country can do for you—ask what you can do for your country." I wonder if this president will say something equally profound.

"We understand that the Information Age has fundamentally altered society, and the way the government conducts business must change with it," the new president reads from the teleprompter on his makeshift dais.

"No longer can we be mired in the bureaucracy and subjected to the endless stalemate in Congress. Americans demand timely action, a swift resolution to their problems, and above all, strong executive leadership."

The crowd gathered around the Capitol erupts into applause at this decree of presidential autonomy. It reminds me of when Chancellor Palpatine addressed the Senate in *Star Wars: Episode III—Revenge of the Sith*, prompting Padmé to say: "So this is how liberty dies...with thunderous applause."

"Is he for real?" Vince asks, feeling much of the same vibe I am picking up. "I thought these speeches were supposed to be about history and patriotism."

"Typically, they are. At least the ones I have read or watched on television."

"The Founding Fathers of this country, and the Framers of the most enduring constitution in the modern age, could not have foreseen the challenges our great nation faces in the twenty-first century. Life, liberty, and the pursuit of happiness are universal ideals in theory but far different in modern practice than they were when those great men codified them into our governing documents. It is our responsibility to rise and meet those challenges and overcome the obstacles of progress for the benefit of all the American people."

"Are you listening to this crap?" Cisco exclaims more than questions, arriving in our office during another long spectator ovation.

"It's one of the bolder Inauguration addresses I've ever heard," I say honestly.

"It sounds like a declaration of war on Congress to me."

"We cannot afford any delay in bringing America forward into this new age. We cannot stand idly by, confusing the spectacle of politics for progress. We cannot wait any longer for those sworn to conduct the business of the people to end their procrastination and make hard choices to address the issues of our time."

"Ooh, he's calling you out, Congressmen," Vanessa taunts while the president waits for the applause to subside. The network we are watching switches to a long shot of the Capitol to show the enormity of the crowd before zooming in on several attendees decked out in red, white, and blue.

"Yeah, along with the five-hundred thirty-four members of Congress," Chelsea adds in for good measure. They are trying hard to get me all wound up, and it's working.

I should be honored. In the president's first address to the people, he's making direct references to what I was saying at the press conference before Bernard started trying to kill everyone. I had mentioned how a line of presidents had advanced the supremacy of executive power and my desire to reinstate the balance the Framers had envisioned. Our new president doesn't feel that way.

"The oath of office I recited here today is a pledge to our country and its people, not any faction or political party." Chelsea starts coughing, and we all chuckle. He is the most partisan president we've seen in decades. "I will faithfully execute that pledge in my duties to the American people as we unite to steer this country back on the course of liberty, back on the course of prosperity, and back on the course of adhering to our time-honored values and ancient ideals. God bless you all, and God bless the United States of America!"

"Well, this will be an entertaining couple of years," Cisco practically spits while saying. "If dealing with all the money sloshing around this town isn't bad enough, now we have to deal with this?"

"So much for electing a president who wants to reach across the aisle," Vince laments.

"So much for reaching out to Congress, period. It sounds like he wants to rule by executive order," Chelsea comments.

It's an astute analysis because that is precisely what he wants to do. Whether he can get away with it is another issue.

When I finally pry my eyes off the screen, I notice everyone in the room is looking at me. I'll need to get used to that feeling because much of the House of Representatives will be doing the same thing. Somehow, I have gone from complete obscurity to becoming the most influential member of Congress in less than six months.

"Michael, Congress allowed every president over the past seventy years to expand his power. This is the next natural step, and it's a dangerous one. He's going to do everything he can to make the whole legislative branch irrelevant and usher in the era of the imperial presidency."

"It's worse than that, Congressman Reyes," Vanessa explains. "Americans are going to eat this up. They won't realize the consequences of going along until it's too late."

"Which makes our work that much more important," Chelsea argues. Again, every pair of eyes turns to me.

"The very notion of coequal branches was designed to stop exactly the type of hegemony the president is advocating. Checks and balances exist to divide the power of government for the benefit of the people. He dreams of having the powers of an elected king because he feels Congress is no longer equal to the task. He is also hoping that through apathy, or silent consent, that the American people go along for the ride. We are going to start working on shattering that dream tomorrow after we finish nursing our post-Inaugural ball hangovers."

-SIXTY-FOUR-
KYLIE

"He extended his vacation."

"What?"

"You heard me," Terry says on the other end of the line. "His secretary is saying he will be in Hawaii for another six days."

I would like to think I have at least some virtues, but patience is not one of them. It didn't take long to track down the name of the firm Phillip Bernbaum was employed by, but the timing couldn't have been worse. The big cheese that runs the shop has been off sunning himself in the Pacific during the holidays.

"Terry, we've already lost three days waiting for him to shed the lei and get back to work. Did he extend his stay because he knows we're waiting for him to return?"

"No, I don't think so."

Well, if Mister Conspiracy Theory doesn't think he's avoiding us, I'll accept that. Nyguen sees a nefarious plot hiding in every shadow at sunset.

"Will your think tank splurge for a flight to the tropics then?" That's an unlikely dream but worth the inquiry.

"No sooner than your paper will. I made an appointment for five days from now. It's the first day he'll be back in the office."

"Damn it. We are so close."

"Kylie? I'm sorry to interrupt, but the boss wants to see you in his office," one of the young reporters assigned to the Washington desk informs me.

"Terry, I have to run. I'm getting called into the principal's office."

I end the call and pocket the phone in my suit jacket. I thought dressing up would be a nice touch, especially given my considerable absence from the office, so I wore a pantsuit. I feel weird in it. I do my best work in a pair of blue jeans.

The door to my editor's office is open, so I watch him jot some notes on a legal pad when I give it a good rap or two.

"You wanted to see me, Carl?"

"Yeah, come in. Close the door behind you."

I oblige, getting an uneasy feeling about this. Closed-door meetings are not a good thing on this floor. Tongue lashings are usually a public spectacle here.

"I saw your report on the Capitol Police investigation into the shooting. It was good, but also pretty apparent you don't think much of their work. I don't know if we'll ever get the chance to run it with everything else going on in this town these days. It's not exactly a must-read."

"It has been a hectic couple of months. And no, I don't think much of their performance. They are competent men and women, but they have settled onto their narrative of what happened and aren't willing to consider alternatives."

"You know, I gave you a lot of leash after the shooting. The only thing I asked in return was that you didn't interfere with their investigation. This is too hot to get in the way of them doing their jobs. Do you remember me telling you that?"

"Yes, and I've done what you asked. I haven't interfered." Crap. What did he stumble onto?

"You know, it was against my better judgment to allow you to run around D.C. talking to everybody after the police did. I have gotten more than a few phone calls from Chief Hayes complaining about it. But the investigation is as much of a story as the shooting is, and I knew we wouldn't be the only ones interested in holding them accountable."

"And we are. I have done nothing inappropriate or outside the scope of what you wanted me to do."

"Really? Then can you explain why I got a call from some woman in Manassas, Virginia, named Jennifer?"

The smallest of things can foil even the most thought-out plans. I have used the guise of my current assignment for the *Post* to provide cover for my inquiries around Washington. As soon as those paths diverged, I hoped there would be no way my editor could find out. One phone call just put an end to that thought.

"No? The name doesn't ring a bell? She's a genuinely nice woman who told me all about your visit to her. She believed your promise that her name wouldn't end up in the paper but wanted to confirm it with me. Imagine her surprise after I explained that I had no idea what she was talking about."

"I can explain."

"I certainly hope so."

I give him the lowdown, omitting Terry's involvement and a few key facts. Critics nicknamed us the "Pravda on the Potomac" because of our perceived bias in both reporting and editorials. Once the mighty investigative juggernaut of the nation's capital, we have lost our edge under this editorial staff. Hopefully, the new owner that bought the paper a couple of years ago can eventually restore its former luster.

"Wow. That's one hell of a story," he derides.

"Wait until I write the article."

"Kylie, we are not bloggers or conspiracy theorists. We don't print sensationalized stories just because we have a hunch or because the little hairs on our necks are standing up. If that was the case, we would be running articles about aliens at Fort Knox or how the president is really a cyborg sent back through time to kill John Connor. Hell, we could even run the article on how there won't be a Christmas because Santa Claus won't renegotiate the elves' union contract!"

"Don't patronize me!"

"Then stick to doing your job!"

"I am doing my job! I am doing the job you aren't doing, and the_New York Times_ before you."

"The _Times_ fired you because you wanted to run an article you didn't have the evidence for. Now I see why."

"But I was proven right. Beaumont was a crook."

"That doesn't matter. It's not how we operate. And since I can't trust you to do the right thing...I have to let you go."

"Let me go?"

"You're fired, Kylie."

The words echo in my head. I shouldn't be surprised since this conversation has conjured up some serious déjà vu. It is almost identical to the one I had five or so months before I met Michael and his student campaign staff.

Our political system depends on the media, and the media depends on politics, forming the perfect symbiotic relationship. Politicians blame us for jeopardizing national security, oversimplifying issues, and exhibiting political bias. Of course, they also attempt to influence and control the press to get their messages out to the public.

"You know, our industry enjoys the privilege of constitutional protection right there in black and white in the First Amendment. The Framers included that so journalists could serve as watchdogs of the government without fear of reprisals. It's a shame that guarantee has been squandered by such a cowardly crop of editors and newsmen."

"And it's a shame you are so emotionally caught up in this that you can't see the truth right in front of your face. You are lost, Kylie, just like you were when they let you go up in New York."

"This article is going to get printed, one way or another. It'll be your loss if it's not in the *Post*," I assert, rising to my feet in defiance.

"If you say so. We have nothing more to discuss. You know your way out. We'll mail you your things."

The newsroom is eerily still. Every pair of eyes in the room is riveted on me. I have no doubt they heard much of that conversation through the door, given the decibel level of our heated exchange.

Now I acutely understand Michael's reaction in that committee hearing last summer. I wish I had my own table to flip and put an exclamation mark on my departure. Since I don't, I simply head for the door, my head held high as I leave. This is one more sacrifice on my journey for the truth. I have done more of them than Hercules, and I am more determined than ever to finish this. I will prove them wrong, whatever the cost.

-SIXTY-FIVE-

CHELSEA

"Hey, buddy! How's the leg?" the congressman asks as Cisco manipulates himself into our office on crutches. Given his fierce independent streak, I'm guessing he's tired of relying on others pushing him around and ditched the wheelchair.

"You should have upgraded me to the Lee Majors package when I was at G.W."

"I don't think our health insurance plan covers that," I dispute playfully. "Besides, Lee Majors was the Million Dollar Man, but that was back in the seventies, and I shudder to think what that cost is when adjusted for inflation."

"Amanda could have told us," Vanessa states.

"What does it matter? It's not like the U.S. isn't using China as a charge card anyway. We can afford it," Vince chimes in.

"See? They get it," Congressman Reyes points out as he takes a seat, and the congressman sits on the sofa across from him.

"Can I get you something to drink, Congressman?" I ask, realizing it will take him a half hour to get back off the couch and get it himself with his bum leg.

"No, I'm all set, thanks, Chelsea. But since we're talking about hefty medical bills, how's Blake doing?"

"He's got a long recovery ahead, but he's in good spirits. I think he is kind of enjoying getting waited on hand and foot by an army of nurses."

Blake is a hard worker and very independent. He resents not having the mobility we take for granted but has been on the go for so long that he's making the most of the break. I'm sure he'd rather the respite be under far better circumstances, though. Lying on a beach in Tahiti or strolling along La Rambla in Barcelona comes to mind.

"I'm glad to hear that, Chelsea. Tell him I was asking for him when you see him next," Congressman Reyes says, the sincerity in his voice almost bringing a tear to my eye.

"I will, sir."

"Michael, I heard about Kylie's termination. I'm sorry."

"That was quick. It only happened yesterday," the congressman replies, equal parts surprise and relief that he didn't have to mention it apparent in his voice.

We have all been avoiding the subject of Kylie's firing yesterday. Their relationship is on the ropes, and we are not about to say something stupid. It may be an irrational fear, but none of us wanted to end up in a position where something we say could be the final nail in their coffin.

"Bad news travels fast in this town. How's she holding up?" Congressman Reyes holds no such concerns.

"She didn't have much to say about it. Kylie hasn't had much to say about anything lately." Cisco looks at the three of us, who are all subtly shaking our heads. He gets the point.

"Sorry, I didn't mean to bring it up around—"

"There really aren't any secrets in this room, Cisco. They probably know more than I do."

"Okay, then what's the deal with you two?"

"I don't want to talk about it. I'd rather focus on what's going on here."

That is the problem with them. Neither the congressman nor Kylie wants to talk about what's happening to their relationship. The pressure is building, and when it finally blows, it's going to be horrible. The congressman and Kylie are heading toward an epic fight or far worse. The thought of it really sucks because I like her.

"Fair enough. When did you ditch the sling?"

"When I realized I missed using my left arm. I'll take mobility over pain at this point. Thankfully Bernard didn't have the foresight to use hollow points instead of full metal jackets. What brings you to casa de Miguel?"

"God, your Spanish is terrible. I just got through talking to some of the icongressmen. They are all pretty worked up about the inaugural address.

They're livid at the president's plans to bypass Congress and want to fight back. Hard."

"We were just discussing that," Vince interjects. "The media are buzzing about it, too. Most of them are sounding an alarm on what they're calling, and I quote, 'a dramatic overreach of executive power,' unquote."

"Parts of the speech went viral on YouTube, many of the popular videos using the president's speech as a voice-over for footage from Nazi Germany. There is no shortage of voices crying foul on Facebook and Twitter, either," Vanessa adds. "People are talking about it, but they don't know what to think yet. I think a lot of our supporters are expecting us to weigh in soon."

"Stop looking at me like that, Cisco. I've avoided making any substantive tweets or posts until I figured out what I wanted to say."

"And?"

"And I still don't know. That's why I'm glad you hobbled in. Did you know James Madison worried that the balance of power within government tilted toward the House of Representatives? He believed that our chamber's control over taxes and spending and ability to work with the Senate to legislate away the powers of the executive and the judiciary made us the real epicenter of federal power."

"Madison never could have known that Congress wouldn't be able to agree on what color ink to use printing a bill, much less concur on the content of one," Congressman Reyes scoffs.

"How does the president think he'll get away with this?" Vanessa asks.

"Easy. The executive branch is responsible for working out the details of a bill when we do manage to pass something. The Oval Office gets to implement the law and chooses what agency oversees that implementation."

"Thus, the tendency for Congress to allow the unchecked expansion of presidential power."

"Yeah, but it's more than that, Vince. There are five hundred thirty-five separate voices in Congress, whereas only one in the White House. They have the advantage of a single message and a strong platform to pronounce it from," I add to the conversation.

"Where does this end then, Chels?" Vince laments.

"It doesn't. If it ever did, it would have by now."

"Chelsea's right. Billy Joel didn't have a dearth of material to write *We Didn't Start the Fire*," the congressman concludes, evoking the name of one of his favorite songs from class. That brings me back.

"Billy Joel? Really?" Cisco questions with an eye roll.

"Just because you can't salsa to it doesn't mean it's not great music, my friend."

"Well, we have no shortage of allies. The caucus is itching for a fight now that it's up and running. I'm not sure how many fronts we can fight on. Between lobbyists and their cash, political parties that hate us, ideologues that will scream about every compromise, special interest groups, an aggressive president..."

"There are obstacles in our path, but we do have one thing going for us."

"What's that?"

The congressman looks at me. For most of my time here, I have felt we were never on the same page. Now, I feel like we are in step with each other. Now, it's game time.

"We have the will of the people."

-SIXTY-SIX-
KYLIE

Accounting is handled by a single treasurer or professional CPA in most political campaigns. Depending on the race, it may be a trusted volunteer or family member responsible for wading through the quagmire of regulations that define the dos and don'ts of campaign finance reporting. Learning and abiding by these rules is crucial since the simplest mistakes lead to fines and public embarrassment.

To assist with these requirements, there are accounting firms in Washington and around the country willing to help a treasurer prepare compliance reports, develop a budget, track fundraising totals, and provide other basic support. This firm in northwest D.C. does precisely that, among many other things, I'm sure.

"I told the police everything I knew, which is nothing," Jim McAllister blurts out defensively as we sit across the large cherry finished desk from him. From what we have seen so far, cherry furniture is a favorite of this Washington power player.

"The police were here?"

"Yes. There is some vicious rumor floating around town that Jerold Todd Bernard worked here."

"How long ago?"

"He never worked here."

"No, she means how long ago were the police here?" Terry asks in his typical businesslike approach.

"They were at my house when I got back from the airport. Getting greeted by men flipping badges in my face wasn't exactly what I had in mind when I returned from Maui."

The information is a surprise considering what I know about the Capitol Police's investigation. Everything has led me to believe the chief ordered them to go through the motions, but if they contacted the high-powered head of a big-time accounting firm based on a rumor, they're being more thorough than I am giving them credit for. Maybe Deana Hayes took my warning seriously.

"Why would that rumor start?" Terry presses.

Nyguen plays his cards close to his chest, even with me. He has let me take the lead in sniffing out information from people throughout most of our inquiries. Now he's focused on Jim McAllister like a Doberman gnawing on his favorite bone. Terry sees the finish line ahead of us, and he's as determined as I am to reach it.

"I don't know. I heard that Bernard was a Gulf War vet, and we've hired a lot of veterans over the years. We've added dozens to our firm following the War on Terror, but that's all I can think of. There is no employment record for him on file, and I certainly didn't interview him."

"Do you interview everyone in your company?"

"No, it depends on the position, but I do like to interact with my employees. I'm telling you, I never saw him in our offices." He's lying, or at the very least, holding something back.

"Did you handle the accounting of campaign finances for Marilyn Viano when she was running for the Senate?"

"What does that have to do with anything?" McAllister snaps. He's taken aback by the sudden change of direction and isn't accustomed to this kind of interrogation, given his perceived station in life.

"We will explain if you indulge her question, sir," Terry answers. Nice touch adding the "sir" to give him the illusion of control and superiority that he craves.

"We do accounting for a lot of politicians, candidates, bureaucrats—"

"We are only interested in Senator Viano. Did you work with her campaign?" Terry asks a little more forcefully.

"Yes, it was a long time ago, but I'm pretty sure we did. Why?"

"Are the accountants who worked for her campaign still on your staff?"

"Some of them are. Since I took this meeting out of respect for Miss Roberts's employer, I will only ask this again before ending this discussion. What is this about?"

Control freak. Unfortunately, there is no disputing what he said. He doesn't need to talk to us and would be less inclined to do so if he knew I no longer work for the *Post*. I'm not about to offer up that information, though.

Terry pulls his copy of the photograph out of his jacket pocket and hands it to Jim. He puts on his reading glasses and looks down his nose at the photo. A hint of recognition flashes across his face, and I know we've got him.

"You recognize him, don't you?"

"Yeah, it's a picture of a clean-cut and healthier Jerold Todd Bernard." We let him study the picture for a few moments before he looks up at us. "Where did you get this?"

"One of Viano's former staff members gave it to us. Mister McAllister, are you one hundred percent certain he didn't work on your staff?"

"I'm certain. I'm telling you that Bernard has never been an employee of my firm."

If he is lying, it's well-rehearsed. His tone, cadence, and pitch all contain just the right amount of firmness without being defensive. After all these years of investigative journalism, I have a good sense of when people are telling the truth and when they aren't. I'm not sure what to think right now, so I need to jar him by trying a different tactic.

"Does the name Phillip Bernbaum ring a bell?" His head shoots up. That did the trick.

"Yeah, I know that name. How did—"

"That's Bernbaum," Terry informs him, pointing at the picture he is studying. "Or at least a guy portraying Bernbaum who went around claiming he worked for this firm."

Jim places the paper on his desk, pulls off his reading glasses, and drops them on top of it. He rubs his chin and then his thinning hair with one of the deepest stress-relieving exhales I have ever heard.

"Care to revise your passionate denial about him having worked here, Jim, or should we just call the police now?"

"You don't get it, Miss Roberts. I didn't lie to you."

"All evidence to the contrary," Terry points out.

"Believe what you want, Mister Nyguen, but I never actually met Bernbaum. I knew him by his name and reputation, but I could have stood next to him in line at any Starbucks in the city and would not have known who he was. He only interacted with the accountants we had advising various campaigns, including Marilyn Viano's."

"Interacted...how?"

"Mostly in the areas having to do with campaign fundraising and contributions."

"If your function is accounting and reporting, why would you have anybody involved in fundraising on your payroll?" I ask, confused as to why this guy would be an employee of a firm whose job it is to account for campaign funds, not raise them.

"I told you, and I cannot be any clearer about this. Bernbaum wasn't on my payroll. He didn't work for my firm."

"Okay, if he didn't work *for* your firm, who did he work for?"

Jim is very uncomfortable with this conversation. He's cornered but still isn't eager to tell us what he knows. Finally, after what seems like an eternity, he exhales and resigns himself to his fate.

"Ibram & Reed."

-SIXTY-SEVEN-

JAMES

"Okay, I understand," I say into the phone. This was a call I never expected to hear. "Thanks for letting me know, Jim."

I hang up the phone and rotate my high-back executive swivel chair to face the window looking out at the city I love. It has been a long, wondrous journey since coming here forty years ago. It's a trip that I feel the end of creeping up on me.

"Excuse me, Mister Reed? I am heading out now. Can I get you anything else before I leave, sir?" my secretary asks over the office intercom.

I check my watch and wince. Marcy has already worked much later than I should have asked her to. I feel guilty about holding her up longer, but I need to talk to someone since the sensation of the walls closing in on me is overpowering.

"Please come in for a moment," I respond after pressing the talk button. A moment later, she enters the office.

"Yes, sir?"

"Close the doors and take a seat for a moment."

"Is there something wrong, sir?" Marcy asks innocently.

"Did you know that when the Constitution was crafted by the Framers, they intended to design a system where it was impossible to subdue the general will? James Madison believed special interest groups and lobbyists could lead to tyranny if their control over government became too great."

"No, I didn't know that. If they were so scared, why bother to ensure the right to petition the government was protected by the First Amendment?" she queries after a pause.

"I don't think the modern incarnation of political lobbying is what they had in mind. Do you know where the term lobbyist comes from?"

"Didn't President Grant coin the term by referring to the petitioners as 'those damn lobbyists?'"

The legend is widely circulated, but untrue. It's a great story to tell the countless thousands of tourists that visit the landmark Willard Hotel where he allegedly uttered the phrase. President Grant absolutely visited the Willard Hotel, but he didn't invent the term there.

"Actually, no. The usage of 'to lobby' predates Grant's presidency by at least thirty years. It originated in the British Parliament and referred to the lobbies outside the chambers where the real deal-making took place."

"Oh, I didn't know that," she says, still wondering why she's here instead of on her way home.

"Corruption back then would make even the shadiest politician of today wince. No office couldn't be purchased, and no man above being bribed."

"So why do so many people say it's worse now?"

"Transparency. What used to happen in the shadowy halls and dark rooms transformed over time into a system of legalized bribery. Because of social media and the Internet, groups have a widely adopted forum to point out how we are distorting democracy. Their words and stories feed mistrust by taking advantage of an intuition most Americans hold—don't trust anything when money is involved."

"I don't think I understand what you mean," Marcy meekly states.

"The presence of money concerning a set of results makes people less confident about those results. If a scientific study funded by the coal industry shows the earth isn't warming as fast as scientists say, we immediately question the legitimacy of the results because of its funding source. The same is true for the other side of the equation. Americans perceive that the conclusions of such research, legitimate or not, are skewed on purpose to placate those paying for them."

"Are they?"

"Good question. The fact that you asked it proves my point," I say, feeling the sudden need to stand and stretch my legs. I move to the window and gaze down on the park below. The illumination the lampposts provide does little to puncture the darkness on this January evening.

"What makes Michael Bennit and his band of independents so dangerous is they have earned the public's trust. By not taking huge donations from special interests, they have immunized themselves against public cynicism. The perception is that they are for the people, and something drastic will need to be done to destroy that. Something *very* drastic."

"Sir, you're worrying me. What is this all about?"

"Nothing to concern yourself with, my dear," I respond, turning back to face her. "In the morning, a woman named Kylie Roberts is going to come to the office with an Asian man and demand to meet with me. When they arrive, please cancel my appointments and immediately show them in."

"Okay, I'll do that. Sir, do you want to tell me what this is all about?" I force myself to smile.

"It's getting late, so don't let me keep you any longer. I'll see you tomorrow."

"Yes, sir."

"Marcy?"

"Yes?"

"Thanks for listening."

Marcy leaves me alone in my office to once again gaze at the majestic view of our capital. I fish for the keys in my pocket and sit to unlock the bottom drawer of my desk. My staff has access to every file cabinet and desk drawer in this office except this one. It is reinforced and double-locked, and although not impenetrable, would take someone considerable time to get into it.

I open the drawer and remove the brownish-yellow clasp envelope containing the bulky object inside. There is no reason it wouldn't still be here, but I just wanted to check anyway. I'm going to need it tomorrow.

-SIXTY-EIGHT-

MICHAEL

It is a little like watching the same movie on an endless loop. After a while, you learn all the lines, know all the scenes, and have no anticipation for the ending. You already know what's going to happen. After experiencing the decline and subsequent end of my relationship with Jessica, I already know where this is going.

Kylie and I have been avoiding each other for the last couple of weeks now. Since the shooting, we have been walking on separate paths. As they have diverged farther away from each other, so have we. I have no illusions as to what that means. The last time I felt this way, Jessica tossed me the ring I bought her and marched out my front door. I half expect Kylie to do the same. This could be the last night of our relationship.

When we communicate, we use the same tired platitudes Jessica and I did before our engagement ended. Kylie and I both have things to say to each other, and we're both afraid of what that will mean. The day of reckoning is coming, so it's only a question of how long the fuse is before things go boom.

"How was your day?"

"It was fine. You know, typical work stuff." By work stuff, she means her investigation in which she has not given me a reasonable update on in some time.

"Work stuff? What work?" Okay, that didn't come out right. I know this because her slamming the dish she was washing back into the sink was an unmissable indication.

"You really want to go there, Michael? Fine, let's go there."

"I didn't mean it like that."

"Yes, you did! Poor Kylie lost another job because she didn't listen to me. Go ahead and say it."

"I wasn't going to say that at all."

"Maybe you'll let me come to work for you now since I'm unemployed."

"Why? You think that you're close enough to the staff to join it? You didn't bother coming to the rally, and you couldn't even be bothered to say goodbye to the kids a couple of weeks ago. Your crusade is more important to you than they are, and now even me."

"Is that why you saw your ex a few weeks ago? Looking for an out?" The gloves are coming off early in this fight.

"I told you it was a chance meeting!"

"Yeah, right, sure it was. Are you telling me that Jessica hasn't called or e-mailed since then?"

I don't say anything because she has, and I won't lie about it. I know Jessica is trying to work her way back into my life, and I have done nothing to stop it. She hasn't crossed any lines, but she is waiting in the wings hoping for my relationship with Kylie to end.

"No, I'm sure she has. If you want to go running back to her, go. You've never completely gotten over her."

Kylie has an astounding number of insecurities because of the beautiful Jessica Slater. She once shared with me that when Blake knocked on the door of her New York apartment a couple of days after the election, she thought it was my ex coming back to plead with me to get back together. As irrational as that sounds, her biggest fear has always been my leaving her to go back to Jessica. Now she's willing me to do it.

"I'm going to see this through, with you by my side or not," she continues with her defiant proclamation.

"Why? This started off as you needing to protect me—but there is much more to it, isn't there? You have a pathological need to do this."

"Yes, I do. And it is for you, regardless of what you think."

"I don't think it is anymore, Kylie. You wouldn't be willing to sacrifice our relationship if it was."

"Is that what I'm doing?"

"You tell me."

-SIXTY-NINE-
KYLIE

"Michael, I watched you get shot! I almost watched you die in my arms. I thought I had lost you! I'm not going to ever let that happen again."

"You don't get to control that, Kylie. Even if you're right and there is some mastermind at work here, it doesn't mean I will never be threatened or endangered by someone or something else."

"Maybe not, but I do know of one threat. I couldn't live with myself if whoever it was manages to succeed next time. You almost died—"

"But I didn't die. I'm alive and well and standing right in front of you. Only you don't see me like you used to. Now I'm something that needs protecting, not someone who needs to be loved."

Damn, I hate arguing with this man. Does he not see that the two are the same? And who is he to lecture about being loved?

"Me? The only thing you have cared about since the shooting is your damn caucus. We're all struggling with what happened that day. Chelsea, Blake, your other students…but you've been too busy sticking your head in the sand to even notice."

"Everyone seems to be dealing with it just fine," he says. It's a lame defense. He really doesn't see it, does he?

"Wow. It's amazing to me that you can be that blind."

The silence between us is deafening. So much hurt and so much pain, but neither of us knows how to explain it to the other. As much as I love him, I feel like we lost the thing that made us, us.

Bill was right. My crusade might cost me what matters most. Michael's attention to his job isn't helping matters any. I have a decision to make. I need to either find a way to get through to him or spend the rest of my life regretting it.

Seconds tick by, and neither of us knows what to say next. It is a good, old-fashioned Mexican standoff, at least in the popular usage of the term. Neither of us wants to pull the trigger.

"Why are you so fixated on this caucus?" I finally ask, my voice softening to convey curiosity more than an accusation. It's a small olive branch, but I also know if I don't say anything, our combined stubbornness will have us standing here in silence for hours.

"Because this is it," he explains, matching my calmer tone and edging us away from the brink. "Everything we have worked for since the day you joined our campaign comes down to the success of this moment. It's the only chance we have."

"Why would you say that?"

"Social media candidates are not the wave of the future, Kylie. We will never have more numbers than we have today."

"Why not?"

I'm a little confused. I have always thought that the movement we all started together in a small coffee shop in little Millfield, Connecticut, would only continue to grow. I never considered the possibility he thought differently.

"Because people are going to eventually lose their fascination with it. Every movement ends. Hell, the hippies only lasted a decade or so, and they were about drugs and free love. If that doesn't last forever, nothing will."

"Yeah, but that was years ago."

"Exactly. Fads and trends don't last anywhere near that long anymore. There is too much competition for the attention of the American people. I need the icongressmen to show what can be done when money is removed from the equation in the short time we have before this trend ends. I need America to learn the lesson to demand change because we cannot make it happen on our own. If they don't see the difference, then all of this was for nothing."

"What if you're wrong? What if social media is how we elect all our leaders in the future?"

"Then, the message after my first campaign failed." Ouch. I hadn't thought about that.

After his first campaign, Michael had me write a scathing article about using social media as the sole method of campaigning. He nearly beat a popular incumbent based on what people had read on Facebook and Twitter, seen on YouTube, and heard over web chats. During that time, Michael didn't shake a hand, hold an event, meet a voter, or take a stand on a single issue. He was determined to let the people know just how wrong that was. His students repeated that message during the press conference he set up for them.

Since then, the icandidates have used social media as a foundation for accessibility and as a platform to spread their campaign messages. They also spent a great deal of time talking about issues directly with the people. It's the expert mix of the two that made them so successful.

"What do you want?" I summon the courage to ask, causing him to exhale deeply. I brace myself for the words I fear are about to come out of his mouth.

"I want you to finish what you need to because I want the woman I'm head over heels in love with back at my side. I can't do this without you, Kylie. I don't want to do this without you. You've been with me when damn near everyone else was against me, and I don't want that to ever end."

"What about Jessica?"

"We were engaged to be married. She's always going to be a part of my life."

"She's going to be a part of your life in the flesh or as a memory?" I ask, unable to mask the hurt and concern in my voice.

"It doesn't matter, and I'll tell you why. Neither of those means that Jessica could ever begin to replace you or how much I love you."

Tears begin streaming down my face. I know we have a lot to talk about and a long way to go to get back where we were, but at least I know he wants to make the journey with me. This isn't going to end all the hurt and frustration between us, nor will it cure my insecurity over his ex-fiancée, but it is a start.

I rush into his arms and share a kiss and a long, warm embrace that is way overdue. Even though I am crying, I experience a moment of peace for the first time in weeks. There are no anthrax scares, crooked politicians, controlling lobbyists, near-sighted editors, or crazed gunmen. That is the effect he has on me. At this moment in time, everything is once again right with the world.

"Is Reed behind this?" Michael whispers as we finally break our embrace.

"Terry thinks—"

"I don't care what Terry Nyguen thinks. I don't care whether he is a SEAL, spook, or the gray-haired guy who lives in the core of the Matrix. You're a brilliant investigative journalist with incredible instincts. I care about what you think."

"Yeah, he did it. He gave the order."

"Then what are you waiting for?"

"Are you telling me to take him on?"

"We have been traveling on our own roads long enough. I want the love of my life back, and if you think your road back to me goes through James Reed, then go get him."

-SEVENTY-

CHELSEA

"You're running late," I tell the congressman as he hurries into the outer office dressed in his long, dark, wool overcoat to protect against the bitter wind now whipping around the city.

"I know. I need to get to the Floor," he says, walking into his office and grabbing the files I put on his desk. "Come for a walk with me."

"Do I have to?" I complain, reaching to grab the coat and scarf hanging in my small office. It's cold out, but the wind chill is making it feel downright arctic.

We head out of the office and toward the elevator, the congressman with a noticeable pep to his step. Curious, I speed up ahead of him enough to get a good look at his face.

"Are you actually smiling, Congressman?"

"It's not unheard of, Chels."

"Yeah, recently it is. Did you and Kylie make up last night?"

"No, we had one of the most epic fights I have ever had."

"So, why are you smiling?"

If it's because they broke up, I will hit him in the head on the way to the Capitol and let him freeze to death on the sidewalk.

"Because for the first time since the shooting, I think we finally understand each other." Thank God for small miracles.

"Are you going to elaborate or just keep me in suspense?"

"If I told you now, what fun would that be?"

"More fun than what's going to happen when I find out you dragged me outside to freeze my ass off just for kicks," I say, meaning it.

"I need you to do something for me. Coordinate with the Speaker Albright's office and set up a press conference for later this afternoon."

"Okay. Any particular spot you have in mind?"

"Not outside," he says with a wink. "Book the highest capacity press room that the media office has available. Time it early enough for the network news to have time for plenty of questions before the primetime news airs."

"You have a plan or something you want to let me in on?"

"We are going to take the fight to our enemies."

"Which ones?" I ask sarcastically.

"All of them. Tell Speaker Albright to meet me for lunch. He can choose the place since I know he's picky."

Congressmen Bennit is not one of the power lunch types. He is usually either on the Floor or up in the office hard at work. Lunch is often at his desk and, unlike the rest of ours, typically something healthy.

"Sure, consider it done. Do you have anything for Vince or Vanessa?"

"Yeah, have Vince start telling the press that they aren't going to want to miss this. Tell him not to elaborate, no matter how much they push him. Give them a taste only."

"That won't be hard since we have no idea what this is about. And Vanessa?"

"Once you get it set up, have her put the press conference information out to everyone she can via social media. E-mail the other icongressmen and have their staffs do the same. I want as many people tuning in as we can get."

"What are you going to do?"

"The elites are not going to give up the reins of power in this country without a fight. There are too much money and prestige involved. If the president wants a war with the legislative branch of this government, then by God, that's what he is going to get. Damn the torpedoes and full speed ahead."

"Congressman?" I ask when we reach the bottom of the steps, near where we were attacked. "You're not going to do something stupid, are you?"

He winks at me before starting up the stairs toward the House chamber. I was afraid of that.

-SEVENTY-ONE-

JAMES

"You are not a lawyer, and this is not a deposition. I do not need to answer your questions, Mister Nyguen."

"I think you do," Kylie says in her counterpart's defense. "And you will."

"It takes a rare amount of arrogance for y'all to barge in here and make any demands of me," I say, switching my stare between the two of them.

Kylie and Terry were shown into my office barely ten minutes ago. The pleasantries were nonexistent as they launched into an interrogation worthy of a CIA black site. Just because I know where this conversation is going to end up doesn't mean I need to make it easy for them to get there. I look at my watch. It's almost time.

"I know you think you're slick, Mister Reed, but you're nothing more than a shady heroin dealer in an expensive suit. Only money is your drug of choice in this town, and once you get a politician hooked, they are beholden to you forever."

"I perform a service to my clients, one that is Constitut—"

"Save it. You can pretend all you want, but we all know exactly what you do in this town. And soon enough, the American people are going to as well."

"And you can save your threats, Miss Roberts. Nothing I do is illegal, and as I'm sure Terry here will attest, nothing is going to ever be done to make it that way. Y'all know it, and I know it."

"That's why you must be so scared. You watched a large percentage of icandidates get elected this past November without your help."

"It is nothing more than a minor inconvenience."

"Minor? Don't you mean one worthy of killing over?"

"Miss Roberts, as I have already told you, I had nothing to do with the shooting. I did not order—"

"Don't lie to me! The game is up. We can link you to the shooter, and once the police see that, they are going to uncover the proof they need to build a case against you that will land you in prison for the rest of your life."

"You are so sure of yourself, aren't you? You think you have all the answers pieced together. Let me clue you in on what's really happening here. Whatever proof you think you have is irrelevant, and it's a shame that such a talented journalist like yourself can be so far off base."

"Our evidence is far from irrelevant, Mister Reed," Nyguen states. "It points to you as the mastermind behind the shooting."

"Is that so?" I pull out the letter-sized resealable yellow envelope from my desk drawer and drop it on my desk. She's right. The game is up.

"What's that?"

"It is the key to what you're really here looking for. It is the answer to the question, 'Who tried to kill Michael Bennit?'"

I let the weight of my words hang in the air for a moment. Kylie and Terry stare at the envelope like it was some alien artifact from another planet. I figured one of them would seize it and rip it open, but they continue to sit there like statues.

"What's in the envelope?" Kylie finally croaks out.

"Open it. The contents inside prove my innocence. You see, I did not order the assassination of Michael Bennit, but I know who did."

I tap the bulge in the envelope with my fingers for dramatic effect. There's no reason I can't have a little fun by being theatrical about this performance. It is my swan song, after all.

"Who?" Terry insists.

"Are y'all sure you want to hear this? Y'all aren't going to like the answer."

"Who?" she demands in an even firmer voice than her counterpart's. Quite the testy one, isn't she?

"You were right about one thing, Miss Roberts. I had a lot to lose with the success of Michael Bennit and the icandidates in November. Only there was one man who had far more to lose than I did."

-SEVENTY-TWO-
KYLIE

I realize who he is talking about but can't admit it to myself. It can't be true. It just can't...

"That's right, Miss Roberts. It was Johnston Albright."

"Bullshit!" is my defiant reaction. "You're lying."

"I'm not."

"There is no way the man who is third in line for the presidency ordered the assassination of one of his colleagues!"

"He wasn't going to be third in line for much longer, was he?"

"He didn't know Phillip Bernbaum," Terry offers, struggling with his own denial.

"Oh, he knew him. Do you know how Albright won his first race all those years ago? I arranged a cash infusion to him that put him over the top in the waning weeks of his first campaign. I have been doing it ever since, including this past election. Do you know who I had work with him during most of those elections?"

"Bernbaum," Nyguen mutters, thinking as I am about the consequences of this if it's true.

It's not just the effect it would have on us, but the chilling consequences it would mean for our government in the eyes of the American people. I'm not ready to accept that yet. It's too convenient.

"You're trying to deflect blame for this and weasel out of it. Bernbaum was still your employee."

"No, he wasn't. At least administratively, he wasn't. Y'all won't find the name Phillip Bernbaum anywhere in my employee records."

"And what about Jerold Bernard?"

"Him either. He was a contractor and was paid off the books for his services. Phillip Bernbaum was the name he used when dealing with campaigns to provide plausible deniability in case of an investigation."

Well, that explains it. There has been a black hole in the police investigation from the very beginning. Bernard has no surviving relatives or friends that have come forward. The police also were unable to uncover the means of how he was able to support himself.

He was off the grid, had no credit cards, bank accounts, or recent employment history. Other than renting an empty apartment in the squalor surrounding the glitzy part of Washington, the man was a ghost. His lack of ties to the community only fed the police's belief that he was a drifter looking for his fifteen minutes of fame by killing a congressman. Or, trying to kill one, at least.

"That's why the police never ended up coming here during the investigation. There is no way they could have learned he was employed by you."

"That was the idea. Jerold Todd Bernard was a troubled man. I don't know what happened to him, but he wasn't right in the head. It's why I eventually cut my ties to him two years ago."

"Wait a minute. Just because Albright knew Bernbaum...or Bernard...does not mean anything. You've already admitted to at least a half-dozen crimes in this conversation."

I'm still refusing to buy into this, but the voice inside my head is getting louder in warning me we have a big problem.

"Yes, I have, but murder and attempted murder aren't among them. Y'all said that there was a call received by Jerold right before he started shooting at the press conference, and that call came from the Capitol Building?"

"Yes," I say, my eyes now fixated on the envelope sitting on his desk and begging to be opened.

As if reading my mind, he snatches the envelope and opens it. He reaches in and pulls out a plastic bag with a phone in it. He lets it dangle in the air for a moment before placing it on the wood surface between us.

"The burner phone," I say to Terry, who begins nodding slowly.

"When the police get around to checking the last number dialed, they'll find it is a match to the number received by Bernard. The prints the investigators find on it will be Albright's."

"Where did you get this?"

"I learned decades ago that the best way to watch Capitol Hill is to place loyal people on political staffs. I have spent an inordinate amount of time mentoring students in college and then getting them employment in the offices of members of both houses of Congress and even at the White House."

"And this came from the guy on Albright's staff?"

"One of them," he says with pride.

What a scumbag. I mean, it's a brilliant tactic, hard to pull off and even harder to keep quiet. Reed must be paying a fortune to buy both their silence and loyalty, but then again, he can afford it.

"So, you're trying to convince us that Speaker Albright not only gave the order but was stupid enough not to destroy the phone he made it from?"

"He tried to get rid of it. That's how my guy on his staff ended up with it. Johnston must not be a fan of spy novels. Y'all have to ask him why he didn't do a better job."

As a reporter, I usually have a litany of questions. Right now, I'm at a loss for words. Reed is equally content to let me make the next move, so an awkward silence grips the room for what feels like hours. Finally, a question cuts through the fog in my brain.

"Why are you doing this? You know you're going to prison."

"Yes, I know. I never expected anyone to link Bernard back to me, but you did. So now I'm making lemonade out of lemons, so to speak."

I look at Terry apprehensively. Reed is awfully cavalier about going to jail. The man is undeniably an opportunist, but he is also a survivor. I know when you implicate one of the country's most powerful politicians in an unspeakable crime, you need to go all in. Reed is willing to allow himself to go down in the process. The question is, why?

"I know what you're thinking, Miss Roberts, so let me answer the question for you. I wasn't going to beat Michael Bennit using any of the traditional means. He's survived fake scandals, staged bribery attempts, and even managed to manipulate the political parties to avoid expulsion. No, to beat him, I need to martyr myself to deprive him of his greatest strength. And in, oh, two minutes," he says, checking his watch, "I will have succeeded."

"I'm not sure I follow."

"Miss Roberts, I thought you were more astute than that. Your boyfriend is about to go on national television with Johnston Albright to implore the American people to trust them. They are going to lead the charge in reeling in the political power of lobbyists, special interest groups, and the president himself. It's the reason why Michael swayed the votes to install Albright as Speaker of the House. How do you think the people will react when it breaks that Michael's most powerful political ally tried to arrange his murder?"

-SEVENTY-THREE-
CHELSEA

"We're all set to go, Congressman."

"Excellent. Thanks, Chels," he replies almost absentmindedly while staring at the sheet of paper with prepared remarks printed on it.

Press conferences are a common occurrence around Capitol Hill, but we never held any formal ones because of our situation last year. In fact, the only one we attempted to set up since the congressman was elected ended with a hail of gunfire. I'm hoping for a less dramatic result this time.

"The room is packed, so whatever you say had better get their attention," Vince says as he arrives back from his recon of the room. "Most of the cable networks are carrying this live."

"Oh, I think it'll get people's attention, Vince," the congressman replies.

This happens to be Speaker Albright's preferred room for holding press events. His staff insisted it be held here once we determined it was available. I balked at first, thinking about the karma of the room itself. This was where he announced that Congressman Bennit would be hauled in front of a special committee to answer bribery allegations.

I still don't know how I feel about joining forces with Congressman Albright. On the one hand, he is an experienced legislator and was once one of the most powerful men in the country. He has years of experience and would make a valuable ally if I could only get past this one thing—I simply don't trust him.

For once, Vince is in my corner on this. Always the loyal consigliere, he has been surprisingly restrained in voicing his opinion to the congressman. Despite his silence, I know he feels as uneasy about this as I do. Unfortunately, he has no more insight into why than I do. Working with

Albright doesn't feel...right. Now we are metaphorically jumping into bed with him and hinging our futures together.

I feel the phone in my jacket pocket vibrate, and I pull it out to see who is calling. Normally I would send it to voice mail, but considering the caller... I accept the call and cover my other ear while trying to relocate to someplace a little quieter.

"Hey, Kylie, this really isn't a good time —"

"You have...press conference!" That's the only part of the harried response I can make out over the crackle and static.

"I can barely hear you. Where are you? Hello? Kylie, are you there?"

I look at the phone and see that the call failed. I have four bars, so it must be an issue on her end. She sounded frantic, and I am starting to worry whether she is okay.

"What was that all about?" Vanessa asks as concern creeps across her face.

"I have no idea," I say, trying to call Kylie back.

It goes straight to her voice mail without ringing. Wherever she is, it's not a place Verizon's dorky spokesman who used to walk around asking, "can you hear me now?" ever visited. I punch end without leaving a message and give Vanessa a shrug.

"If she doesn't call back, try her in a few minutes."

"Yeah, I'm going to."

"This is a historic day, Michael, and one that is long overdue," Speaker Albright proclaims as he arrives.

"They are all set and ready for you, sir," one of his staffers tells him.

"Let's do it."

"Wish us luck," the congressman says to us as he follows the Speaker into the press room.

"Good luck!" the three of us chime out.

My phone vibrates again. "Kylie?"

"Chelsea! Can...hear me?" Kylie asks, with that same frantic tone to her voice.

"Yeah, sort of. You're cutting in and out."

"You need to...the press conference! Don't let Michael...stage with Albright!"

"What? I still can't understand what you're saying. Where are you?"

"I'm leaving Ibram & Reed. Is this better? I'm almost outside."

"Yeah, much better. What's going on?"

"We've been set up!"

"What do you mean 'set up?'"

"There is no time to explain on the phone. We're on our way there. Do not let this press conference happen. Keep Michael off the stage with Albright."

A shiver runs down my spine as I peek out and see Albright settle down the press and start making his opening remarks. As much as I want to jump into action and interrupt, I'm not about to do that on live national television.

"Kylie, it's too late. The press conference already started."

-SEVENTY-FOUR-

MICHAEL

"Congressman Bennit!" a chorus of reporters repeatedly calls out until I point to one for his question. How reporters ply their trade this way will never cease to amaze me.

"Congressman Bennit, are you saying that you don't recognize the president's right to dictate the direction of the country?" Do journalists always embellish statements for dramatic effect?

"I don't believe it was ever the Framers' intent for the executive branch of government to be *solely* responsible for setting the legislative agenda."

"So, he does have a say?"

"The president is the highest elected official in our land and can propose any legislation he wishes. However, the House members are the voice of the people and have the closest relationship with them. It is our job to raise and debate the issues of national and local importance to them."

"Is one of those issues campaign finance reform?" a woman shouts out from the middle of the group. I didn't call on her, but everyone is content to let me answer her question.

"Campaign finance is one of the most difficult issues we face. Americans widely believe there is too much money in politics today. The Supreme Court has also ruled that it is protected as free speech, and we respect that decision. Therefore, the best way to reduce the impact of money is to rely on those people elected to this body that pledged their allegiance to the American people and not the big-money donors."

"Are you alluding to the icongressmen?"

"I am alluding to any member of this chamber willing to put the welfare of Americans before the welfare of their campaign's checking account," I respond, pointing to another reporter waving his arm so hard I'm afraid he'll dislocate it.

"Speaker Albright, aren't you being a little hypocritical supporting this today? You were one of the biggest obstacles to legislation in the last session."

"Yes, I am very hypocritical," he says, eliciting an audible gasp from the room. "I have learned a lot over the last year. Congressman Bennit and the other independents have shown me the type of representative I want to be. I have spent my entire political career doing what was right for my party. Now, my allegiance is for who it should have been all along—my constituents and the American people."

"Are you really asking us to believe you have had a change of heart?" a skeptical man challenges from the front row. If the White House Press Corps is the most jaded group in the country, the reporters covering the U.S. Capitol rank a close second.

I can understand their reluctance to go along with this. Every question the media have asked has been good ones. If I were a citizen watching from home, that's what I would be asking too. Of course, being a longtime hater of lawyers and politicians, I wouldn't believe what he says anyway.

"No, I don't want you to believe me. Politicians have been asking people to do that for decades, and look where it has gotten us. I am telling you this today because from the moment I leave this room, I'm going to start showing you."

"What happens when a bill you don't like gets introduced? Will you allow it to come to the Floor?"

"As of this instant, I will never use the Hastert Rule, or any other parliamentary trick, to suppress legislation. So long as it passes committee, the House will have an up or down vote for all Americans to see."

The reporters can't hide their surprise. After dealing with the partisan political tides for so long, they've grown accustomed to the games both sides played to suppress each other's voices. Now, Speaker Albright and I are not just changing the game. We are throwing the whole board out the window.

"What about amendments?" another reporter shouts at the two of us. I defer the answer to the Speaker.

"I think Americans have the right to hear what amendments their representatives are offering. So long as they are related to the topic of the proposed bill, and not meant to poison it through the introduction of an unrelated and untenable provision, amendments will absolutely be considered during debate on the Floor."

"Congressman Bennit? You and Speaker Albright have a colorful past together. He is widely attributed as being the architect of the effort to expel you from the House. Are you really going to be able to work with him?"

"I think we are going to have our share of disagreements. In fact, not every member of the House is going to agree on every piece of legislation. We're going to change the status quo in Washington and give the American people the Congress they yearn for. That starts with talking to each other and working out our differences. It starts right here, right now, with me trusting the Speaker of the House. I think you all should too."

-SEVENTY-FIVE-
KYLIE

When Michael used the "trusting the Speaker of the House" line, I felt like I was going to throw up. We arrived at the press briefing just in time to hear that, so I told Chelsea I would meet them all in Michael's office when it was over. Terry and I watched the rest of the horror show on the television in the conference room. It didn't get any better. Each question he answered about cooperating with Johnston Albright was another nail in his coffin.

With the presser over, the current panel of pundits discusses what this means for the country. Their opinions are a mix of optimism and skepticism, not that it matters. When James Reed turns over that phone and tells the Capitol Police his story, any changes Michael hoped to bring to Washington will be ignored as another sensationalized scandal takes root.

"Hi honey," Michael says, walking into the office, Cisco right behind him. "Terry."

"Congressman," Nyguen replies, adding a nod and quick handshake.

"Between Chelsea's urgency getting me up here and the looks on your faces, I can tell this can't be good. Is this about the meeting with Reed?"

"Yeah, it is. You're going to need to get everyone in here and close the door." Michael looks at me apprehensively but complies.

"Is it really that bad, Kylie?" Cisco asks me earnestly.

I don't get the chance to respond before Vince and Vanessa both glide in, still buzzing about the success of the press event. I feel bad that I'm about to burst their bubble. Chelsea follows them in and closes the door. She is acting the dourest of the three of them, somehow sensing that what I am about to say will ruin their day.

"What is it? Did Reed actually meet with you?"

"Yeah, he was almost eager to."

"It must have been one hell of a compelling defense to put you in this mood. Did he do it?"

"No, I don't think so."

"Okay, that's not what I was expecting to hear," Michael laments. I was adamant in my assertion that Reed was behind the assassination attempt last night, and he took me at my word.

"So, if he didn't give the order, who did?" Vince demands.

"That's why we were so urgent to get over here and stop the press conference," Terry says, stealing my thunder.

I inform them of what we learned from James Reed about the mysterious and nonexistent Phillip Bernbaum. I stop just before the good part. Or the bad part, depending on your perspective.

"Okay, you're killing me here, Kylie," Cisco admonishes. "Enough with the suspense."

"Who was it?" Michael whispers, as he often does when he knows a bomb is about to be dropped.

There is no putting this off anymore. I have no idea how everyone will react, but it's time to come clean with what I know and find out. I take a deep breath.

"You just got off the podium with him."

Everyone reacts with the same expression of shock. For a few moments, nobody utters a word. Jaws hang open. Everyone is speechless, except Michael, who quickly launches into the first stage of grief.

"Albright?" Michael's incredulous response is the precursor to denial setting in. "No way. I don't believe it for a second. Reed is just trying to drive a wedge between us to advance his own goals."

"I thought that too. In fact, I had the same reaction."

"He has proof, Michael," Terry warns. "He has the phone that made the call to Bernard right before the shooting. He claims it was Albright's."

"And you guys believed him?" Vanessa asks the two of us.

"We won't know for sure if he is telling the truth until it gets turned over. The police run will check for prints on it, but I don't think he was lying."

"Why? Why would he do this now?" Vince asks, still working his way through his own sense of denial.

"To destroy me," Michael says, now seeing the big picture. "I just went on television and stood shoulder to shoulder with Albright. I told the American people that I trusted him, and they should too."

"If it comes out that he tried to have you killed…" Chelsea adds, coming to the same realization of just how bad this is.

"I look like a fool, or ignorant, or—"

"Like the prototypical politician willing to do anything to advance your own agenda," Terry finishes.

Michael exhales deeply. I have seen him deal with a lot since the day I met him—the anxiety over the campaign, the lies Beaumont spread, false accusations of accepting a bribe, almost getting thrown out of the House, the anthrax scare, and even getting shot. Through it all, he's been nothing but resolute. However, at this singular moment in time, he wears the stress of what this means all over his face.

"Reed was going down and knew it. So, now he's found a way to take you with him," I say before the knock on the door to Michael's office interrupts the discussion.

"I'm sorry to interrupt, Congressman, but you have a visitor. He said it was important," a junior staffer meekly says from the doorway.

"Who is it, Sarah?"

"Speaker Albright."

Acknowledgments

I owe everything to those who have spent their hard-earned money to follow Michael Bennit's journey. There are hundreds of thousands of books to read by thousands of great authors, and I appreciate my readers more than simple words can express.

To the love of my life Michele, you have my continued undying gratitude for all the time you spent listening to me rant about this book and the sacrifices you make to help me pursue my dreams. Your encouragement keeps me going, and I can never fully express how much that means to me.

I have been blessed with one of the best families a person can ask for. My parents, Ronald and Nancy, and my sister, Kristina, share every up and down in this journey with me, and I could never ask for more love and support than you give.

Authors may write books, but it's the people behind the scenes that make them a reality. Thanks to my editor Caroline, her husband Gary, and the staff at BubbleCow for making this book the best that it could be. Special thanks also go out to Diana for the copyediting job on this book. Last but certainly not least, I asked my cover creator Veselin Milacic to execute the difficult task of creating a specific cover for *The iSpeaker*. I hope my readers liked the cover art as much as I did.

A Note from the Author

As I promised at the end of the last novel, Kylie made her triumphant return. I think we are finally getting to see a side of her that may not have been apparent in the first two books of the series. I was thrilled to be able to bring her back as a part of the first-person narrative.

The aftermath of any traumatic event affects people differently. I tried to bring that out and apologize if anyone thinks I wasn't up to the task. The intent was to show that each character reacted differently and am aware that the reader may or may not find those reactions believable.

As was mentioned in the novel, good-byes are rarely ever good. It was hard for me to write the staff out of the book, but their involvement had run their course. While I can beg the reader's indulgence in my keeping them involved while in college, there comes the point where it just stops being remotely believable. They contributed so much, but it was time to move the story on without them. It was hard for me to write.

Michael Bennit is finally starting to get his bearings in Washington, but that doesn't mean he will be unchallenged. He is a different kind of politician and will face a lot more obstacles before his journey ends. Some of them will be professional, and others personal. As I mentioned at the end of the last book, his old flame Jessica made an appearance right when he was most vulnerable. Michael may have smoothed things over with Kylie, but I wouldn't expect the tension between the two of them to end there, especially with Jessica waiting in the wings.

Chelsea grew the most throughout the last three books. Many readers thought it was implausible that she'd be Michael Bennit's chief of staff. Hopefully, by the end of this novel, you begin to see her strength just like Michael does and understand his motives for giving her that position.

My editor was quick to point out that she didn't understand Blake's role in this story. Indeed, he wasn't a prominent character in this novel like he was in the first two because he spent most of it in a coma. However, part of understanding Chelsea's maturing is to understand her developing feelings for Blake. Much of this will come into a little more focus in *The iAmerican*.

About the Author

Mikael Carlson is an award-winning political fiction author, including a silver medal from Readers' Favorite, National Indie Excellence, Top Shelf, Book Excellence, and Global E-book Awards. He was named one of the '50 Great Writers You Should Be Reading' by The Authors Show in 2018.

This is his first novel. He authored the four political dramas in The Michael Bennit Series, the Watchtower Thrillers, and the Tierra Campos political suspense thrillers.

Mikael is a former U.S. Army Paratrooper and retired Army National Guardsman. He conducted over 50 airborne operations following the completion of jump school at Fort Benning in 1998 and has trained with the militaries of countless foreign nations.

Mikael graduated with a Master of Arts in American History in 2010 and a B.S. in International Business from Marist College in 1996.

An avid traveler and unabashed political junkie, you can find him at www.mikaelcarlson.com.

Made in the USA
Las Vegas, NV
14 August 2022

53265318R00197